WOMEN AT WAR

WOMEN AT WAR

Inspired by a true story

Christine Lord

Dedicated to all women and children

affected by conflict or war.

ACKNOWLEDGEMENTS

Thanks to everyone that supported me during the many years of collating, researching and then writing my book *Women at War*. It has been a journey of mixed emotions and revelations.

My daughter Emma, my sunshine, who experienced a lot of my moans and struggles as I wrote and re-drafted my book. Living under the same roof as a writer can be challenging.

I'd like to thank Sarah Cheverton for editing my book. I appreciate your expertise and input.

Thanks to Dale McEwan for his technical and editorial skills. A great journalist and proofreader. I appreciate all the hours you sat listening to me during the writing process, and your steadfast encouragement and support.

The stark and beautiful photograph used for the front and back cover of my book was designed by Samuel Carter-Brazier using vintage Soviet film, and added a poignant dimension. The ghostly image represents so many lost lives and futures, but also a doorway of hope. Thank you, Sam, for producing such an amazing book cover.

I also want to thank Alan East for his ongoing technical support and website design. What would I do without my colleagues who have become good friends?

I would also like to thank from the bottom of my heart all the war veterans, camp survivors, eye witnesses, German civilians and allied service personnel I interviewed. Their stories are still shocking, their resilience awesome and their testimonies an important part of our global history.

I must also mention my late parents William and Audrey Lord. My father served in the RAF during World War Two, age 19 years old, and my mother served in the WAAF during the Berlin Airlift. Their stories of what happened to individuals and families in the UK and across Europe in 1945/1948 gave me yet another window of understanding of what it meant to live during and after a world war.

Finally, I want to say what a privilege it was to meet and talk to the

German women who grew up under Hitler's regime and made their homes in the UK and USA after the war. Their honesty and openness to my questions gave me an insight into a time of great change and terror. Listening to their stories and experiences was profound and moving, especially the woman who I have called Greta in my book, allowing me to sit for many hours as she talked about her family life in Germany and what it was like to experience so much death, destruction and heartache. What I learnt from all my contributors was that hope and love are eternal.

I hope my book *Women at War* will give readers a good understanding of the many shades of conflict and how individuals can react and respond when faced with death. Millions of people were killed during World War Two and millions more men, women and children who survived were left traumatised and broken.

What would any of us do to survive?

Christine Lord, Hampshire, UK, 2020

CHAPTER 1

The first time my mother was raped was on my 14th birthday.

We'd been on the road for five days and five nights fleeing the invading armies.

These were the early days of our journey, before we lost all sense of time or place.

The soldier appeared out of nowhere like a dusty, grey ghost. Blood-splattered and smelly, even from a distance. Cradled in his arms was a gun.

My mother squeezed my hand so tight it hurt. We stood still and silent as the soldier shouted something in Russian.

He was young, no more than twenty-two. Weary blue eyes peered out through dirt ingrained on his skin. He barely glanced at me, skinny, short, and flat-chested. A child not a woman. Instead he stared at my mother, straight-backed, still plump-cheeked, her blonde hair shining in the pale sunlight. In the grey landscape she looked like an angel.

He walked towards us and then gestured with his gun for my mother to move into the adjoining field.

I could feel the pumping of her heart through our joined hands. Bending to my ear, she whispered, 'If you hear gunfire, run and keep running until you find a place to hide. I will come and find you.'

She let go of my hand.

Shoulders hunched, my mother walked into the field with the soldier, into tall brown grassland where a few daisies nodded their heads in the light breeze.

My younger brother Hans turned to me, as our mother disappeared from sight, his eyes wide with panic. I attempted a smile trying to reassure him. Instead he became distracted by a swarm of flies buzzing around the putrefying body of a dead fox. I watched him swatting flies with a piece of wood he had found beside the path. He caught a stray fly in his hands and began pulling off its wings and legs. I looked away and into the field towards the swaying grass. There was no sign of my mother or the Soviet soldier.

I listened intently for a scream, the crack of a bullet, ready to run with my little brother into the horizon, just as my mother had instructed. My heart thumped an unsteady beat almost drowning out the sounds of the few birds circling and calling overhead. The daisies continued to nod in the watery sunshine.

I stood watching and waiting, ready to run, for what felt like hours.

Yet it could have been no longer than twenty minutes later when my mother appeared, pulling down her top and adjusting her skirt. When she saw me, her mouth twisted into a tight grimace and she walked towards us. Behind her the Soviet soldier followed, slinging the gun over his shoulder.

Mother was unsteady, her legs shaking as she grabbed my hand in her own and, with her other hand, reached for my brother. I saw the Soviet scramble onto the path.

My mother, walking at speed, dragged us away, trying to put as much space as possible between us and the solider.

Suddenly from behind he shouted in German.

'Halt!' and then yelled, 'Helga!'

I was shocked that my mother had given her name to the Soviet as well as herself.

We had no choice but to stop, the gap between us and the soldier was still close enough for a bullet in the back of the head. I could hear heavy footsteps crunch nearer and nearer.

Slowly we turned to face him. As he came closer, I saw how young his face was, though his body moved like an old man. I would come to see this combination of old age in the bodies of young men many times before the war ended. Soldiers bone weary with the stain of war soaked into their skins. The horrors they had caused and witnessed etched into

2

their faces, reflected in their eyes.

Perhaps in other times, I would have felt sorry for him, but this man with his gun had the power of life and death over my family. He knew it and we knew it, so my family stood in line as the Soviet came towards us swinging his weapon.

My mother pushed back her shoulders, standing tall and defiant, though her face was blanched like chalk. Her fingers, clamped around mine, dug into my skin. I felt Hans tremble next to me, and we watched transfixed as the soldier came closer.

He searched impatiently within the many pockets of his uniform.

Reaching us, he brought out a wizened apple and from a blood-stained pouch pulled out a piece of cloth revealing a slice of cheese moving with maggots. Smiling, he bent forward, offering the apple to Hans and the cheese to me. Mute, we took the proffered food. The soldier then patted Hans on the head, nodded to my mother, swung his gun over his shoulder, turned and walked away.

For a long moment we stood frozen, before mother jerked us into life and began to half-walk, half-run us along the pathway.

She repeatedly checked behind, making sure the soldier was not following us. He never glanced backwards and soon disappeared into the ever-fading distance.

We kept moving until the sun was overhead, then my mother steered us off the path into a wood where there was the sound of running water. We traipsed through tall thin trees until a small stream appeared.

My mother smelt strange, sweat of course, and she also smelt of a man, of the soldier.

She sat us down on a rock near the silver flecked water, and told us, 'We will wash our hands, have a drink, and rest. Greta you must share the apple and cheese, half each, with your brother.'

'Don't you want something to eat too?' I asked, stopping short at saying 'mother'. I didn't know why.

I offered the apple and stinking cheese.

We had not eaten for two days and she must have been hungry, but mother didn't reply. Instead she took off her dress, washed her underwear and waded into the water. It must have been freezing, as the winter snows were still dusting the high mountains.

She turned her back to us and began to wash again, then again, and again. Hans and I picked maggots off the mouldy cheese and shared small pieces of the gnarled apple as we watched our beautiful mother try to clean the soldier from her skin.

I would never celebrate my original birthday again. For the next seven decades, my date of birth would remain hidden until it faded even from my mind and became just another number on the calendar.

CHAPTER 2

My mother continued washing herself for a long time and Hans became bored, laid down on the grassy bank and slept.

I sat next to my brother and slowly felt my mind drift loose, into the past.

I tried to make sense of how we got to the riverbank and the terrible happenings of that morning.

From as early as I can remember, our charismatic leader, Hitler, dominated our daily lives. His promises of a renewed, powerful Germany reborn offered hope to a broken people still reeling from the economic devastation of the First World War. I was only 3 years old when Hitler declared himself Führer, and as I grew, so did his power. Hitler seemed to offer all the answers to the economic woes that troubled my father. That the answers came at the cost of strict regulations and rules didn't trouble anyone, at first.

The rise of the Nazi party brought more jobs and stability as the Führer announced investment after investment in new public works. We celebrated with a party when my father, a policeman, came home one day and announced he had been promoted. My mother danced and praised the Führer's wisdom. To my parents, it seemed the good times had returned.

My early school days were filled with outdoor sports and summer camps as children all over Germany were taught to eat well, exercise, be proud of being German, proud of our country.

Life felt exciting and carefree, but not for long. I was at first too young to realise that the new jobs and the extra money all came at the expense of thousands of Jews and others deemed 'undesirable', as they were taken away in droves to concentration camps.

I would learn years later about Kristallnacht and the earliest warnings of what would become the horrors of the Holocaust, but the reality of the Nazis' intentions first came into my life when I was just 7 or 8 years old.

The only tailor in our small town was run by the Hindlebergs, a well-respected Jewish family. They made all the local men's suits for funerals, weddings and other events. It was said that the tailor's wife, Sarah Hindleberg, designed dresses as grand as any seen in Berlin, or even Paris. The wealthy ladies of the town paid handsomely for her exclusive gowns. My family were not quite wealthy enough to be concerned with high fashion, but I knew the Hindlebergs' only daughter, Ruth, from school.

When the school day finished, some of us would gather in a farmer's field just outside the town. At its wooden gate, we would sit in small groups, talking and playing. It was our special place, secluded from watchful parents and the main road. For me, it was a place of picnics and play; for the older children, it was a secret corner for trysts and young, innocent romance.

Everyone knew Ruth, who was often found legs swinging, sitting on the wooden gate after school, surrounded by adoring boys and envious girls, all competing for her attention. She was a few years older than me, but to my young eyes she already seemed grown up. Black-haired, dark-eyed and strikingly beautiful, I thought Ruth Hindleberg looked just like a film star. Many of the boys were madly in love with her. I would see them hanging around the Hindlebergs' shop, making eyes at Ruth as she packaged jackets, suits and dresses ready to be delivered to wealthy land owners.

It would take only a few short years for those admiring looks to turn to contempt, disgust, and then pure hatred.

One summer day, I was walking my dog Mia and I saw Ruth sitting on the gate. Unusually, she was alone. She sat watching the cattle as they wandered up and down the field, lazily grazing. Plucking up my nerve to talk to her for the first time, I went over, hoping she would not dismiss me for being too childish.

Instead, the lovely girl with the dancing eyes accepted my shy attempt at friendship. She invited me to join her on the fence and we began to talk, about our families, our school friends, our dreams for the future.

'I want to be a nurse one day, in Berlin,' Ruth told me, 'I want to look after children and old people and make them well when they are sick.'

I stared at her, wide-eyed and nodding. I didn't know anyone who had moved out of town, certainly no women who had left to take jobs in the city.

Glancing around quickly, Ruth put her fingers to her lips and looked at me with a serious expression, 'You mustn't tell anyone, but really I should like to be a doctor.'

I looked at her quizzically, not understanding the secrecy.

'When I told my mother I wanted to be a doctor, she cried and said it wasn't allowed. I tried to ask her why, but she told me to never talk about it again. Don't tell anyone, Greta, promise?'

'I won't tell anyone Ruth!' the words rushed from my mouth. Not really understanding why Ruth's mother got upset either, I was more consumed with the fact that this exotic, older girl was confiding in me, boring little Greta. Most of the women I knew were traditional wives and mothers. Those that did work helped out in the local shops or on the farms. Perhaps this was why Ruth's mother was upset at her dreams of becoming a doctor.

Shyly, I took Ruth's hand, 'I promise, Ruth,' I reassured her, 'Friends don't break promises.'

My shyness dissolved as Ruth's face lit up with delight. Squeezing my arm, she jumped down from the fence and pulled me along with her, into the field. We ran around for a while with Mia, then, growing tired, idly collected daisies as we carried on talking. Collapsing onto the grass, we transformed a pile of daisies into crowns and Ruth laughed as I placed one onto her head.

'Let's hope this crown is kosher!' she said.

I laughed too, but I had no idea what kosher meant. My giggles sent my own daisy crown flying from my bobbing head and Mia caught it in her mouth before it hit the floor, only to drop it in disgust after a couple of bites. This made Ruth laugh even more, a tinkling musical sound like rain after a hot day. I longed to be just like her when I was older.

I was an introverted child, and whilst not unpopular exactly, had few close friends of my own, so that afternoon with Ruth stayed in my memory. I longed to make her my friend. A few weeks later while out shopping with my mother, I saw Ruth outside the tailor shop. I waved to her brightly from across the road, and I wanted to ask her back to my house for tea.

Ruth put her hand up in response and the beginning of a smile began to appear on her face, only to be extinguished a moment later as my mother, suddenly furious, rushed down a side street. I had to run to keep up with my mother's brisk march.

Glancing back at Ruth, her face was downcast as she scuffed her shoes into the dirt. Passers-by continued walking past, giving her drooping figure a wide berth, without even looking at her. It was almost as if she wasn't there, as if she were a ghost.

I skidded into my mother as she came to an abrupt stop.

'We don't talk to them, Greta. We don't talk to them ever!'

I had never seen my mother like this. Her voice angry, her face afraid.

Scared, I asked, 'What do you mean?'

She took my hands and told me,

'You are not to speak to Ruth or any members of her family. Their shop has been closed and they will be moved on.'

There was no time to question as she pulled me back towards the main street. As our neighbours went about their business, my mother announced loudly to anyone passing,

'The Jews are very bad people, Greta. That's right, very bad.'

An old couple walking past both nodded in agreement at my mother's outburst. The man tipped his hat in response and then spat a huge gob of phlegm into the gutter.

I felt mortified that Ruth had seen all this. As I looked over, I saw her mother Sarah pulling her back inside the shop. In a heartbeat, she was gone.

My mother never said an unkind word about anyone and she was known for her sweet nature. I remained shocked and deeply confused.

I decided not to ask any more questions about Ruth, the Hindlebergs or the Jews.

As we trudged home, I began to realise that it wasn't just my mother who had changed. We passed a group of soldiers, then another, and I realised that their appearance had become more and more commonplace over the previous months. The military were now frequent visitors to our cafes and shops as they strolled around town with their girlfriends.

I thought about the whispered conversations I heard late at night from my parents' room. I looked up at the whining plane circling above, one of many that had lately started to appear in our skies.

At school, more of our lessons seemed to centre on Germany and the superior talents of our people. One day, Ruth and her brothers stopped coming to class. At first, I thought perhaps the Hindlebergs had decided to home-school their children because of their religion. It was only as our teachers began to parrot my mother's words about the Jews being bad people that I realised they had been banned from our school.

I realised that the Jews were no longer welcome in my town or anywhere in Germany. For a long time I didn't understand. I thought of Ruth and making daisy chains, and I remembered her parents giving out treats to the children of the town from their shop on holidays.

At home that night, my mother and my father sat me down at the dining table in our best room at the front of the house. It was only used on very special occasions and important family meetings.

I stared at the white tablecloth bright against the heavy wood, a single ray of light shone through the thick dark curtains. The room was heavy with a feeling I didn't understand. I was afraid, but did not know why, or of what.

'We need to explain some things to you, Greta,' my mother said, 'very important things that you must not forget.'

My father lifted his hand to my face, and gently but firmly, raised my chin to look him in the eye. His expression was stern.

'Life is going to get even better for us and Germany, Greta,' he said. 'The Führer is making a lot of changes and we need to understand our place.'

I looked at him, puzzled.

'Greta, as a police officer I now belong to the Orpo, which is headed by the SS. This means I work for the Führer. It matters very much that people see us following his orders. This includes you.'

In his uniform, I had always been intimidated by my father. He looked so large and menacing, more like a soldier than a police officer. I was so young and did not understand the significance of my father's increased powers. All I knew was he was now an important person who had to be obeyed.

'Herr Hitler's orders are to make sure all Jews in the area are identified and moved out. The Führer says they are no longer German citizens and have no rights. It is my duty to see this happens.'

My father's words made no sense. The Hindleberg family had been part of our town for generations, and surely my father knew they were not bad people. Why would the Führer think that Ruth and her family were not good citizens? Why would my parents believe that too?

He pointed to a family photo on the mantelpiece: my father's arm proudly around my mother's waist as she stood smiling behind Hans and me. My brother and I laughing and relaxed.

'As a family, we must respect the Führer's wisdom and authority and you all must do as I say, without question.'

I nodded at him, wanting to cry.

'Greta, from now on, you must never talk to any Jews.'

'Not even Ruth? Not the Hindlebergs?' The words burst out of me before I could control my mouth.

My father frowned and banged the table, hard.

'No Greta! Not the Hindlebergs, not their filthy children. No Jews, ever!'

My eyes filled with tears and I turned to my mother, appealing for her help. She was cold and silent as my father continued.

'If a Jew speaks to you, let me know straight away, or our family could get in very serious trouble.'

As my father brushed his blonde hair away from his brow, I noticed for the first time his forehead was furrowed with lines. He had aged.

'If Hans was older and not asleep, he too would be given the same instructions,' my father told me, his voice softening. With a wave of his hand, my father signalled to my mother and me that the conversation was at an end and suggested I went to bed.

After that night, everything seemed to change. I became watchful and measured. I listened as my teachers began to tell us in every lesson that German children were superior. Our obedience, self-sacrifice and discipline, they told us, would make our country the greatest in the world. I was proud to be a German. But in the corner of my mind was an uneasy feeling that never quite left me alone. It fluttered around my head like a bird flapping its wings against a cage.

I heard whispered conversations among adults – my parents, teachers, shopkeepers and customers – about people disappearing. After the day I waved at Ruth, talk about the Jews as 'inferior' and as 'enemies' of the German people seemed to be everywhere – on the radio, in newspapers, at school, even in the newsreels at the movie theatre. Or perhaps, because of Ruth, I just noticed it more.

As Germany began to change, so did my father. Once cheerful, caring, just and compassionate, he seemed to be always brooding, always on the edge of anger. I began to forget the last time I had seen him really smile or scoop my mother into his arms as they both laughed with happiness.

Weeks after they had talked to me in the best room, I woke late at night to hear hurried footsteps outside. Doors banged and engines revved. Headlights from one, two and then three large vehicles lit the ceiling of my bedroom, one after another. I heard sharp words spoken in anger and the scuffling of feet, followed by the sound of women's muffled voices cut off mid-flow, then men shouting and a baby crying. Finally came the sharp crack of doors closing as the vehicles moved away into the distance.

My bedroom was at the very top of the house. As I heard the vehicles move away, I desperately wanted to go to the window, but I was too fearful. Some of the voices shouting seemed familiar. I was worried that if I had been seen at my bedroom window, I might be taken away too. I hugged my favourite doll, Ingrid, and tightly shut my eyes. I eventually fell into a fitful sleep.

The next morning, my father was not at the breakfast table and I nervously asked my mother why he was absent. I did not enquire about the sounds of the previous night.

'He has been working all night on party business, Liebchen, he'll be back later. You know what an important man your father is.'

Her tone was soft, her eyes never left mine as she spoke. I knew she didn't want me to ask any more questions. She looked exhausted, and the conversation was abandoned as she encouraged my brother to eat his breakfast.

I ate in silence and left for school, walking slowly through the town.

As I turned into the street where I had last seen Ruth, I stopped short. The Hindlebergs' shop was closed, shutters at all the doors, windows smashed. Splinters of glass and shards of wood decorated the floor.

I looked around and saw the cafe run by a husband and wife called the Cohen's was also boarded over, as was the house next door and one opposite. On the doors was painted a yellow star and just one word: 'JUDE'.

I never saw Ruth, her family or the Cohens ever again.

CHAPTER 3

I jerked awake at the sound of water splashing. My mother was wading out of the stream. I had no idea how long I had slept. I rolled onto my side, blinking. Hans was already awake and building a fort out of the mud on the bank. I watched my mother finally getting dressed. Her back was red and, in places, scratched and bleeding. As she put on her coat, I saw that it was splattered with mud from the field.

I thought of the animals on the farm outside town and how, on the way home from school, we would often laugh as they mated. Heat filled my cheeks as I realised why the soldier had taken my mother into the field.

My mother met my father when she was only 17, and he had been her first and only boyfriend. She had been a virgin until they had married in the local church.

Hans was too young to understand what rape was, but he knew that our mother had been terribly hurt by the Soviet soldier. My brother stopped playing and waited for our mother's instructions.

As she buttoned up her coat, mother beckoned to us and we continued on our way. This time we kept off the path, heading back into the woods.

'We're travelling north,' said my mother. Her eyes downcast.

My brother opened his mouth to speak, but I put my fingers to my lips, looking at mother and shaking my head.

As mother walked ahead, I took Hans' hand, leaned toward him and whispered.

'We must be quiet now little one, so no one else finds us. We must be very brave, Hans. You must be a strong little man.'

Hans nodded with a grim determination I had never seen before as he began to march behind our mother. I sighed in relief that there would be no idle chatter or questions from my young brother.

As we walked, I wondered how my mother knew we were heading north. Every tree and bit of green looked exactly the same. After the sunshine in the clearing around the stream, the dense woodland felt sinister. The trees loomed above and around us, their branches rustling and sighing in the wind. Hans felt it too, and instead of looking for solace from our mother, he took my arm, holding it tightly.

We walked for hours until the trees thinned and a light scattering of wild flowers sprayed the floor like a fallen rainbow. Hans and I started to pick them and, as a distraction, I encouraged him to try to remember their names.

I put a flower in my hair and one behind Hans' ear, and he gave a tiny giggle as I teased him about mispronouncing the name of one of the plants. This unexpected signal of childish fun jolted my mother out of her thoughts, and she stopped to watch us. I moved towards her with a handful of wild flowers and tried to place one in her hair. Suddenly furious, she pushed me away.

'No!' she said in a low voice.

Dropping the flower, I chose a prettier one and offered it to her.

'But mother, you will look so pretty!' I tried to sound light, but my voice trembled.

Her anger gone as suddenly as it had arrived, mother closed her eyes for a moment and when she opened them again, there was not a trace of emotion to be found in them.

With a steady voice, she met my hopeful gaze and said flatly, 'I will never be pretty again.'

She turned away and continued walking.

Hans and I looked at each other and began to trail after her. Without a word, we both dropped the small bunches of flowers in our hands to the ground. I took the flower out of my hair and threw it aside. Hans pulled the flower quickly from behind his ear and began to remove the petals, one by one. When only the stalk was left, he looked pleased. The whole time mother strode ahead, oblivious.

We continued onwards, the sun began to dip and the evening shadows grew. Suddenly we heard a voice carried on the wind.

A low gruff timbre – a man.

We stopped. I held my breath and listened. The moaning of the trees seemed to fill the whole world. My mother gestured to me and Hans to hide behind a tree, as she began to move stealthily towards the voice.

When she disappeared into the trees, I remembered her words before the soldier took her into the field.

'If you hear gunfire, run and keep running till you find a place to hide. I will come and find you.'

I knew if there was a shout, a scream or a gun fired I would have to escape with Hans, but to where? Nowhere in this country I had always called home seemed safe.

Five minutes, ten minutes, fifteen minutes passed. I counted every second of each minute to quell my fear, holding Hans close. Petrified he barely moved and remained mute.

My mother reappeared with another tight-lipped smile on her face. She was with an elderly man who wore a jaunty hat, brown jacket and crumpled trousers. He looked friendly enough, but my heart began to hammer as I saw he was carrying a shotgun. Then in an instant, a tiny bundle of fur moving at great speed shot through the woods towards us.

A small dog jumped into view, furiously wagging its tail, then sat at my feet begging for attention. Both Hans and I relaxed as the old man cleared his throat and said,

'This is Georgie, children. He very much wants you to make a fuss of him.'

Hans and I knelt down and began to pet Georgie, who rolled on his back in delight at the sudden attention. Our fears disappeared as both Hans and I stroked the little dog, his soft face nuzzling into our hands.

The old man continued, 'My name is Rufus, I live with my wife in a cottage just ahead of those trees.'

His mottled brown hand pointed to three huge trees a short way behind us. They seemed to stretch endlessly to the sky. With a quick nod from mother, we all followed Rufus into a clearing where a one-storey tumbledown building stood. A few chickens scratched the dirt out front and a bent old woman swept dust from the front door.

Looking up, she jumped in surprise as she saw my bedraggled family, but visibly softened as Rufus came into her view.

'Well, well!' she said, with a laugh, 'We don't get many people passing this way!'

As we reached her, she stepped aside and gestured to the front door and its newly swept step.

'Come in, come in!' she laughed again, 'We are so glad to welcome you to our home.'

Hans and I sat down on a couple of stools, while my mother accepted a comfortable chair by a fireplace where a few embers glowed. Georgie curled up at her feet and was immediately asleep.

The room had a stone floor and wooden walls. At its centre was a huge bed, piled high with blankets and goat skins. The bed dominated the room and I began to feel tired just imagining its softness. Floral curtains hung at the windows. Jugs and ornaments filled the shelf above the fireplace. This was a home, cosy, lived-in and loved.

The old woman interrupted my observations by placing a warm cup of goat's milk in my hands, offering the same to my mother and Hans.

'Here drink this, I've just milked Jenni,' she said. Then, seeing our confused faces, she added, 'our goat!' and giggled.

Satisfied that we were all sipping contentedly, the old woman took a step back and smiled, then suddenly burst out laughing.

'I've told you the goat's name but not mine!' she exclaimed, 'that's how unaccustomed we are to guests these days!'

Shaking her head, she introduced herself.

'I'm Joanne,' she took Rufus' arm and patted his hand, 'and we're both very glad to welcome you to our home.'

I drank the creamy liquid so quickly that I felt sick almost immediately. I willed myself not to vomit and I didn't. After days with only the soldier's stale apple and cheese, fresh food was too precious to waste.

I watched my mother sip her milk, and saw the tension leave her body. She closed her eyes and within a few minutes was asleep. The gentle breathing of the little dog at her feet matched my mother's tiny snores.

Joanne got a blanket from the huge double bed and tucked it around my mother as if she was her baby, smoothing the material over her sleeping body and taking the empty cup out of her hand with great care. For the first time on our journey, I felt secure.

While mother slept, Joanne took me and Hans into the kitchen and store room. She gave us chunks of homemade bread and goat's cheese and we ate until we could barely move. Only when we were completely full, did we win Joanne's approval.

As we returned to the main room, Joanne said, 'It's so good to have children in the house again.'

Rufus sat in the corner smoking his pipe, his ragged hat tipped over rheumy eyes.

'What an adventure you've had, walking like explorers through the woods,' he said, 'what did you see?'

Hans and I looked nervously at one another. Neither of us wanted to speak about the soldier.

Perhaps Rufus saw our discomfort, because he quickly interrupted his own question, 'What wildlife did you see?'

Relieved, Hans leapt up and replied,

'I saw a fox! But it was dead. But it still counts, doesn't it? We saw a cow, it was still alive!'

Rufus chuckled, 'Yes, little one, it still counts. Did you see any wild flowers?'

As Hans told Rufus about every plant and animal he had seen on our journey, I leaned back next to the now blazing fire and listened. Between Hans' excited observations, Rufus taught him the proper names for the plants we had forgotten. He told us that for decades he had been a gamekeeper for the big houses and mansions nearby.

Rufus was a man of the land and knew everything there was to know about the countryside. He had been born at the cottage and had raised his family there with Joanne. Living simply with a small number of animals and Rufus' knowledge of the countryside meant they had enough food to eat, even at times when the war left Rufus with no work. The cottage was so deep in the woods, they had never been discovered by soldiers or fleeing refugees.

I listened to the gentle sound of Rufus' deep voice telling us all about life in the woods and slowly, though I fought against it, my eyes and limbs quickly grew heavy. Joanne noticed our energy was flagging and fetched extra blankets to make us a bed. That night my family slept on the floor of the main room, with earthy goatskins piled on top of us.

For the first time in weeks my mother cuddled me and Hans as we drifted into sleep. It felt as if she had finally returned from that dark place the soldier had taken her to, when they had disappeared together into the long grass.

My eyes were so heavy with fatigue, I could barely open them, but I felt my mother's lips on my cheek and heard her kiss Hans before I fell asleep. Nestling into the warmth of the blankets, I heard her sigh gently as she whispered, 'Goodnight, my darlings, sleep well.

'Sweet dreams.'

I couldn't help but feel comforted. This was the first time my mother had said those two words since we had left our home, a much-loved ritual for our bedtime throughout our childhood.

There were no dreams waiting for me that night, good or bad; instead only an exhausted blackness awaited me, from which I awoke still tired. I was the last up. Hans was already outside helping Rufus with the goats, and my mother bustled around Joanne in the kitchen, aiding her with the cooking and preparation of food.

'Come help us, Liebchen,' my mother smiled across the kitchen, 'look, we're making preserves.'

She seemed more content than I had seen her for months, even before we fled our home. Although I was still tired, I soon forgot my aching muscles as I lost myself in Joanne and my mother's gentle chatter, and the calming repetition of stirring a saucepan bubbling with chunks of vegetables and herbs.

As my mother strained the last of the preserve into jars, she sent me outside to help with other chores. I went outside into the watery sunshine.

Hans was in front of the house, with Rufus.

'Greta, Greta!' cried Hans, so excited he almost dropped the axe in his hand, 'I milked the goats and collected the eggs! Now Rufus is teaching me to chop wood for the fire, come and see!'

Hans struggled to raise the axe before striking the wood. He barely made an impact with its blade alone, and Rufus helped him lift and strike the wood to create logs for the fire. When Hans became tired, I took over and found that physical work had its own rewards.

The next day at the cottage was much the same, as were the many days that followed. Over the next month we learnt the everyday life of

Joanne and Rufus' woodland existence: helping the old couple with their animals, chopping wood for the store, cleaning sheds, digging another vegetable patch. It was hard work, done mostly outside, but, divided between us, easily managed. Each morning we woke to a predictable routine: breakfast, milking goats, collecting eggs, tending the animals, sowing, weeding, and preserving food for leaner times. Our days closed with a nourishing dinner each evening, shared around the large kitchen table.

Hans loved being with Rufus, and though he was only 11, a young man's muscles were starting to form as he became accustomed to the physical labour. Working outside made me stronger too, but my favourite times were with Joanne in the kitchen: making bread, jams, and sometimes even small biscuits or cakes.

My mother swapped recipes with Joanne as we worked, gossiping about household matters and life before the war. My mother became more like her old self and I welcomed her return.

Joanne adored her, and often hugged my mother to her ample bosom. Her sympathetic glances and whispered words of consolation made me suspect my mother had told the old lady about the Soviet.

The simple daily chores in the woodland homestead were exactly what we needed to heal the trauma of fleeing our own home and the incident with the soldier. Painful memories and fears for the future could be put on hold. It felt like the cottage had magical powers as it seemed so removed from conflict. The ending of the war and all its atrocities seemed far, far away, along with our past.

But neither would remain distant for long.

CHAPTER 4

Each evening after dinner, mother would make our excuses to the elderly couple, and take us for a short walk in the woods. Only then were we able to speak of the topics our mother had forbidden us to discuss in front of Rufus and Joanne: why we had left our home, our plans for the future, and the one subject my mother made clear we were never to mention, our father.

Strolling through the countryside in the gathering dusk, mother explained, 'We must not talk about your father and his work for the party, even with other Germans. Telling people about your father could put all our lives at risk. We do not know who is safe for us, who we can trust, not even people as warm hearted as Rufus and Joanne.'

I hated deceiving the two people who had been the most kind to us since we left our town. Rufus and Joanne never asked about our past or pushed for information about my father, so my mother said it wasn't really lying.

I urged my mother to think again and said,

'Rufus and Joanne are so good-natured, mother, perhaps they would understand? Father didn't do anything wrong, he was a policeman not a soldier.'

My mother's expression was a mixture of pity, fury and fear. When she spoke, it was through gritted teeth.

'Greta, Hans, your father worked for the Nazi party. It is true that he never chose to, he never signed up as a soldier, but the Nazis made the police part of the SS. The Allies are now chasing down members of the party. We are no different to the families of senior Nazi officers, no different to the wife and children of Goebbels himself!'

I dared not defy my mother's instructions. I had seen enough people disappear from our town to know there was reason for us to be afraid. My feelings about my father and his role within the Nazi party were confused. My mother always presented his job as if my strong, resourceful father had no control over his actions. I wanted to believe in this version with all my heart. There was no denying that whatever my father had done for the party he had been clearly very good at it.

After the disappearance of the Hindlebergs and other Jewish families in our home town, father was promoted again. Along with this promotion came a much bigger house – still opulently furnished with the previous family's furniture – which had belonged to the town's Jewish bank manager before he and his family were removed. Men dressed in high ranking Nazi uniforms would visit for coffee and schnapps. An expensive gramophone was given to my father by an SS officer, and, as it played, my mother's simpering words echoed upstairs. My brother and I would often creep down from our bedrooms, sit on the stairs and watch the adults through the spines of the bannister.

The German Commandant was a frequent guest at our new home, and he was clearly enchanted by mother. She seemed to love our new station in life and appeared oblivious to the price others might be paying for our success, as she laughed and chatted to the same men in Nazi uniforms who had taken away families that were once our friends. Underneath, a strange tension crackled. Often my mother's laughter was too loud, too high, and brittle.

My father was a respected member of the Orpo, and, as such, was influential and valued. Yet Father had vanished too on a night time mission with the Nazi Commandant and had been missing for over six months.

The good times and parties ended and the sound of my mother's giggles over the music of the gramophone stopped. People in the street would ignore us whenever we ventured outside. Everyone watchful, suspicious and scared.

I sensed mother's fear grow with each day of father's absence. She never admitted that he could be dead, and barely spoke of him. Any remarks made by me or Hans about father's absence were swiftly negated by mother's firm tone and mannerisms.

Within a few months, the Allies invaded and our lives would never be the same again.

Each day, we were greeted by the sounds of bombs in the distance heralding the Allies' advance.

One morning, mother made the decision for us to leave, a bag packed at her feet.

'We are going to visit our relatives in the mountains, your aunt and uncle,' she announced lightly, as if telling us of a quick trip to the grocers.

Hans and I stared blankly. We had never heard of family members in the mountain regions.

'Why mutter? Why can't we stay here, at home? I don't want to go!' burst out Hans.

Mother's face was instantly full of rage.

'It is not safe, Hans! Why can't you understand? The Allies are coming, foreigners, to end the war and they are looking for people just like us! They would not understand that your father was not a real Nazi, that we are innocent. We must find somewhere safe where we can hide. And we must go now. The Allies will be in the area in only a few days.'

Once on the road, she censored any mention of our father or our past.

That very day, we set off from the town where I was born. My mother painted with the colourful brushstrokes of her imagination the idyllic life that awaited us with relatives in the mountains. As the days went by and we ran out of food, our aunt and uncle's simple abode became a paradise in my mother's description, growing more lavish by the day. She talked as if life there would be utterly untouched by the war.

Although we did not speak of him with my mother, Hans occasionally talked to me about our father with the hope of his return. I was more pessimistic. I did not want to believe he was dead, but my father was organised, precise, and disciplined. I knew if there were any way to do so, he would have sent a message or found a way back to us long before now. I feared my father was probably lying in a ditch somewhere with a bullet in his brain.

So now we were at the cottage, it was Rufus and Joanne who fast became the steady rudder in our crumbling world.

Once a week, Rufus would take me and Hans out with him to set traps for rabbits. Away from the cottage and from Joanne, the old man talked about his son Jon and grandson Dietrich. Both had been soldiers in the German Army, killed in the early years of the war.

Joanne never talked about them again, the grief too large to ever be spoken.

But Rufus loved to tell us about his 'beloved boys'. For him, it seemed a way of keeping them alive.

'Jon always combed his hair to the right, then to the left, then right, then left again,' he laughed, 'It had to be just so!

'And Dietrich, ah, you remind me of him, Hans, how he loved to sing and dance. He helped me all the time when he was little, just like you do.'

Rufus taught us all their favourite songs, and we sang them on our trips to set the traps as we meandered through the woods with the sure-footed old man. These were often the times Rufus seemed happiest, and I was glad that we could be the audience for the stories he so desperately needed to tell to keep 'his boys alive' in his memory.

One afternoon, as Hans dozed next to me after a long walk, Rufus quietly shared with me,

'I can still see my boys walking out of the cottage in their uniforms, Greta. Ah, they were so desperate to go to war, so certain they would be heroes.

'Young men can be so reckless, Greta, so full of ambition, they do not realise the reality of battle. That war, even if it lets you survive, will fill your heart with a blackness that can never be lifted again.'

There was nothing to be said.

As week followed week, I hoped we would stay with Rufus and his wife forever.

It wasn't to be.

The unseasonable warmth of early spring brought fresh life into the woods but it brought more work for us. The vegetables had to be watered more often, weeds grew and birds and other woodland animals tried to steal and eat our crops or kill the livestock.

Hans and I enjoyed the extra work. It meant more time outside with

Rufus, who we both had come to adore like a grandfather. As we learnt more about the countryside, our skills improved and we needed no prompting for the set everyday tasks.

Rufus would joke, 'Soon I will be able to retire!' as we busied ourselves chopping wood and caring for the livestock.

But a man like Rufus could never stop working. His heart belonged to the land to which he had devoted his life. Instead, he began to spend more time hunting, particularly in the deeper parts of the wood, tracking deer to kill and preserve for the store. He would often be gone for most of the day, returning with a doe slung over his shoulders as the sun dipped low.

After setting off early for one such hunting trip, none of us was concerned at his absence throughout the day. But when night fell and Rufus had still not returned, we all knew something terrible had happened. Rufus had not spent a night away from Joanne since the deaths of his son and grandson.

'It's OK, Joanne, he's probably just fallen asleep next to the fire,' Hans told the old woman.

Joanne patted his head softly, saying only, 'Good boy.'

As the hours stretched with no sign of the old man, Joanne refused to go to bed and sat on a stool facing the door, waiting. At first my mother busied herself in the kitchen, made us all a weak tea and then prepared for bed. There was still no sign of Rufus.

Eventually Hans and I fell asleep on our blankets, but Joanne and my mother were still awake as we slipped into dreams.

I was woken by a scratching at the door. Joanne rushed to open it from her watching place at the hearth, and Georgie sped into the room, issuing short, urgent yaps that soon lengthened into howls. The first rays of light were dusting an ink blue sky.

With desperation in her eyes and knowing she could never navigate the woods with our speed, Joanne urged us, 'Please, follow him!'

My mother, Hans and I didn't hesitate in following the little terrier into the spring morning, as Joanne waited anxiously in the doorway.

We tore through the woods, Hans sprinting ahead after Georgie, with me next and then mother behind.

Georgie led us to the edge of the ravine at the top of the river. As Hans reached the little dog and picked him up, he must have seen what lay beyond. He screamed.

Skidding to Hans' side, I looked below. Rufus lay, face down, his body spread over a granite shelf by the river side. He was clearly dead, his neck twisted into an unnatural angle. My mother appeared at my side and gasped, covering her mouth and turning away for a moment.

Hans, his face streaming with tears, paced from side to side, trying to work out a way down to reach Rufus. Helpless, I joined him, but try as we might, there was no safe way to navigate the jagged rocks and dangerous outcrops of stone and mud. After ten minutes, my mother gently pulled us back from the edge, and said, 'We must go back to Joanne.'

At that moment, Georgie jumped from Hans' arms and achieving what we could not, scrambled down the perilous rock face and reached Rufus' tangled body. Georgie licked Rufus' blue face, yelped once and then stood sentry by his master's body. Despite our encouragement, Georgie would not budge from Rufus.

Resigned, we trudged slowly back with mother to the cottage.

The thought of telling the old woman that she had lost her husband made my stomach feel like a stone. When we arrived, mother signalled to Hans and me to stay outside.

My brother and I stood in silence as a terrible wail rose from the cottage, full of love and longing for Rufus, her life-long companion. With her remaining family gone, Joanne now had no living blood relative.

For the next two days, Joanne cried and cried, barely speaking. My mother kept close vigil on her whilst Hans and I continued the daily chores, clinging to the illusion of normality to stave off our own grief. Despite my mother's efforts, Joanne refused to eat, taking only small sips of water.

Hans and I returned to the ravine every day in an effort to bring Georgie home, hoping that the little dog would want to comfort Joanne.

Standing at the edge – but never looking over – we would call and call the little dog, but he refused to leave Rufus' side. The terrier remained like this for weeks, until the forest claimed his life and, eventually, the bodies of the old man and his dog were reclaimed by the wild animals, ever lurking in the woods for an easy meal.

While mother took responsibility for the cottage and caring for Joanne, it was left to Hans and me to carry on feeding the animals, taking care of the goats and their kids, and making sure the fruit trees and vegetables were thriving.

The days lengthened and the countryside slowly flowered, ripening in the warming, spring sun. Soon, the forest was buzzing with life, insects, birds, and buds.

As the forest came to life, Joanne was shrinking, becoming smaller and smaller. Shortly after Rufus died, she caught a cold, which she was unable to shake. The old lady barely ate and the cold developed into a hacking cough deep in Joanne's chest. It was difficult for her to talk, so her usual chatter faded to nothing.

Every day and evening, she sat wrapped in blankets before the fireplace, staring blindly at the front door, as if waiting for Rufus to return with Georgie at his heels.

Several nights after Rufus' death, Joanne suddenly spoke and asked my mother,

'I need you to go and get an old suitcase from the attic, Helga. It's full of Jon and Dietrich's clothes.'

My mother looked shocked, and sent Hans, who quickly returned with a small, brown and dusty old case. He helped Joanne to open it and sat down at her feet as she gave him a small, rare smile.

She picked out pieces of fabric, shirts, and trousers, all carefully and neatly packed inside.

'These bits of material are all that remain of my son and my grandson, Hans.' She showed him a cream plaid shirt, then looked up at my mother.

'Please use these clothes, they are no good for anyone but the living.'

Joanne raised the shirt to her nose and smelled the material, shaking her head.

'Once I could smell my Jon and Dietrich in the fabric,' she took a long breath. 'Did you know each person has their own smell? Our individual perfume envelopes our clothes and identifies us like a fingerprint. My Jon smelt like the pines in the mountains, Dietrich like the dew on flowers at daybreak.'

She began to cry, 'Even the faintest scents of my son and grandson have gone, as they have gone. Rufus is gone. Soon I will be gone, too.'

My mother rushed to Joanne's side.

'Your cough is getting better, Joanne. I will not allow you to talk this way. You will recover your strength, you have to be well. Hans and Greta need you.' In a plaintive whisper, my mother said, 'I need you too, Joanne.'

The old lady stopped crying and touched my mother's stricken face as if to reassure.

'Please help me into bed, Helga.'

My mother ushered Joanne under the goatskins. She lay back on the pillows and, for the first time in days, slept for hours.

I knew we were all hoping this was a turning point, and that the Joanne we loved so well would come back to us.

The next day, Joanne was up early and was pottering in the kitchen.

As I scrambled out of bed, so happy to see the old woman back on her feet, she smiled at me and said, 'I've a fancy to make some soup, Greta. Do you know where the wild garlic grows in the wood?'

Racing to her side, Hans burst out, 'I do! I know where it is, Greta! It's the one with the pretty white flowers and the funny smell that -'

Rufus had shown us the garlic and I knew my brother stopped himself saying the old man's name to spare Joanne.

Joanne nodded and carried on, 'Well, it's very good for coughs and colds and I think it will make me feel much better. Can you both gather some for me today?'

Hans and I agreed happily, delighted to see the old woman back on her feet. After our morning jobs, we set off into the woods at lunchtime. Mother offered to tend the goats and was singing to herself as she started to clean the sheds.

Joanne came outside for the first time in days to chat to my mother. Whether it was an accident or by design, somehow the old lady set the billy goat loose.

The male goat was large, fierce and fleet of foot. He could run for miles and had led Hans and I a merry dance on many occasions through the rutted paths and steep banks surrounding the cottage.

My mother raced after the billy, leaving Joanne to prepare the vegetables. The old lady waved her off from the doorway, laughing at the antics of the goat. My mother told me later that the sound of Joanne's laugh returning had lifted her heart.

An hour later, Hans and I neared the cottage, laden with water from the spring, wild garlic, and herbs for the soup. Only fifteen minutes' walk from our destination, we met my mother leading the now captured and sullen billy goat.

'He escaped!' mother explained, 'It's taken me over an hour to catch him, but it was worth it just to hear Joanne laugh again!'

We made the short journey in high spirits, filled with thoughts of Joanne's cooking and returning laughter, and looking forward to sharing a meal once again, together at the large, old kitchen table.

As the cottage came into sight, we all suddenly stopped. Instead of the clanking of pots, there was an odd silence and atmosphere. Something was very wrong.

My mother threw the string holding the billy goat into my hands, hoisted up her skirt and ran towards the cottage. Hans and I followed, pulling the reluctant billy.

Joanne was hanging from the low beam in the kitchen, an upturned chair at her feet, her shadow moving gently over the table-top, which was set for only three. Her eyes bulging and below her a pool of urine steam rising from its puddle on the stone floor.

My brother and I froze where we stood in shock, while my mother climbed onto the table and cut Joanne down, her tiny body sliding from my mother's arms onto the table. The same table on which Joanne had given birth to her son and fed her family for decades.

Her neck was bruised, scorched with rope burns. My mother laid Joanne on the dirt floor and admonished her for killing herself, tenderly pushing hair out of the old lady's sightless eyes.

Taking Joanne into a close embrace, my mother rocked back and forth.

'Why? Why?' she shouted to the empty air, weeping. But we all knew why. She could not live without Rufus, without her son and grandson.

A long time seemed to pass. The three of us frozen in one moment, then jerked back to reality as my mother began to remove Joanne's jumper.

Placing it to one side, she started to untie the laces to remove the old lady's shoes. Still crying, she held each shoe up to the light and turned them over, checking for holes.

'What are you doing?' cried Hans, rushing to her side and trying to take the shoes out of mothers hands, 'Stop it! Leave her alone!'

Not looking at him, my mother coldly pushed him away.

'My shoes are getting worn; these are the right size for me. We might have to walk many more miles yet. The jumper will keep you or Greta warm.'

Her voice was flat, but my mother was still crying as she said, 'I need her shoes, I need her shoes.'

My mother looked at me and said, 'We need her clothes, they are no use to the dead.'

I pulled Hans to my side, but instead he moved towards the billy and hugged his matted skin, burying his face into his fur and hiding his eyes from the spectacle of our mother robbing a dead woman of her clothes.

The usual feisty billy goat stood as still as a stone effigy.

We wrapped Joanne in an old, white sheet which made her look like a wizened bride, and placed her carefully on the small, wooden cart. Hans insisted on pushing it all the way along the broken tracks into the woods.

We buried Joanne deep in the countryside, not far from the ravine where Rufus died. None of us cried; even Hans was stony-faced.

As we calmly stood by Joanne's graveside, all three of us dirty with sweat and earth, there was no room for tears or emotions. We all had to go into practical mode, to keep surviving.

Inside though, I was screaming and screaming.

I was learning to separate myself from feelings to push them down deep, deep inside of me into yet another darkness.

CHAPTER 5

Despite the loss of Rufus and Joanne, we all wanted to stay. Not only did the cottage offer everything we needed, it retained an atmosphere of kindness that none of us wanted to leave.

The house was a home and, more importantly, it seemed to be secret from the outside world. During the time we had spent with the old couple, we had all learnt new skills and been given specific chores.

A few nights after Joanne's suicide, my mother told us,

'If we all work hard and continue taking care of the animals and copying everything that Rufus and Joanne taught us, we will have enough food. This is a good place to live away from all the madness of fighting.

'Just think, in a few months when the war is finally over, how beautiful the mountains will look then. Think how many hugs you will get from your aunts and uncles.'

I glared at my mother. I didn't believe in the house waiting for us in the mountains. It seemed at best implausible and at worst a fairy story.

Sensing my scepticism, she looked away and told my brother brusquely, 'Hans, you will weed and tend to the vegetable plot, and take care of the hens. Also check the traps for rabbits.

'Greta and I will look after the house, outbuildings and the goats. Hans, you can help us to milk them. Of course, we will need much more water now the weather is becoming warmer. We have to make cheese and preserve food so that we always have a store, just in case of harsher times.'

So, from dawn until dusk we toiled relentlessly to store, salt and preserve as much food as possible. Each night falling into bed exhausted.

My mother had transferred all of the goat's skins from our bed on the floor to the double bed where Rufus and Joanne had shared their married life. Instead of feeling squeamish, Hans and I loved smelling the familiar tang of Rufus' tobacco and the floury perfume of Joanne's hair.

One evening before bed and over cups of weak tea, Hans and I sat at the fireplace wriggling our toes.

'You've grown, Hans, your trousers barely cover your ankles!' I teased.

All of the fresh air and hard work was making us both stronger, and Hans, nearing puberty, was growing fast. My mother noticed and brought over the suitcase full of clothes that once belonged to Joanne and Rufus' dead son and grandson.

She shook out a wool shirt, a couple of white shifts, vests, three pairs of tweed trousers and three jumpers, laying them out in the flickering light of the fire.

'These clothes are big, but we can roll up the sleeves and double over the material.'

I glanced at Hans, worried he would protest, but he was lost in the flames. We had both learnt to forsake sentimentality. Clothes were of no use to the dead.

Life once again settled into a pattern of sorts as the three of us began to settle into our new life alone in the cottage as a family. But within a couple of weeks of Joanne's death, the animals began to sicken.

Rufus and Joanne had kept only a modest selection of livestock: three nannies, the Billy, three kids, some hens and one rooster, but each played a vital role within the small farmyard's ecosystem.

Slowly, each group of animals stopped eating and drinking. Then the goats stopped giving milk, producing a green discharge around their teats and stomach. The baby kids could not suckle and died.

Even the billy was affected with green gunge hanging in ribbons around his stomach and tail.

The hens and then the rooster sat down and hardly moved.

I kissed Jenni, the eldest nanny goat and Joanne's favourite, and begged her, 'Don't die, please don't die, we need you so much and I will miss you!' But she only stared back at me as I stroked her velvet face.

My mother kept her focus on pragmatic concerns, though her growing desperation became obvious as the animals worsened.

'Perhaps we need to keep the animals even cleaner,' she told us, washing the vile, green slime from the goats' coats. She shouted to Hans, 'Get some fresh water and clean out the whole area where the hens sleep at night.'

'But I've already done that!' Hans answered in confusion.

'Clean it again and again!' came her reply.

By the end of the third week, despite our best efforts, all the livestock was dead or dying. Only a few chickens remained. My mother became scared that whatever had killed the animals might transfer to us. We buried the carcasses deep in the ground, away from the house. The chickens that remained, my mother killed with her bare hands.

Burying the last of the animals, Hans complained, 'Now there's no meat to eat at all.'

'We don't know what ailment killed the animals, Hans,' my mother glared at him. 'It could be anything, so I won't risk us eating any of their meat. We all need to stay healthy.

'We can probably just get by with the vegetables and fruit and the small store of food that Joanne left us in the cupboard.'

Hans ran off into the woods and mother looked at me, appealing for support.

I didn't answer her as I was hot and tired, digging yet another grave, placing a shovel of earth over our livestock.

Hans returned a moment later with a few stray flowers, white ones from the wild garlic. I felt sad and so did he; somehow it was easier to get upset over the goats and hens than it was people.

My brother spluttered through trembling lips,

'Did the animals die because they missed Rufus and Joanne?

'You know how much Joanne loved Jenni and told us she was her favourite goat in the world.'

'I don't know, Hans,' I replied, hugging him to my side. 'Rufus and Joanne taught us a lot of things, but it might be that we just don't know enough about taking care of the animals without them.'

Patting Hans on the head, my mother said, 'But now they are all having fun together in a field full of sunshine, eating lots of grass. Jenni and the others will be so glad to be with Rufus and Joanne again.'

There was a short pause before Hans said, 'Where are they?'

'It's a safe place, where there is no war, lots of food to eat and no fighting,' she said slowly. 'It's called heaven.'

I looked sharply at my mother. We had been told so many times that the Führer did not approve of religious teachings. Hans had little knowledge of the Bible and I could only just remember Sunday school.

Hans said, 'Can we go to heaven, too? Can we go there now? I don't like it here without Rufus and Joanne.'

My mother kissed him on the cheek and led him slowly back to the cottage, changing the subject to bedtime matters.

Perhaps it was naïve of us, but I think all three of us believed that even without the animals, we could remain in our secret cottage home. The preserved food and vegetables would be challenging, but enough to survive.

We were wrong.

A week later, the storms came: days and days of lashing rain and wind made mush of the vegetable patch and washed away the tiny flowers and seedlings that would have grown into fruit. The earth became quicksand beneath our feet and all efforts to save the crops were impossible.

We each eyed the larder with worried eyes, but no one spoke the words: the small store of pickled food, jars of preserved vegetables and a few packets of essentials that Joanne had left would not last long.

One night, I was awoken by a howl of wind. Accustomed to the sound that had haunted our dreams for several nights, I burrowed deeper into the blankets and tried to get back to sleep. I was startled when I heard movement in the kitchen and sat bolt upright.

Checking to make sure I did not wake Hans, I slid out of bed.

My mother was tipping out every cupboard and drawer, pulling back the rugs and moving the furniture.

She barely glanced at me.

'I'm looking to see if Joanne hid anything of value which we could sell on our journey or in a town.'

My heart sank. We were going on the road again.

My mother spent all night arranging clothing and food into piles of supplies for the next part of our flight.

In the morning, Hans and I carefully stacked and tied the bundles onto the small handcart we had used to take Joanne's body into the woods.

I worked quietly, the silence broken only by Hans' sniffles.

My mother looked over at Hans and, for a moment, she seemed defeated.

'We have to leave here as soon as the wind drops and it becomes dryer. We must take as much as we can carry. You both know we will not survive now the animals have died. The few vegetables left are mouldy, the fruit harvest this year will be non-existent.

'We will leave for the next village or town, find work and stay there until we can find transport to the mountains.'

I looked at her and said nothing, as the wind screamed through the eaves like the crying of lost souls.

CHAPTER 6

After the shelter of Rufus and Joanne's cottage, it was a hard task to resume the endless walking with no clear destination. For two days and nights we didn't meet a soul as we weaved across bare fields or wooded areas. Occasionally we would venture onto a small road to find what looked like bundles of clothing. Closer inspection revealed them to be rotting corpses.

In other places we saw the marks of vehicles and boots where tanks and soldiers had been, other times muddy paths covered in footprints showed the route taken by others like us, trying to flee marauding men. Only the distant booming of guns and the whining of planes overhead broke the quiet.

We may not have known where we were going, but our mother had a clear sense of where we were not to go, as we skirted around desolate or dangerous looking settlements that bore the heaviest scars of war.

The first person we met was a solitary woman, in a vivid mauve shawl with more holes than wool, foraging in the grass and debris thrown around by battle. She barely glanced upwards as we approached.

'We're just passing through,' said my mother.

The stranger sniffed and wiped her nose on the sleeve of her encrusted dress and said,

'I've seen far more dangers than you these past months.'

Mother offered her some water. It was a friendly act that expected information in return.

Between gulps of water the stranger needed no prompting and told us,

'They come in waves, the soldiers – some running away from the war, some looking for it. Soviet, English, Canadian, American. So many soldiers.' She looked into the distance, her eyes empty.

'Even our soldiers, so desperate now, so few. They fire their guns and ask questions later, if they ask at all.

'So many soldiers, so many,' she murmured. 'They all look the same after a while, whatever uniform they wear.'

The woman had drunk enough and gave the bottle back to my mother who placed it quickly into our cart.

The stranger started to move away, but my mother stopped her and asked,

'Is there a safe town nearby where my family could find some work?'

Spittle flew from the stranger's mouth and the shawl untwisted from her spiny arms to reveal weeping sores and black bruises. She then took my mother's sweet face in a vice-like grip as she pleaded,

'How can we be safe here or anywhere? There are soldiers everywhere, but not to protect us, just to take.'

Gasping she said, 'If it's not soldiers, it's people like us. Where is there to go?'

My mother prised dirty nails and hands from her face, revealing livid spider-mark shapes on her cheeks. The woman was clearly crazy. Distracted, she moved towards the debris before offering us one more piece of information.

Warning us,

'Don't got into that field. It's full of mines, probably left by our soldiers to dissuade the enemy.

'Yesterday I saw a young man urinating against that tree. The next minute, he was no more as his legs flew this way and that.'

Grimly she moved away and began her relentless task of rooting around for spoils in what was once a small hamlet.

Giving the field a wide berth, we continued our journey, mother's body language closed to any questions, so there was little conversation.

It was a monotonous day of putting one weary foot in front of another. When evening fell, my mother spread her coat under the trees and all three of us crawled beneath. The nights could be very cold.

The next day, we woke covered with dew, our spirits low. I could hardly bear another day of walking, and, from the look of Hans, he was reluctant to move an inch.

As mother prepared to leave, Hans leaned over and whispered to me, 'Does she even know where we are?'

I had been asking myself the same question and feared that mother was lost. Pulling myself together and becoming the big sister, I stretched my cold lips and whispered back,

'Of course she does. Mother always has a plan, and it won't be long now.'

As if just realising that we were over half way up a steep hillside, Hans, now more positive, said, 'At least later today we'll be over the top of this hill and going downwards, so we'll all be less tired!'

Relief washed over me. I didn't know how I would have answered him if he'd asked anything further. If mother did have a plan, she didn't discuss it with me either.

We set off, Hans darting to the left and right of the path, looking for interesting things in the scattered trees and bushes. Though I was tired and my clothes damp, it was good to see Hans behave like the child he was, as this was now a rare sight.

After a couple of hours, mother told us to stop and put her fingers to her mouth to warn us to be quiet. On a track below us, a group of people were walking. It looked like a family of sorts. There was a middle-aged woman, her clothes almost rags, a small boy who was better dressed, and two men walking with two very thin girls about my age.

My mother bit her lip. I saw her reluctance as there were men in the group.

'Wait here,' she said, making up her mind. 'Stay hidden.' She looked at me and nodded, silently signalling to me to watch over Hans.

'But…' Hans began,

My mother was firm, 'I need to talk to them, Hans. They may have information, they might help us.'

We crouched down out of sight as the slight figure of my mother made her way down the hillside.

The group stopped as they saw her and one of the men in the group stepped forward, pushing the others back.

He stood, hands on hips, his head thrust forward. Fear began to dance in my stomach and I shifted my gaze to the rest of the group. They looked menacing.

'They're filthy!' observed Hans.

'Perhaps they've been on the road much longer than we have,' I answered.

My mother spoke first, walking slowly towards the man in front, her hands spread in a friendly gesture.

There was a short exchange between her and the man.

I pulled Hans closer to me and we crouched further down behind a rock covered with lichen and brown grass.

What came next happened so fast. As my mother turned slightly towards the horizon – perhaps asking about where we were – one of the teenagers darted quickly behind her and hit her with a piece of wood across the back of the head. Mother dropped to the floor and the rest of the group encircled her prone figure.

Hans made to get up and help our mother, but I held him in a tight grip and placed my hand over his mouth, pulling us both further behind the large rock, trying to blend in and not been seen.

We watched as mother tried to stand up, but this time the middle-aged woman knocked her down again. She and the teenage girls quickly dragged off mother's shoes and made short work of removing her clothes. The girl who had hit her first, kicked my mother in the ribs, hard. It was over, the men already strolling away as the women shared their spoils between them, the little boy jumping around excitedly.

They continued to meander into the distance.

I waited with my hand over Hans' mouth until the vicious family were just a spot on the horizon. We then hurried down to the seemingly lifeless body of our mother. She was trembling and dazed but alive. Gently I raised her head and told Hans,

'Hold mother, comfort her whilst I run back and get some clothes from the cart.'

My brother, white with shock, did as he was told.

I raced up the hill and retrieved items of clothing and fresh water to clean her wounds.

My heart burst with the sudden exercise as I re-joined my brother and my mother, who was now desperately trying to talk and raise herself up from the ground.

'Mother,' I said firmly, 'you must do as you're told until your strength returns.'

She watched through bleary eyes as I removed my jumper and skirt, and then I dressed her as if she was a broken doll.

I took my own shoes off and gently eased them onto her feet.

I changed into the tweed trousers and jacket that had belonged to two men that went to war and never came back. I placed the dead son's boots onto my tiny feet, stuffing grass around them so they fitted better.

When I was dressed, I offered my hands and strength to mother. She stood, at first swaying in pain, but eventually, with my support, we all set off on the road once again.

Days and nights merged into each other. The changing colour of my mother's bruises the only clock to note the passing of time.

I began to fear we were walking in circles. The empty barns, overgrown fields, and trickling streams from which we drew our water, all began to look the same.

Our focus soon shifted to the aching hunger in our stomachs. The food from the cottage was running out and mother eked out the rations to us in smaller and smaller handfuls. Then we had no more.

Hans and I then had the job of hunting for food along the roadside, spending all day searching for berries, vegetation such as edible leaves and even grass.

One day, I found Hans standing over three dead rats in the undergrowth.

'Can we eat these?' he asked. I didn't hesitate and picked up the vermin and took it to our mother.

That night she made a fire and cooked the rats, before handing us pieces of flesh she stripped from the bone. For a moment, we chewed in silence.

'This chicken is cooked to perfection, mother!' Hans suddenly announced, and even through our low spirits we tried to laugh. Though rats were rare findings, it was not the only time our diet depended on feral creatures.

One evening, mother brought a scrawny cat to the fire.

'Look what I just found. It seems to have only just died,' she said excitedly.

I looked at the cat's twisted neck, its matted tortoiseshell fur, fresh blood oozing from its mouth, eyes glazed in terror. I touched its paw and it was still warm. My mother had hunted the cat and killed it. I was far too hungry to care and ate the dead feline with relish.

The impact of our journey was beginning to take its toll on our health. My hair thinned, my gums became sore, and downy black hairs now covered my arms. One day, Hans pushed his hand through his thick thatch of blondeness to reveal a clump of hair in his hands.

Another day, my mother wiggled one of her back teeth and pulled it out.

'Pity it's worthless and can't be eaten or sold,' she said as she threw the tooth away into the grass.

Hunger was not the only challenge, as planes often soared in the sky above and our tiny figures could easily be spotted in the open fields.

As we prepared a small fire to warm us during yet another night's sleep outside, mother told us,

'We need to keep to the paths and small roads, stay in the wooded areas as much as we can. There are dangers in the sky as well as on the road.

'There can be no safety for anyone in a country in defeat,' she told us sadly, as Hans drifted to sleep in my arms. 'At the end of a war, the only winner is chaos.'

The defeated tone in her voice made me depressed. I tried to distract myself with more cheerful thoughts.

'Could there be others, mother?' I asked as the dim fire light made the shadows dance around us. 'Other like us? On the road? People like us, who would not harm anyone?'

She clutched the coat we used as a blanket closer around us.

'Perhaps. I suppose yes, there must be,' she said slowly.

I remembered our home town, before we embarked on this terrifying journey.

I tried to focus on my early childhood, the happy times when I had never thought that one day we would have to flee.

As if reading my mind, my mother interrupted these thoughts,

'We had no choice but to leave, Greta. You understand that, don't you?' Her eyes were closed, her face tense.

'Because of father's job and what he had to do for the party?' I asked. In a low voice she said,

'Yes, because of his work with the SS. The Soviets would have blamed your father for associating with SS. It wasn't his fault! Your father didn't want to join them. It was war. Everyone had to do what they were told.'

The words fell from her mouth in a rush and the acid in my stomach rose to meet her panic.

'I know, mother, I know it wasn't our fault,' I said quietly in an attempt to calm my mother.

Inside, though, was deep uncertainty and shame. I had spent months longing for my mother to confide in me and even now she was giving her version of events.

I remembered my father's pride in his new uniform, strutting around our town full of importance and bravado.

I did know that my mother's horror of retribution was true. I had seen enough on our journey to confirm that, had we stayed in our home town, we would have risked being executed, either by the invading armies or being murdered by the relatives of the people my father had sent away to the resettlement camps.

I loved my father, but I felt guilty about what he had done. I had anger towards both of my parents. Nagging feelings that somehow mother and father had put all of us in danger.

Watching my mother sleep that night, anxious dreams chasing across her face, my anger shrank.

War had changed my mother from a graceful, peaceful woman into a sullen shadow of the woman she once was. Our flight had brought her many traumas, her sole focus now to protect her children at any cost.

Better to focus on the next meal, the next place to sleep than to allow our past history and the precarious nature of our situation fill every waking moment. The practical was essential for survival, our past irrelevant.

Drained, I stared at the embers of the fire until eventually sleep eased me into a blackness of nothing.

CHAPTER 7

The next morning, I was sluggish and withdrawn, trailing behind Hans and my mother. The landscape was a vast empty space with scant agriculture. Domestic animals such as cows, goats and pigs had been either eaten by ravenous people on the move or merely killed. Hedgerows had been destroyed by tanks and armed vehicles, trees stripped or cut down for wood.

Our stomachs were now in a permanent spasm. Starved and deflated, we could walk no further.

So, when rooftops came into view, we all kept moving towards the buildings.

We trudged through a small lane, empty of people, its gabled houses broken and shattered.

The first thing we heard was a terrible collective rumbling of voices.

'There are lots of people here,' mother said, her head tipped to one side.

'They are Germans, they won't attack us,' and to reassure, 'It's not like before.'

I wasn't sure. Our hands entwined, we moved towards the noise.

The end of the lane opened into a square, clearly the centre of the village. People were clustered together in a group at the far side, their backs to us. Lots of them were booing. I could hear screaming.

Others were leaning out of windows above, hollering and swearing. Awnings from shops unravelled like bandages to the floor.

My family, with tentative and slow steps, went to the edge of the crowd.

A gap appeared to reveal a group of middle-aged women and a few young men in farm workers clothes throwing bricks at a heap of rags on the floor.

Hans and I turned puzzled faces to our mother.

I then let out a short gasp as I recognised the bundles on the ground were in fact a dozen or so women huddled tightly together, barely moving as the stones landed on and around them.

A tall man, who in different circumstances I might have thought good looking, seemed to be in charge. He egged the crowd on, pointing at the women with jabbing motions.

A scrawny and rabid looking old woman waved a knife and screeched at writing bodies.

'You scum! You dirty scum. You slept with the Cossacks to save yourselves! Slept with the enemy! Dirty whores!'

She rounded on the crowd, who were already baying in agreement.

'I saw them!' she shouted, almost with triumph. 'I saw them all with the Cossacks in the back room of the bar, doing everything and anything for a pot of stew. You disgrace your family!'

The mob roared in agreement, looming closer to the women once more. A few rocks were thrown but a man suddenly broke from the heaving mass to stand beside the women. He started shouting.

'Freda is an innocent! You know her, you all know her!' his voice cracked, pleading.

'She is just fifteen, what choice did she have? Do you think she could have said no? It was sleep with the soldiers or be raped and then murdered. You know that! Why are you doing -'

His voice disappeared as one of the young farmers landed a sharp punch to his face, ending his protests.

A woman with a headscarf moved forward. She took the hand of the tall, distinguished-looking man. He flinched and snatched his hand away as she began to speak.

'You know me, Herr Brahams. You taught my daughter, Grace. You know that she is a good girl.' The woman appealed to the crowd, 'You all know her! You know all these girls!'

Herr Brahams flushed a deep red and stepped away from the mob, but it was too late. They surged forward in anticipation, as the old hag started to chop at the long, auburn hair of one of the young women huddled on the ground, who stayed completely still as her ragged tresses tumbled around her bleeding feet.

'Grace! Grace!' her mother screamed, but Grace didn't look up, even once.

My family watched as, one after another, the young women had their hair removed from their heads. A cheer went up from the crowd, as if something wonderful was happening. I looked slowly around the square, feeling empty with shock. Nothing felt real.

When all their scalps looked like plucked chickens, another man raised his arms to the crowd. The terrified girls shrunk even closer together as the mob hurled mud, splattering their scalps and stricken faces. Many of the girls wet themselves.

I prayed it would soon be over, but the crowd were not satisfied.

As the people of the town started to punch and kick the young women, my mother dragged us away.

'How many more lives will be ruined needlessly in this war?' she murmured as we half walked, half ran back towards the lane. 'Surely they know there are few virgins in Germany these days. There will be none by the time this is all over.'

She pulled us into a shop doorway, but it did not drown out the noise or stop us from seeing the blood-spattered faces of the town's citizens, and the teeth-bared faces of ordinary people gone mad. Blow after blow continued to rain onto the girls.

I tried to put my coat over Hans' head, shielding his eyes, but he pushed it away, transfixed by the unfolding horror. I saw real fear on my mother's face as she tried to claw her way inside the locked shop, scratching with bleeding nails at the entrance. Terrified that the escalating aggression might then be directed at strangers.

The door did not budge. My mother's hands were bruised and red with the effort.

A gunshot broke through the shouts, leaving a sudden and devastating silence. A well-dressed man on a horse was trotting through the scattered crowd a rifle in his arms.

'That's enough!' he shouted. Some of the young farmers tipped their hats at him. Perhaps they worked for him. Behind him were two other men on horseback, also carrying guns, who I took for his servants or employees.

As quickly as it had begun, the violence stopped. It seemed as though the townspeople began to wake one by one from a nightmare, looking at each other with dazed expressions, visibly shaken. A few gave a cursory glance at the bloody, tattered mess on the ground that was once a group of young, living girls, straightened their clothes and hurried away.

Others with no shame spat on the broken bones and shouted,

'They got what they deserved,' and, 'My boy didn't die in battle for those tarts to lie with Cossacks.'

The man on horseback looked disgusted. He urged his horse onwards and sped away, his servants following more slowly, making sure the townspeople had dispersed.

Grace's mother fell to her knees. In heaving gasps, she searched the bloody pile for her child. She gave a sudden scream as a hand met hers, and a few people ran to help. Somehow, Grace had survived.

The small group carefully carried the shattered young girl to the other side of the square, and gently propped her up against a wall. A terrible crack echoed across the square. As Grace tried to lift herself up, part of her arm split, bone gleaming white through skin. She slumped forward, unconscious, and as the parents of the other girls ran towards the bloody mess, Grace disappeared from our view.

Jolting us back to reality, Hans suddenly ran from the doorway and into the street, vomiting and projecting green and yellow bile into the gutter. Slumping onto the floor, he sat with his head in his hands, dry retching again and again.

My mother's face was now an expressionless mask.

A frail, old woman we had not seen before shuffled over, a mangy dog sniffing around her heels. The elderly woman was dressed in a man's jacket with large black boots. She sat in the gutter beside Hans, while the stray dog ate the pool of vomit.

Looking up at me and my mother, she said, 'Those young girls went to the village school. Some of them worked in the local shops. They only did what they did to live and now they are dead too!

'If they had refused to bed the soldiers, there would have been reprisals for all of us.'

The old woman started to weep, a terrible racking sound.

My mother sat down next to her and pulled her close.

We soon learnt the woman's name was Rosa and she used to run the Post Office.

'A couple of weeks ago, Cossacks on horses came to our town,' she told us. 'They terrorised us, taking anything of value, making us cook for them and serve them. They raped the women, and if they fought them, they killed them afterwards.'

Shaking her head, Rosa told us, 'The Cossacks left only yesterday. They were going to Berlin.'

Speaking softly, she confided, 'There are many rumours that we're nearing the final showdown of the war.'

Looking at my mother with tear-stained eyes, Rosa howled,

'Those monsters dressed as soldiers leave and as soon as they are gone, we become the monsters!'

'Come, Rosa,' said my mother, 'Let us take you home.'

Suspicion edged Rosa's eyes. We could see her weighing us up. Would we rob her? Or worse, kill her?

I don't know what she saw in us. Perhaps it was Hans still shivering beside her, but in that moment, Rosa made a decision that probably saved our lives.

'Alright,' she said, 'Come, I'll make us some tea. It'll be weak though, there's hardly any left.'

Paralysed with what we had witnessed, in a slow gait Rosa led us across the square and down a narrow road. Only two houses, heavily damaged, were left standing among the debris where once a street must have stood. As the old lady ushered us indoors, she apologised for the state of her home. The two-up-two-down had no lavatory and just a water pump in the yard. But it was quiet, and, for the time being, away from the madness that was happening outside.

'I only have one chair, so you'll have to sit on the floor. All the other furniture was burnt to keep me warm. Last winter was so cold, the trees around the town were used either for firewood or patching up property. Well, the trees that were not destroyed by the tanks, fires and bombs.'

Raising her voice as she had in the square, she added, 'Even the land is weeping!'

Scattered at her feet and grateful to be eating real food with a roof over our heads, we sat listening as Rosa told us stories about her town before the insanity of war took over. With her hazelnut skin and lined face, she looked much older than sixty. Over more tea she reminisced,

'There were balls and dances in the square all the time back then. This was a wealthy, happy town!'

Her face darkened, 'We were good people,' she said quietly. 'Those people in the square, they were good people. Nowadays I just rely on my next door neighbours. We keep away from those in town. They behave like wild dogs.'

Noting our weary faces, Rosa gently bid us a goodnight. I watched the light from her candle fade as she went to her room next door.

That night, my mother, Hans and I snuggled together on the floor, a filthy carpet for a blanket and splintered floorboards for a bedstead. It was the most luxury we had experienced in weeks, but I only managed a few hours of sleep.

When I dozed, images of the girls in the square haunted my mind, and I woke gasping at the memory of the crack of Grace's arm. Questions, images and thoughts buzzed round my mind, keeping me at the edge of sleep and far from rest.

I no longer recognised my country, its people or my mother, Hans or even myself.

Every one of us had become such a different person, our personalities bent and twisted by terror and need.

What would become of us in this chaos of advancing soldiers and fleeing Germans? Was anyone really in charge of this war? All I could see was marauding men cutting through town after town, leaving more destruction and death.

Even if my little family of three survived, we would have nothing left to our name. Was this not punishment enough?

So many questions flew around my mind, but I had no answers. My mother, sensing my worry, embraced me with a warm hug.

I let loose a long sigh. There was no need for me to be fearful, as my mother had protected us this far. She would know what to do.

Finally, I slept. But my mother did not.

CHAPTER 8

There was little food in the town. Though Rosa gladly shared her few rations, we never had enough to eat. Hunger during the first week is monotonous, then there is a strange feeling of elation. At first, Hans and I talked about food and ate imaginary dinners together, discussing morsel by morsel how the meat, vegetables, and puddings in our minds tasted, looked, and smelled. We soon stopped. Our pretend dinners made the vacuum in our stomachs worse. But none of us ever stopped thinking about food.

It eventually controls every action and thought, a constant and overwhelming need.

Further down the line come the physical symptoms of malnutrition: loose teeth, peeling skin, always feeling cold, my thick hair gradually thinning. My arms became covered in a light, downy hair, my nails broke loose, and my feet shrank. I had to stuff grass and paper into my shoes to make them fit. The uninterrupted pain in my belly reverberated through my body and mind, a gnawing emptiness I couldn't escape.

It's often the overwhelming emotional connection with food that dominates. Food eaten when plentiful is never far from mind or memory. I would picture meals I had in the distant past and salivate like an animal.

We were slowly starving, often going days with no food at all. Physical tasks became more of an effort. Weight fell from my mother's body, her once apple-cheeked face was sharp and pointed, her head too large for her body. Strangely, Hans and I grew a little taller, but this only accentuated how thin we had become.

Rosa looked almost transparent. Her generosity reminded me in darker moments that even in the insanity of the war, people could be kind. None of us spoke of it, but we all knew that her meagre food store, small vegetable garden and two scrawny chickens would not last many more weeks. The whole town was starving, Germany was starving. The few shops that remained open bartered in goods or possessions in exchange for small rations, and we had nothing to trade.

What saved us was not what I would have expected, in fact it was what I had come to fear the most: another battalion of soldiers.

The rumbling of guns and shell fire had been a backdrop to our lives for weeks, as the bombardment of Berlin by the Allies took hold. Plumes of smoke smeared the sky as noisy planes moaned their way to the capital.

One morning, as Rosa and I were preparing another sparse breakfast of tea and a thin gruel, the ground beneath our feet began to vibrate to the familiar crunch of an army's tread. They were heading towards the town.

My mother, Rosa and I stood frozen to the spot, as Hans came rushing into the room waving a large bar of candy, his mouth smeared with chocolate.

Excitedly, he shouted over the noise, 'The Americans are here, and they gave me this and this and this!'

Beaming, Hans emptied his trouser pockets to reveal a pack of chewing gum and a tin of something labelled '*Spam*'.

Alarmed, my mother grabbed his shoulders, demanding, 'Where are they?'

'I was by the field,' he said, still talking through a mouthful of chocolate. 'I was trying to trap rabbits when a big group of men marched past. One of them saw me and came over. He said his name was Hank and he gave me all of this.'

Hans' face was split from ear to ear with the most enormous grin. I could not help but laugh and nor could Rosa. My mother was silent and looked at the floor.

Snapping out of her thoughts, mother took hold of the bounty and quickly hid it at the back of the kitchen cupboard.

She quizzed Hans again, 'Are you sure they are Americans?'

Subdued, he muttered, 'Americans maybe, or Canadian.'

'What did the soldier say to you?' mother demanded, raising her voice.

Hans thought for a moment, still licking his lips.

'He said hello and a few other words in German, but I didn't hear the others talk. They've got vans with them, come and see!'

Mother pinched hold of my brother's arm.

'What vans? With guns?'

'No, not tanks,' Hans said, as he tried to pull away.

Mother did not let go.

'Are you sure?'

'There are soldiers but not tanks, I promise mother! Come on, please! Let's see what's happening, they're not scary. They might have more food for us!'

Hans was hopping from foot to foot, his eyes never leaving my mother's face.

She let go of him and went to the open kitchen door. We all followed.

Dozens and dozens of men, legs and arms swinging in unison, were striding towards the square, followed by jeeps, ambulances and trucks. Hans was right, there were no tanks.

Some of the soldiers waved at children playing in the street, and they shyly waved back. These men seemed good-natured.

I had vague memories of seeing photos of some American movie stars and their homes in a few magazines that my mother had before the war. America always looked like a friendly place.

Many of the townspeople had left their houses to follow the soldiers, and we joined the end of the throng. Before we even got to the square, Hans was violently sick, deep brown vomit spraying over his shoes.

Oblivious, my mother hurried us along, holding on to Rosa's arm so the old woman wouldn't be swept away in the sudden swell of people.

The American soldiers lined up on one side of the square as their lorries parked on the other. The soldiers stood to attention and waited.

So did we. For the next hour, there was a lot of speculation in the crowd, alongside remarks about how the Americans were too sure of themselves, and that the Führer would save us all.

Then, on the balcony of the battered town hall, the mayor appeared with an American officer, an older man in his forties. Beside them both was a young soldier, a private. The officer spoke to the private, and the private spoke to the mayor.

The mayor then turned to speak to the assembled crowd, 'This is Colonel J. K. Jeffery 111 from the United States Army. He and his men are now in charge of the town.'

Colonel Jeffery smiled at us all and spoke again to the private, who then relayed the conversation to the mayor.

'Colonel Jeffery's men will be running a field hospital nearby. They will stay here to care for the Allied soldiers, who are liberating Germany from Hitler. The colonel wants to address you directly now, and this young soldier will translate.'

The private, looking slightly nervous, stepped forward onto the balcony and began to translate as the colonel spoke quietly next to him.

'The Allies are marching on Berlin, and Hitler will soon be defeated.'

At this, a cheer went up from the American soldiers. The townspeople were at first quiet, then, at first in a whisper but slowly louder, came comments about what the Nazis would do to these Americans. The muttering became shouting and swearing. A few pockets of people began to push towards the Americans.

At a shout from an officer, several soldiers moved across the square, guns raised. The crowd parted until the people who had been shouting moments before were left standing alone, defiant. The Americans gestured at them to move and led them from the square. The crowd was silent.

Colonel Jeffery spoke again to the private, offering no reaction to the sudden disturbance. The private continued with his translation.

'Whilst we are here, we will help you as long as you work with us. We expect and demand your cooperation. The war is nearly over. Colonel Jeffery wants to go home to his family and knows you only want your lives to return to how they once were.'

The private took a breath. He was beginning to look and sound tired. I wondered how many other similar speeches he had given as he and his Allied comrades made their way across the decimated towns and villages of Germany.

'Your town is in a strategic place, especially for Berlin and other cities. I don't need to tell you that the USA army will treat you better than some of the other armies making their way across the German countryside.'

The translator gestured for the colonel to slow down as he was finding it hard to keep up. He looked no older than early twenties, his hair cut so short he almost looked bald. But he had a good grasp of the German language and his accent was perfect.

'Our men will be posting leaflets through your doors about the curfew, which will be from 8pm until 6am daily. The literature will tell you about the other requirements I expect from you all. Anyone trying to undermine our work here will be severely punished.'

A few younger farm hands in the crowd started to jeer but fell silent as another group of soldiers advanced with guns and took them in the same direction the others had gone.

Despite the interruptions, the US private informed us,

'Here is a goodwill gesture for you all. There are some sacks of seeds for you to grow vegetables, and shortly our kitchen will be making soup. Every one of you can have a bowl of soup and bread, and, in exchange, you will give us your name, address, age and occupation, then present your papers.'

I turned to see a table had been set up in the corner of the square. Motivated by the promise of food, people were already queuing to give their details to four seated soldiers. I noticed a few of the younger men move to leave the square, but they were stopped in their tracks by soldiers and pushed into a truck. A group of older men and women, perhaps their parents, shouted angrily as the truck drove away.

I recognised some of the young men as part of the group of farm hands who had joined in with the mob-led murder of the young girls when we had first arrived. Later, I heard comments in the village that they were really Nazi soldiers who had run away from their posts as the Allies advanced.

I was distracted by the young private finishing his speech with an assurance that every person who gave their details would get some food. My mouth drooled at the thought of hot, thick soup, as I watched the American soldiers cut potatoes and carrots and place them into huge tureens on stoves set up in the centre of the square.

I was desperate to eat. Rosa hobbled over to the ever-growing queue. Instead of heading for a much-needed meal, mother rushed me and Hans towards a tent that had been erected at the entrance of the town hall.

'Agree with everything I say, stand tall and look strong,' she ordered.

She whisked us into the tent where a medic with a stethoscope around his neck was shouting instructions. A couple of gangly, young soldiers were moving equipment inside from the vehicles. Bandages covered a table in the corner, and across from us a row of beds was being assembled.

My mother approached the medic, and in halting English told him, 'I was a nurse before the war. I can help you and so can my children. They are capable and need work. We come from a small village on the borders and had little to do with the war.'

Luckily, Hans and I were too tired to react to our mother's sudden stream of lies. We stood and looked ahead as she continued,

'I can speak good English because I had an old school friend whose mother came from England. Lottie and her family returned to England several years before hostilities broke out. My friend wrote me long letters in English for many years, which I used to read to my children, so they too have a good understanding of the language.'

Hans and I gave weak smiles on cue. This part of our mother's story was actually true. My parents had believed that knowing a little English was a good skill for Hans and me to acquire. Through Lottie's letters about her life in England, our mother taught me and my brother rudimentary English. Then war got in the way and she never heard from her school friend again.

The doctor replied in fluent German, and my mother looked surprised.

'I admire your audacity, Frau. Everyone I have met in Germany has had nothing to do with the Nazis and hates Hitler.'

He gave a wry smile, 'But that's what I would expect from a country on its knees before the Allied forces.'

Behind her back, I saw my mother's hands clench into fists. The doctor rocked back and forth on his heels, looking us over.

When he spoke, his voice was sharp, impatient.

'What are your names? How old are your children?'

My mother lied again, 'Our name is Brunn. I am Helga, this is my son Hans, he is thirteen, and Greta my daughter is nearly sixteen.'

She rushed on, barely pausing for breath, 'Both my children have experience of working in a hospital environment, kitchens too. They work hard and are respectful.'

Apart from helping in the kitchen at home and looking after Hans when he had the measles, this was another exaggeration of our skills.

'I am Major Steve Simpson,' said the doctor, looking thoughtfully at our sunken faces and scruffy appearance.

'Where are your papers?' he suddenly barked. 'How do I know you are being truthful?'

My mother's hands remained tightly curled behind her back.

Yet when she spoke, mother's voice was soft. The major, who in my mind had become Dr Steve, leaned forward to hear her.

'We ran from the advancing armies, we were afraid, we have no papers. I just want my children to survive and have a future.'

Dr Steve looked hard at her for a moment. Would he give us a chance?

'Our General, Dwight Eisenhower, has commanded us not to fraternise with German families, especially women.'

My mother's shoulders slumped as Dr Steve stepped over to a table which he appeared to be using as his desk. Mother straightened her back and looked at him in that desperate, beautiful way she had with men.

He said, 'It's true I need as many people as possible to get this hospital up and running. However, you could be collaborating with the Nazis.'

My mother began to speak, but he held up a hand to silence her and looked down at Hans, with his chocolate stained face, and sighed.

'I have a young kid just like you at home. His name is Pete.'

With weary eyes, he stared at us for a long time. 'Dwight may have ordered that there must be no friendships between the US Army and the defeated, but us guys on the frontline have found that most German people welcome liberation from Hitler and the end of all the carnage.'

Sighing again he said, 'We're not even supposed to give food to the German people. It's OK for the big guys in Washington to have those strict ideas, but our chief, Colonel Jeffery, knows the reality of war, and when occupying towns and villages it's only humane to offer some help to the defeated.'

My mother nodded in agreement, but her fists remained tight balls of fury.

'I will give all of you some work, and trust that you are not going to cause trouble,' said Dr Steve. 'If you do, all of you will be taken from here and handed over to the guards. I could not vouch for your lives. Is that clear?'

We all said in unison, 'Yes.'

'My first and only priority are my patients and my men. You better not let me down.'

My mother gave Dr Steve her sweetest smile, 'Thank you, I swear we will not betray your trust. All I want is for my children to be safe. Like you, we want this war over and to go home.'

My whole life, I had seen my mother charm men with her beauty. Even as unhealthy and bedraggled as she looked, Dr Steve was no exception. He melted. The major had made up his mind and briskly gave us our first chores.

'More tents like this will be going up today. Some will be operating rooms, others will be for the recovering wounded, and another will be a mortuary. There will also be a kitchen. Your boy can work there, and you and Greta can help me and the hospital staff.'

Dr Steve repeated his warning for the last time.

'If I find you are here to make mischief, instead of to help, I will not only be very disappointed, but you will then become the property of the US Army. Are you clear about that?'

My mother, Hans and I nodded, heads bowed.

'There are more vans arriving tonight, so there is a lot to do. You will all work for as long as it takes to get the hospital ready. Understood?'

'Yes,' we all replied.

'You will be paid in food and maybe some US dollars. You will wear this as a uniform.'

He crossed the room and pulled some brown coats from a kit bag.

'You will start now. I assume that is suitable?'

My mother dropped her hands to her sides, then folded them meekly in front of her and replied, 'Of course.'

Dr Steve's steely eyes scanned us all from the top of our heads to our toes, telling mother,

'You are all underweight. I assume food has been very sparse. A warning from the doctor: when you have dinner later tonight, don't eat too quickly or too much.

'Your stomachs have shrunk, and your bodies need to adjust to nourishment again. It will most likely hurt when you eat. Be patient. It will take time for you to get used to regular meals.'

And with that, Dr Steve set us to work: at first unpacking cases and assembling beds, then moving medical equipment and supplies. It was hard work, but we did not stop until we were told to go and get some food, and we came straight back after eating.

It took us and the soldiers all night to make good the mobile hospital. The next morning, as we wearily headed back to Rosa's, I glanced around. Overnight everything had changed again.

There was now a tented town within the town.

CHAPTER 9

After the shock of the US Army's arrival, the days began to speed past, filled with a brand-new routine. Dr Steve was as good as his word and kept us busy.

My mother, Hans and I left early each day for work and got back to Rosa's in the late afternoon. If we were needed to work after curfew, we had to snatch some sleep in a chair at the hospital or on the rough ground outside the tents. There were a few female nursing staff who kept their distance from my family. The majority of the medical team were male, made up of army personnel, orderlies and civilian medical doctors and surgeons who had been seconded into the army.

Each time there was a new intake of wounded soldiers, we worked through the night and into the next day to treat them all. My mother and I emptied bucket after bucket of faeces, burned bloodied bandages as they were removed, and changed beds soaked with blood and death. We carried containers of amputated fingers, toes and limbs to a furnace set up in a nearby field.

The work was tough, physically and mentally, but we had a purpose, and more than enough food to feed ourselves and Rosa.

Initially, we were treated with suspicion, and Dr Steve and his staff made clear that if there was the slightest hint of us working against the Allies, we would be imprisoned and face even worse. But as the days flew by, they saw how hard we worked and that we wanted the same thing they did: for the war to be over and some normality to return.

Hans and I, starved of company, quickly built tentative friendships with the cheery medical staff and wounded men who were often desperate to talk about their experiences and their lives back home.

At first, the Allied soldiers were shocked to hear our accents, but my mother added another lie to our story and said we were part Swiss, and this softened some of the animosity. The troops gradually became more relaxed, even helped us with our faltering English. Our language skills were improving every day, and before long even Hans was having long conversations with the troops. As my English improved, I read letters and magazines to the wounded. Most were not much older than I, in their late teens or early twenties. They seemed too young to fight and far too young to die. Many had never tasted alcohol, had a girlfriend or even been away from home until they signed up for military service: virgin soldiers in every sense of the word.

Mother and daughter were also learning a great deal about the craft of nursing during war. This included bandaging wounds, stitching gaping holes, setting broken limbs and the necessity of keeping infection to a minimum. There were times when the tents were crammed with injured men, stretchers lined up outside the three working theatres. Then my mother would help Dr Steve and Dr Frank during many operations, and Helga – as they knew her – soon proved an able assistant.

Eisenhower's command for troops not to form close bonds with Germans, or the 'defeated', was unworkable at the mobile hospital. We all had to get along and work together to survive. Tentative working friendships were formed between my family and the Allies, and bonds were made with our patients. Many of the soldiers who arrived at the hospital were often delirious with pain or gravely ill, so anyone holding their hand was welcome.

I sat with many of the injured as they spent their last minutes, hours, or days in that tented town, all hoping to make it back home. These boys and men were frightened, and cried out in pain and distress, asking for their mother's help and a hug. Instead, they held the hand of a fourteen-year-old German girl who was frightened, too. They would ask me, 'Am I dying?' Outwardly calm, I would make them comfortable and keep talking and grasping their hand until it relaxed with sleep or fell away with death.

Inside those canvas rooms, divisions and differences faded. I became just another young nurse and sometimes it felt like we were all on the same side. We all wanted to live our lives and have a peaceful future. We all wanted the fighting to stop, to go home, though I wasn't sure where home was or what it felt like anymore.

Meanwhile, Hans was busy in the kitchen: running errands for the men, peeling vegetables, dishing up food for the soldiers and generally helping out. The cook showed him how to make special soups and broths for the very sick, and my brother delivered them to the stricken soldiers, often sitting to chat with them. It was good to see Hans blossom under the care of the cook and the kitchen staff. They treated him like a cheeky younger brother. When it was quiet, the cook and other orderlies would play football at the back of the tents and let Hans join in, deliberately letting him score and revelling in his glee. Some of the recovering patients would come and watch, cheering as they smoked cigarette after cigarette.

The soldiers that we nursed were mostly from the USA but we also took care of Canadians, French and English personnel, alongside other nationalities caught up in the mayhem that was the ending of the war. With each new influx of patients, we received more news. We learnt that the German army was now in full retreat, whilst Hitler remained incarcerated in his bunker in Berlin.

The war may have been in its dying days, but it didn't stop the dying. Landmines littered the countryside, along with booby traps, bombs and pockets of Germans fighting to the last. The US soldiers told me they had encountered German battalions supported by boys as young as twelve.

Despite the horror of the last days of war, within the canvas walls of the hospital there were also many light-hearted moments. Between shifts, there was time to chat, play cards or read magazines brought in by the soldiers. There was alcohol available if a GI had enough dollars or goods he could barter. Recovering patients mixed freely with staff and soldiers in the canteen and with those men who were just passing through.

Hans enjoyed working in the canteen, preparing the food and chatting to the guys. The soldiers made him paper airplanes and always managed to find him some candy. Most days, my brother and I shared a meal at one of the canteen's long tables, eating and talking with the troops. Our mother rarely joined us.

It was during one of these meals that Hans introduced me to Chuck, a southern boy with immaculate manners. Chuck was auburn haired and good looking, almost pretty in that way that young men shine before age narrows their waist and sharpens the jaw. His eyes were the colour of cornflowers, and so striking I found it hard to look away. Officially, he was twenty one years old, but though tall and strong, he looked about sixteen.

I blushed when Chuck took the seat next to me. My brother seemed completely oblivious to the nervous glances Chuck and I kept exchanging.

'Chuck works between the supply base and the hospital,' Hans told me, by way of an introduction. 'He's one of the men ferrying the sick and dying back and forth and making sure food and medical equipment is kept stocked.'

I knew from my time at the hospital that this work could be dangerous, as soldiers like Chuck often worked close to active fighting and the land mines buried by the retreating German army. I had carried the severed limbs of some of the unlucky ones down to the furnace myself.

On the day we were introduced, I asked Chuck if he was ever scared.

'It's dangerous, ma'am, that's for sure,' he smiled. 'But it's safer than when I was on the frontline. And every time I come here and see all the soldiers y'all are helping, I know I'm right where I'm needed.'

My heart warmed to Chuck and his gentle, self-effacing manner, and it was obvious he liked me too. From that night on, whenever I appeared for my dinner, Chuck gave me a shy smile and pointed to the two seats he had saved next to him for me and Hans. I soon came to miss him the nights he was on duty.

One evening over dinner, Hans asked, 'Chuck, how did you end up a soldier?'

'Well, young fella, that's a story I'm hoping to tell my grandchildren one day.'

Gently, he continued, 'I was far too young for military service and I knew it. Now, I'm from a small town smack bang in the middle of nowhere, Alabama, and there was no way I could sign up in my town without everyone I'd ever met knowing about it. But that was not about to stop me, Hans, I'll tell you that.

'One sunny day, I heard tell on the grapevine of a recruitment drive at a town some sixty miles from our farm. Well, I headed straight over there without a word to my folks and told the recruiting sergeant I was twenty years old, though I wasn't a whistle past seventeen. They accepted me on the spot and gave me a date to report to barracks.'

Chuck shrugged,

'I'll tell you the one thing I regret though, Hans, is not telling my folks the truth. When I got home, I told them I had found some well-paid work helping out a farmstead in Mississippi, and off I went!'

There was a long pause. Sensing the lowering of Chuck's mood, I asked, 'What did they say when you told them the truth, Chuck?'

He met my gaze for a brief second then stared down at the table,

'I don't know the answer to that one, ma'am,' he said quietly. 'After some training, I was quickly shipped out of the US and it was too late to go back home and fess up. So I wrote them a letter as my battalion left England. I'm not even sure it reached home.'

I breathed in sharply, struck with sympathy for Chuck and his family.

'Oh, Chuck, I'm sorry. I'm sure they got your letter.'

'I hope so, ma'am. Truth is, I've been too ashamed to write to them since. I feel like I need to say sorry to them face to face. I should never have lied to them.'

He looked over at Hans, 'It wasn't that long ago, but I was so much younger then. The war made me grow up fast, you know how it is. War sure ain't nothing like the movies! I just want to get out alive.'

Chuck's doleful eyes and shaking hands revealed the toll the war had taken on him since landing in Europe. That evening after dinner, he asked me if I would go for a walk with him. Hans tactfully made himself scarce and we slowly wandered through the tented town towards the open fields, but no further, as these were patrolled by burly GIs on the look-out for trouble.

Chuck was very respectful, and I felt safe with him. I was thinking how worried his parents must be back in America. A US guard appeared and warned us not to go further as curfew was approaching.

'Sometimes, when the light is like this, Germany reminds me a little of home,' said Chuck. 'Our farm was a bit like this,' he said, pointing towards the countryside.

'Miles and miles of open fields. I miss it.' He laughed, 'Even the hard work! And Lord, it's hard working a farm. I have two older brothers and the three of us have been working the land since we were infants. Before I became a soldier, it was all I knew how to do. Riding horses, herding cattle, tending the land. Learnt to ride when I was only three! I was made for it.'

'It sounds like a movie to me, Chuck, the way you describe it all. I would love to see it,' I said.

He paused and turned to face me, 'I'd love you to see it, too.'

I blushed, feeling both perturbed and happy at the same time.

'Miss Greta, I know we've met in the craziest way here in this war, but you are the person I look forward to seeing every day and I think that must mean something. Will you be my girl?'

I didn't hesitate.

'Yes, Chuck, of course I'll be your girl,' I replied.

And so my first courtship began. Chuck had witnessed so much, but he was, in other ways, inexperienced. A committed Christian, I was relieved when he told me one night that he wanted to be a virgin when he married. In the insanity around us, our innocent courtship was just what I needed. Chuck and our burgeoning relationships gave me wings.

The other soldiers teased us a bit, but I think they liked seeing Chuck so content. Most days we would try and spend some time together. Often when I finished work, we wandered through the town. Since the Americans had arrived, the town had come back to life. The US soldiers had access to money, food and other items including alcohol, which quickly led to a local black market. A couple of bars opened, alongside some other shops.

Rosa approved of Chuck and asked him round for tea. My mother's only comment was to thank him for the tin of dried egg he had brought to the table. I couldn't tell what she thought, and between work and spending time with Hans and Chuck, I hardly saw her.

I didn't think she missed us. Our mother was busy with her own life. With a regular diet restoring all our health, my mother's blonde shining hair, pretty face and slim form earned her many admirers. The hospital now played a central role in the town and everyone knew the pretty blonde nurse, Helga. Hans and I heard her name so much, even we began to call her Helga when working. It felt professional and right.

At the hospital I sometimes caught Dr Steve looking at my mother the way men do when they are a little in love. I saw them engrossed in long conversations as they sat outside smoking cigarettes. Very occasionally I heard her tinkling laughter and saw her dimpled grin as she looked up at Dr Steve. There was a definite spark between them, but Dr Steve was married, and remained faithful. Disappointed, Helga looked for comfort elsewhere.

Though the Allied soldiers were not supposed to fraternise with German women, relationships – both sexual and platonic – grew. The soldiers were tired and emotionally drained. They needed comfort. A German woman's willing arms and body in exchange for food or cigarettes was always a bargain. Relationships based on what people needed worked well for everybody. It became clear that Helga had noticed this too. She began spending time with a sergeant called Al Malone, a big man, over six feet tall. I didn't take to him, and he made me nervous. He was what my mother would once have called 'rough around the edges'. Rosa called him a gangster. Al seemed to have a finger in every pie.

Al Malone was the 'go to guy' if an individual needed anything from booze to dollars.

He was always coming in and out of the hospital to see Helga, bringing her things and making clear to everyone that she was 'his girl'. Dr Steve was not impressed. Like me, he knew Helga was worth more, and, at first, I did not understand what she could see in such a brute. Then I did. Al Malone was in charge of the transport going in and out of the town. While Hans and I were building a new life in the camp, my mother was always looking forward and usually had an escape plan.

I began to see even less of my mother, catching glimpses of her on Al's lap in a bar as I walked past with Chuck, or seeing her in the hospital tents, but only rarely at Rosa's. Al had his own tent at the back of the town hall, and this is where she was on the nights she did not return. She would arrive at Rosa's an hour before our shift began, and stare defiantly at me and Rosa, daring us to say something. I began to avoid her gaze. I knew she was trying to look out for our future, but I hated Al, and I hated that everyone knew my mother was with him. It was also risky being in a sexual relationship with a bully like Al who had enemies.

There had also been a few attacks on women who had flaunted their affairs with Allied troops in the town.

Those citizens responsible for the violence had been arrested and taken away, but underneath the apparent calm, many of the citizens held a simmering resentment towards the Allies, while benefitting from their presence. The worst men were those who pimped their wives to the Allied soldiers for money, wine and bread and then beat their women in disgust.

Hans didn't like Al either, and we shared nasty jokes about him. Hans had always adored my mother, and he found it hard to see Al's huge paws on her tiny frame. I often saw him balling his fists when the burly soldier grabbed my mother in the mess hall and pulled her into his arms.

Our dislike of the man didn't stop us or Rosa from drinking his wine, eating his food, or accepting his generosity. It didn't stop me wearing the new dress he gave me, or Hans the new shoes.

The war made hypocrites of us all.

For some, the fight for survival was harder. Small queues of women snaked outside the soldier's accommodation tents at night. Some were undoubtedly prostitutes, others ordinary housewives and neighbours. On my way to the showers, I would see women entering the canvas bedrooms and hear the ribald laughter from within. Then, as I was walking back twenty minutes or so later, the same women would come out of the tents clutching their prizes. Dishevelled and adjusting their dresses, they hugged a few tins of food as they walked painfully back to their homes. It was common knowledge that those without a 'regular guy' might be handed around to one, two or even several men in a night. I was grateful it was not me.

My mother's relationship with Al Malone kept me safe from unwanted advances. Men looked at me, but if it started to go further, Chuck, his friends and Al Malone soon put them right. Chuck and I were a young couple in love, and this struck a chord with even the most battle-hardened guys. Perhaps we reminded them of more innocent times.

During our times together, Chuck never asked about my background, and just accepted I had come from a small village on the borders. He did not understand the politics of war and was uninterested in anything but me, home and his family. Neither of us talked about the future, both of us aware that even though hostilities were nearly over, life was fragile, and anything could still happen.

One afternoon as we lay peacefully in each other's arms at the edge of the field by the river listening to the low gurgle of splashing water, Chuck sat up suddenly and reached his hands to the back of his neck. He took off a silver chain I knew his mother had given him, removed the cross and placed it in his top pocket. The sparkling rope of silver chain in his hand he offered to me.

I sat up, shocked, 'No Chuck! You must keep it with the cross. It has kept you safe, and it was a present from your mom.'

I curled my hands in my lap to show him I would not take the precious gift.

'Please, I want you to have this. You are my Greta, and I want you to always have a part of me. My Mom would love you to have this, I know she would. Please, Greta.'

Before I had a chance to say another word, he carefully placed the chain over my head and patted it into place. I looked up at him, smiling with tears in my eyes. We laid back down, cuddling until it was finally time to head back to the tents and work.

A week later, Chuck received word that he and the rest of his men would soon be moving out to fight at the front line. He didn't tell me until the last minute. When he got his orders, I was in the hospital in the middle of my chores, making yet another bed. Chuck's face appeared around the doorway of the tent. I grinned at him, and he watched intently as I tucked in the blanket and asked my patient if he was comfortable.

Dr Steve looked up from his desk, saw Chuck with his kit and in full uniform and guessed what was happening. He yelled across the moans of the sick and the chatter of recovering men, 'Greta take your lunch break. You've not sat down since 6am.'

Delighted, I skipped over to Chuck, but he was quiet, a thin smile on his lips. He led me out of the tent and across the square, into a clearing used to store supplies. I didn't understand why we weren't heading to the canteen for food, and when he pulled me toward him, he smelled of sweat and fear.

'My girl, Greta, I'm leaving,' he began, and I looked up at him sharply, stepping backwards.

'Our orders came in and we are heading towards the fighting,' he reached out and took my hands as his voice broke. 'Greta, I'm frightened.'

His head was on my shoulders as he began to cry, but I remained dry eyed, as always.

'It's fine, it's all going to be fine,' I said over and over, using my calm nurse's voice and gestures.

I knew that Chuck needed so much more from me. I told him how much I would miss him, that I loved him, and I told him he would have a future. But would he? Would he really survive? I didn't know, but I knew it was the right thing to say.

Chuck reached into his coat and pulled out a letter addressed to me.

'This is for you, my love, open it when I am gone. It has my address. Let's find each other when the war is finally over. Tom in my platoon says the war is all but finished, so we could be together again in just a few months.'

Chuck's southern drawl became even rounder the more distressed he became. I tried to smile, but it was stretched and false. He sat down on the ground and held me as I perched on his lap. He lit a cigarette, his first one ever. After a few puffs, he burst into a fit of coughing which made his eyes stream even more.

'Guess I'm not a smoker then!' he gasped.

'One of the guys said a smoke might make my nerves better.' Chuck tried desperately to look brave, but fear was etched in every pore of his face.

'Look, it didn't work.' He held out his shaking hand, and when I took it in mine I could feel his whole body trembling.

Suddenly the booming voice of Al Malone rumbled from his gorilla-shaped chest. Al was standing just a few feet away in full uniform.

'Get moving, Baldwin. Give her a kiss and then head for the truck. You're leaving.'

Chuck picked me up, swung me around and kissed my hand. I realised with a shock of panic I had nothing to give him as a keepsake. I ripped the hem of my dusty threadbare dress, pressed it to my lips and gave it to him, a piece of me. He swung his kit bag onto his back and pulled himself up so he stood tall, sticking out his chin to steady his trembling lips. He kissed me one more time, turned and walked briskly away.

I stood for a few long moments, almost paralysed, and then I picked up my skirt and chased after him. I was too late. Chuck's face, white with fear, stared from the back of a departing truck. He was waving the piece of my dress as the vehicle sped out of town.

Then he was gone.

CHAPTER 10

I could not bring myself to open the letter from Chuck, so I kept it inside my dress, close to my heart. I welcomed the scratch of the envelope against my skin, as he had sealed it with his lips. If I opened it, it would mean that Chuck was really gone.

My world seemed greyer and I felt so lonely. My mother remarked only once about my despairing, pale face and black-circled eyes.

'Forget him, he is just a boy and you have work to do at the hospital.'

I glared at her, my sorrow for Chuck's departure transforming into hate for my mother's cruelty.

'Another group of wounded have just arrived,' she said, dismissing Chuck as if he had never existed.

'There are also ten Jews. They look awful. They're full of lice and can hardly walk. Dr Steve has relieved me of my duties for the rest of the day. He wants you to go straight away to the transitional tent and help nurse those Jews.'

I was glad to leave my spiteful parent behind. I rushed out of Rosa's kitchen without even eating and headed for the tent which processed the intake of new patients. Chuck's letter rubbed against my skin, a constant reminder of the boy with auburn hair and cornflower eyes now fighting on the front line. I focused on placing one foot in front of the other and getting to work. Feelings were not welcome.

When I arrived, the square was buzzing with activity: trucks coming to pick up the men released from our care and being taken back to the fighting, and trucks arriving with even more wounded for us to tend.

I found Dr Steve instructing the orderlies and nursing staff as the new patients came in on a relentless wave of stretchers. He took my arm and pulled me to one side of the tent.

'Greta, some women and children from the concentration camps arrived late last night. They had been found, half-starved, by our men. Most of them are Jews; some may be political prisoners.' He looked sternly into my eyes, 'Greta, I hope this is not going to be a problem.

I screwed up my face, confused, and said, 'Why would that be a problem? My best friend in the village where I lived was a Jew.'

Then I remembered my mother telling me she had been sent home that morning. I closed my eyes as I began to understand what I had missed while so consumed with Chuck's departure. I met the doctor's icy gaze squarely.

'What did my mother say, Dr Steve?' I said.

He shook his head, looking both tired and gloomy, gesturing to the constant influx of stretcher bearers where to deposit the next group of causalities.

'Your mother does not like the Jews and this was made abundantly clear. I was shocked, I had no idea. If another officer had heard her, I could no longer protect your family.'

The doctor's eyes were like flint as he spoke.

'I took a chance on Helga, on all of you,' he said.

There would be no more soft looks towards my mother now. In front of me stood a stranger. I was frightened. Instead of the easy-going Dr Steve I was now confronted by an angry officer of the Allied forces. With a few words he could cut my family off from work, food, safety and turn us out into a battlefield in which none of us would probably survive. In a heartbeat, my mother's words had revealed us as the enemy, not an innocent family caught up in a war that was nothing to do with them.

Panicking, I knew I had just a small window in which to gain back his trust. Without it, my family could be doomed. In that moment, I had never hated my mother more.

I took hold of Dr Steve's hand, pleading with him. 'Dr Steve, I am sorry for whatever my mother said. You must know I am not like that. Chuck's grandmother was a Jew, my best friend back home was a Jew. She was called Ruth.'

A bleak silence stretched between us. I took one last shot and said,

'Dr Steve, I am not my mother.'

The doctor's shoulders dropped heavily. He looked exhausted and beaten. He had hardly slept as more injured men were arriving daily. Men wounded in the fighting but also by random bombs the Germans were planting everywhere as they fled. Amputated legs and arms had been taken out of the operating tent by the sackful and Dr Steve had been operating day and night.

When he finally spoke it was grudgingly tight-lipped,

'I am glad that Chuck shared his family heritage with you. Greta, I don't care who your family is or where the hell you came from, but I've seen the results of what happened in those camps and I won't listen to the sheer hatred that Hitler fostered. I will not have it in my hospital.'

I dropped to my knees with my head bowed. I would beg, do anything to convince Dr Steve that my family were worth another chance.

Glancing at my bowed head he told me, 'I go by my own experience of people and their actions, and I have seen both you and Hans work with many different people. I have been impressed at how caring and considerate you have both been. But I believed Helga was, too.'

Everything hung in the balance, and I pleaded again. 'Please, give us a chance. Hans and I like working here and feel we are doing a good job. I will speak to Helga very severely. I am ashamed of her.'

Finally, I repeated, 'I am not my mother.'

Out of the corner of my eye, I saw Dr Steve's face relax a little. He beckoned me to get up from the floor.

'Greta, I am glad to hear that you do not have the same values or attitude as your mother.' His voice became confiding for a moment, 'I am very shocked and disappointed in Helga. I thought she was, that she was -'

His voice tailed off into another silence.

I knew why he had not seen my mother as she really was. Her feminine, pretty-little-girl act and bright chatter had fooled Dr Steve. Since we had been in the town, I had seen many times how adept my mother was at dazzling men to get her own way. Dr Steve was one of many who had fallen under her spell. So far from home, dreaming of their wives, these men saw what they wanted to see, and my mother helped them by playing the part.

Dr Steve had made his decision and started to talk,

'OK, Greta, here's what we do. I don't want Helga working in the hospital with patients, I can't allow it. Many of the soldiers, like Chuck, come from Jewish families and there may be more people arriving from the concentration camps.'

Dr Steve's face began to darken, his tone hardened once more, and when he spoke, his voice was louder.

'I just don't understand your mother's attitude no matter how much I try. I did not discriminate against you or your family. Yet your mother spouts the same vile stuff as Hitler. So many people have been destroyed because of his lunacy. If your mother says another word, I will make sure she is jailed and punished for racial hatred.'

I accepted the full blast of his fury, the pent-up anger at Helga and the memory of the awful scenes he'd witnessed as a medic in this war. But as suddenly as his temper exploded, it disappeared. The doctor was bone weary.

He sat down on the chair next to the table he called his desk.

'I'll find a place for Helga as part of the cleaning staff, away from the vulnerable.'

Coldly he said, 'Tell Helga and your brother how close your family was and still is to being handed over to the authorities.'

It was a reprieve but not a pardon.

The hospital was busy and I intended to be indispensable. This was my family's last chance.

The doctor walked briskly with me to the transitional tents at the far end of the square. Each tent we passed was full of casualties, and even more wounded spilled over onto the pathways between the tents. It was obvious that fierce fighting was taking place at the frontline and that the hospital was under immense pressure. As we walked, Dr Steve bellowed out orders to the nursing staff and orderlies and they jumped to attention. The doctor could tell almost at a glance which men stood a chance and which had no hope of survival. Those that would live were taken inside; those that would not, stayed outside on the ground.

One soldier, no more than twenty years old with a shock of velvet black hair, lay slumped against a tent post. He was cut open from his chest to the top of his legs. With a determination that belied his terminal state, he was trying to push back the contents of his stomach into the cavity it had left in his body. Entrails spun and oozed onto his trousers, staining them deep red with blood mixed with bile.

Dr Steve took the cigarette he was smoking out of his own mouth, and, crouching down gently, put it into the mouth of the young man. The soldier was British and looked hopeful as the doctor told him,

'Take it easy son. I'll send over my top nurse to sort you out. You will be on your way home very soon.'

Getting up, Dr Steve gave instructions for one of the orderlies to help the dying boy smoke his very last cigarette. The boy would not die alone.

We arrived at the tent I was assigned. Outside, Dr Steve gave me my orders in a brisk, quiet voice.

'As well as your regular tasks, your duties are to help Lieutenant Watts nurse ten German civilians who have arrived from the camps. Help them to adjust to the hospital, make sure they eat very tiny portions and drink little and often. There have been many cases where prisoners from the camps have died through eating too much too quickly.'

He added, 'Our patients have been deloused, washed and are now in clean clothes. None of them speaks any English, so try to find out who they are and if they have family anywhere.'

Pausing whilst gazing at my face, he informed me, 'These women and children are deeply traumatised and have been systematically beaten, tortured, starved and worse.'

Once again, I bowed my head as he told me, 'It seems right that a German girl like you should see what your government and Hitler has done to the innocent people who once were your neighbours and friends.'

I flushed as he delivered his last warning, 'I will check on them and on you later, Greta.'

Before I could answer, the doctor turned sharply and left, leaving me red faced and guilt ridden.

As I stared at his retreating back, I remembered the summer camps with the League of German Girls, and all of the songs we sang about our racial purity. In that moment, I finally understood what had really happened to Ruth and her family, and the lie of the benign resettlement camps mother told us about. My heart pumped harder and harder as I realised that we were fleeing because my father had been a Nazi too, and part of Hitler's killing machine.

Quickly, I pushed those dark thoughts to the far reaches of my mind, determined never to speak about my time as a willing member of Hitler's youth camps.

What is not said is often the most significant part of any refugee's story.

So whenever memories from my past interrupted, I would tell myself, 'Think of the now, think only of the now.'

I stepped inside the tent, where Lieutenant Watts was tending to a young boy. Watts was a wiry soldier with excellent nursing skills. He was known around the town for his sense of humour and quick wit. Leaving the boy for a moment, he came over, shaking his head.

He gestured to the boy and the other patients in the tent, 'They've all come from the same concentration camp. It was abandoned when the Nazis realised the Allies were advancing. Our boys found them on a roadside and brought them here, along with some wounded Polish soldiers they were transporting. Dr Steve said we'd look after them.'

His usual laughter was completely gone, and Watts looked stricken, 'I've never seen anything like these appalling injuries, even on the battlefields.'

He gestured me to assist as he returned to the boy and began to dress a gaping cut on his stick-thin leg.

'This is Reuben, Greta,' he said to me, before introducing me to the boy, 'Reuben, this is Greta.'

The little boy stared at Watts but did not once move or cry out in pain, despite the severity of his wound. Glancing at the beds around me, my stomach heaved. Each bed contained clothes hanging on the skeletal frames of human beings. I had never seen people so emaciated and still alive. The heads of the women and children were shaven, marked with deep cuts and abrasions. Their faces and skin were the colour of custard and each had a purplish tinge to their fingers and lips. I counted six women and four children, aged between five and ten years old. I later found out the children were much older but the conditions in the camp had stunted their natural growth.

I spoke to them in German. I had to lie to make sure that they weren't afraid, but also to protect my family. I judged my mother harshly for her deceptions, but war makes liars of us all.

'Hello,' I said softly, 'I am Greta and I am an Austrian Jew. I have been working at the hospital for a while. We are here to help you get better and regain your health. I understand the horrors you must have gone through. You are safe now.'

My speech was met with absolute silence.

Lieutenant Watts looked at me quizzically. He knew a smattering of German and that I was neither Austrian nor a Jew. He glanced at me and went on with his work.

For the next few hours, we stayed busy: taking temperatures, changing dressings, removing soiled pads, dispensing medication and finally feeding the women and children tiny amounts of bland food with sips of water. Silence continued throughout, despite my soft smiles and Lieutenant Watts' gentle chatter. A few hours later, with no verbal response from our patients, I tried again. I knew that for a long time these women had had no control over their lives. It was vital to let them know what was happening to them and why.

'You can only have small amounts of food, little and often, until your stomachs are able to digest food again,' I explained. 'We are not being cruel. I know how hungry you must be, but if you eat too much too soon it could be harmful.'

I caught the eye of a violet-eyed woman and I jumped at the shock of her voice when she finally spoke.

'Who are you to say you know what we have gone through?' Her eyes were narrow and her voice rough and rasping. Her teeth were ragged stumps of blood and black. It must have hurt her to speak, but she did not stop.

'Who are you to say you know how it feels to be tortured and starved? Have you seen thousands walk to their death every day? Seen babies thrown on fires, mothers hung by their private parts? You with your pretty hair, white teeth and fancy clothes. Your war seems to have been pretty good!'

I stepped back in shock, realising how patronising and trite my words must sound to these people. She was right. I knew nothing.

'I am sorry. Forgive me,' I said. 'I am young and say the wrong things. I am here to help. What do you need?'

Her reply was quick and surprising. I had assumed she would ask for more food or clothes.

'Where are we? Is the war over? When can we see our families again?'

I did not have answers. It was dangerous to talk about the ending of the war. I was employed by the Allies, so had always kept my mouth shut about what was happening outside of the town.

I stepped closer and knelt down by her bed, whispering my answer.

'This town is on one of the main routes to Berlin. I have heard the war is nearly over. I have been asked to find out your names, and perhaps the soldiers here can help you find family or friends that could take you in?'

She glared hard at me for a long time, then painfully turned away, putting her back to me. Our conversation was over.

For the rest of the day and evening I nursed the women and children, cleaning up the mess as their bowels took exception to regular food and water. They suffered terrible stomach cramps as their bodies struggled to take in nourishment, only to reject it. Our patients lost control of their bladders and bowels often and four were completely bed bound and could not make it to the latrine.

Lieutenant Watts and I talked in low voices as they rested. Were the symptoms just the result of starved bodies processing food again, or the mental relief of being safe? I quickly saw that the women had been tortured in the most intimate parts of their bodies, which would probably result in lifelong bladder and bowel issues.

Watts' growing anxiety was that our patients could be carrying a virulent infectious illness. When Dr Steve reappeared at the tent entrance at dusk, he gestured us outside to be updated on our patients' progress. Listening to our report, he shared Watts' concerns.

'This diarrhoea, the colour of it and smell, could be something serious. For the time being I want you and Lieutenant Watts to stay here. Everyone who has had close contact with these patients has to be isolated. I cannot risk something contagious getting out to the rest of the hospital.'

He continued in a serious tone, 'Get samples of their stools and blood and place them at the front of the tent. I will give you supplies to sterilise everything, and you must both wear your mask and gown at all times.

Watts, you know the routine for this sort of outbreak. Instruct Greta, please.'

When he left, Watts filled me in on how the next week or so would go, all sense of humour gone.

'We cannot leave this tent or the immediate area until the sickness has passed. We could be infectious. It's very serious, Greta. Imagine the disaster if this illness struck down Allied soldiers going to the front line.'

My mind was racing as thoughts of lethal bacteria came into my head. Who knew what disease there had been in the camps and what these women and children might be carrying? I took comfort from Watts' calm pragmatism and Dr Steve's instructions, and concentrated on the task at hand, pushing my fear aside.

So began ten days of clearing up bowel movements, testing stool samples and sterilising everything we touched. Our gowns, filthy bedding, clothes, anything that might contain the infection were all burned. In between, we dressed abrasions, fed and washed the women and children, and prayed that none of them would die, that the illness could be cured and contained.

Our patients hardly said a word. Some were so ill that even raising their heads to take a sip of water was an exhausting effort. A latrine for the women and children, plus a separate one for myself and Lieutenant Watts, was dug in the field behind the tent. Only two of our patients had the strength to make it to the outside toilets, the others lay on rubber sheeting and had little control over any of their bodily functions.

When our patients slept, Lieutenant Watts and I would snatch a quick nap on two chairs, or stand outside for a few moments, chatting over coffee in the fresh air. I discovered Watts' first name was Chris and his family were from New York State. He told me about the city and the blocks of buildings, so high that you could barely see the sky from the pavement, or 'sidewalk', as Chris called it. It was hard to imagine such a thing in the middle of a field, but I loved to try.

'New York sounds like a city of movie stars!' I told him over coffee in the early hours of one morning.

'You're not far wrong there, Greta,' he said. 'I met Errol Flynn, from *Captain Blood*, you know? He was just walking through Central Park one day, and do you know, when I waved, he waved back and said hi!

To me!'

We loved talking about the movies, and Chris had so many stories. I'd never seen *Captain Blood* or Errol Flynn, but I soon felt like I knew them all. He made me cry with laughter showing me the famous walk of an actor and comedian called Charlie Chaplin.

Our conversations were often dark, too. Chris told me how much he hated Hitler and the war. It was a welcome surprise as he talked to me as if I was not a German, just another colleague. For that I was grateful. One evening during a break from our duties, we sat holding our steaming mugs of coffee and watching the sunset over the field that was our only view.

I confided, 'I'm frightened, Chris. I'm frightened all the time that this disease might kill us, that we might not survive the war. I'm even frightened of what happens if we do.'

'It's OK to be scared, Greta,' he said. 'Most of us are scared.'

Looking at me, he continued, 'It's normal to feel fear. It's the people that aren't scared who frighten me the most.'

We watched as the red ball of fire dipped behind the trees and was then obscured by the huge furnace used to burn medical waste. Acrid smoke stained the twilight sky and Chris began talking.

'My friend is an army photographer, and he was with the first group to liberate the camps. It was his job to document what they found there for the Allies. He said there were chimneys there that ran day and night to burn the bodies of the Jews they killed.'

He looked at me with wide eyes, 'It wasn't only Jews either, Greta. There were disabled people there, anyone they decided was not 'pure'. In God's name, Greta, I will never understand how this happened. Never.'

Glancing at my scared face, the lieutenant tried to lighten the mood. He offered me half a chocolate bar he had been 'saving for a special occasion'. We both sat eating slowly, savouring the sweetness. Chris talked of his childhood and asked me about mine. I was non-committal, and just kept asking him questions about America and its seemingly endless possibilities.

I shivered as the night guards came into view on their rounds. They marched continually around the perimeter of the town, looking out for anyone suspicious. Every couple of hours, four of them would walk past the tent, and check we had not broken quarantine. We would shout our names and those of our patients from inside the tent. The soldiers would then walk onwards, their guns always ready to fire. These were the same guards that would have taken control of my family if Dr Steve had not given us a second chance.

Once more I shivered, and Watts looked at me intensely, 'Hope you're not sickening? Greta, do you feel OK?'

'No, I'm fine,' I smiled, 'I'm just a bit cold.'

Trying to change the subject, Watts pretended to sniff his armpits. 'I stink. Pity the water in our shower is stone cold. I swear a hot shower gets you cleaner.'

A rudimentary shower a few short yards from the tent had been quickly assembled once Dr Steve's orders of quarantine had been issued. The shower cubicle had been made out of old doors and bits of wood nailed together, with a blanket as a curtain. A stand pipe with a hose was just for our use. Dr Steve had thought of everything to contain the stomach bug. The shower, though cold, was very welcome after a long shift. After cleaning up faeces that could range in every colour from yellow to black, with the consistency of thick oil or watery slime, it was glorious to have cold, fresh water on my skin. My trips to and from the shower were something to look forward to after hours of nursing. One of the orderlies had smuggled in a sliver of soap, which Hans had managed to acquire. I used it to lather my hair and body.

Six days after the women and children had arrived, there was an improvement in their condition. They were all clearly stronger and the food they were eating was finally being processed as nourishment. Both Chris and I were silently relieved to not have to clear up any more smelly waste. We were both ready to drop.

Slowly, the women and children were getting better, but they refused to speak to me about anything but their treatment, with one exception. The woman who had berated me so furiously on my first day in the tent finally told me her name was Dinah and her son was Asa. I felt honoured at even this small confidence.

When Dr Steve dropped the quarantine and made his first rounds, he was happy with the patients' progress. The women and children had not had a loose bowel movement in three days and most of them, with support, had ventured out of bed. Dinah and Asa even managed to get to the rudimentary toilets.

The samples we had sent over had shown no signs of contagious disease. Dr Steve believed the diarrhoea had been caused by the terrible conditions the women and children had experienced in the camps and the shock for their bodies in trying to process food again. His examination of our patients revealed that they were making the first tentative steps towards long-term recovery, though he quietly told Chris and I that none of them would ever return to full physical health.

'I can see from your excellent nursing and care that the crisis is over,' Dr Steve told us.

'To be on the safe side, I am keeping the tent isolated for another week. But you can both go back to your billets for a well-earned sleep once you have showered and changed. There are nurses outside to relieve you of your duties.'

He gave us one proviso.

'I want you both to have two days' rest and keep away from preparing food and from the kitchens for a further week to be on the safe side. And I don't want either of you to mix with the other patients for an additional week after that. Chris, you can help with some admin work over at the town hall.'

Chris suddenly picked me up, kissed me firmly on the cheek and then swung me around and around and said, 'Honey we did it!'

It was the first time a man had touched me in an affectionate way since Chuck left. I felt tears begin to form but stopped them in their tracks and instead gave out a strange, strangled laugh halfway between a scream and a cry.

Suddenly I felt anxious. Why hadn't Dr Steve given me any instructions or jobs to resume? Was he still angry with Helga? Angry with me?

Since my time in quarantine, I had received only one hastily scribbled note from Hans saying he was fine and hoped I was OK. I had no communication at all from Helga and I hoped that she had kept her mouth firmly shut and not talked out of line while I had been gone. I looked in despair at Dr Steve. Both men put my strange behaviour down to needing a good sleep.

Dr Steve told me sternly, 'This is an order, Greta. Go to the shower, change into clean clothes and then go straight back to your family. You are relieved of your duties until you are fully rested.'

I walked slowly to the shower, placed my dirty overalls in the basket outside, as instructed, and eased my tired body under icy water. As the clear liquid hit my bent shoulders, I felt a little better. I put on my new overalls and walked towards Chris who was at the brazier. I watched as our sweat-stained clothing burnt to a crisp. Then I started to shake in realisation.

Chuck's letter and his silver chain! Normally I transferred both straight to my new uniform, but this time I had been so tired I had forgotten. I had left both precious items in my dirty work clothes in the basket outside the shower.

I shook Chris' arm, 'Where are my old overalls?'

'Why honey, that soiled clothing is burning in hell like that bastard Hitler should be doing!' he grinned.

I started to shake as I watched what was left of my clothes, Chuck's last letter to me and his silver chain disappear into smoke and then ashes.

How would I ever find him now? I would never, ever see him again. It felt like Chuck had died; it felt like I was dying.

Everything started to spin. Then it went black.

CHAPTER 11

Two days later and groggy with sedation, I awoke. Narrowing my eyes to focus, I saw my mother dozing in a chair close by and felt her hand in mine. I peered slowly around an unfamiliar room. I was in a single metal bed, covered by a sheet and a thin blanket. The window was open, and warm air rolled in on a gentle breeze.

'Greta, my girl, you are awake,' my mother said softly.

I smiled at her, then fell instantly back to sleep, puzzling about a photo of Dr Steve and what looked like his wife and son, on a cupboard next to the bed.

As my medication was lowered, I slept less and understood more. The next time I was fully aware, I opened my eyes to find Hans sitting in the chair looking through several movie magazines.

Dr Steve, Dr Steve, she's awake!' my brother shouted.

The major was sitting at a small table a few feet away. As he crossed the room toward me, I realised I was in the medics' accommodation where the higher-ranking officers were stationed, in buildings away from the tents.

'Hi Greta, you look much better after your rest.'

I tried to talk, but Dr Steve put up a finger to silence me.

'Greta, you're here because you worked yourself into a state of nervous exhaustion. Your body was under too much strain, that's why you fainted. I gave you medication to help you sleep so your body could repair itself.'

He smiled down at me, 'There's nothing to worry about, you are going to be just fine.'

I let out a long breath, relieved. Suddenly I understood first-hand why the boys and young men Dr Steve looked after in the hospital tents needed him. Alongside his incredible skills as a physician, he had a powerful professional certainty that made his patients feel secure.

Thoughts of Chuck, his letter and the silver chain were banished into the sealed room in my mind where I hid all difficult and painful things. I had to focus on getting back on my feet, re-joining my family at Rosa's and trying to build a brighter future for us all.

Within a heartbeat of Dr Steve's diagnosis, my usual coping skills went to the practical. Work and being useful were essential coping strategies that had I learnt from my mother and father.

'What about the hospital? Are there enough medics and nurses?' I asked Dr Steve.

'The numbers of injured coming in has significantly dropped over the last week,' he told me. He glanced over at Hans and said, 'But there's still work for me to do, so I'll leave you two to catch up.'

As the doctor left, Hans leaned closer and said quietly, 'I've heard in the kitchens that the fighting is now mostly in Berlin. That's why we're seeing fewer casualties. The hospitals at the frontline are looking after the injured. Maybe it really is all coming to an end, Greta!'

I nodded in hopeful agreement. Hans had grown up so much in such a short time. He was taller, his shoulders broader and there was a new confidence about him. In that moment, though, the hope in his eyes brought the boy he still was back into my view.

Lightening the mood further, proudly from behind his chair, Hans produced a cardboard box which he carefully placed on the bed sheet. Tentatively, I opened the lid and discovered inside a sponge cake with my name iced on the top.

'What do you think of my cake creation, sister?'

'Mick, one of the cooks, gave me some extra provisions as he knew how poorly you have been,' he beamed. 'I think my cooking is getting really good. Hey Greta, maybe I could have my own restaurant one day! You can come and manage it for me as you know how to do things like that.'

He held up one of the magazines and pointed at a photo of a place called a 'diner' in New York.

'Perhaps even in America?'

And there it was, a reason for me to hang on to life. My little brother's wish was the echo and hope for both our futures. A business we could both share, a life and a home far away from war and Germany, a place where we could start again, a country thousands of miles away called America. 'Yes Hans, I would love for us to go to America.'

Deep inside, there was the hope that if we went to America – though it was a vast country with millions of residents – somehow, I would be closer to Chuck and his family.

Hans continued chatting and placing the magazines on my bed, and told me,

'Lieutenant Watts delivered these when you were sleeping. He said you really liked hearing about movies stars.'

I began to flick through the pages, when Hans took my hand and said, 'I don't think we should head for the mountains, Greta.'

I looked at him, puzzled, as he gestured to the magazines.

'The more I have thought about it, the more I think we should all go to America! It looks like a great place to live and work. Look, Greta!'

He took another magazine from the pile and thumbed through the pages.

'I would love a car like this,' he said.

Eyes sparkling as he spoke, Hans showed me a photo of Clark Gable in an open top car, the background a sandy beach and, beyond, an ocean stretching to eternity. It looked like paradise. I remembered Clark Gable from my chats with Chris at the hospital. He was so handsome. I thought of Chuck and his cattle farm, and I pushed the thought away immediately, focusing on the photo of the car.

I spent the rest of the day with my brother, talking and whiling away the afternoon imagining our future life. After a few hours poring over the magazines from Chris, I asked my brother to tell me what I had missed while I was ill.

The conversation turned to our mother and Hans informed me that she had been given cleaning duties at the officer's accommodation in the town hall.

I was relieved that my collapse had overshadowed my mother's outburst and we were once again in Dr Steve's good books.

Then my little brother shared his frustration over our mother's behaviour,

'Things are so different than they were before,' he said, sadly. 'Mother is changed. She is angrier, and sometimes the things she says and does are so very cruel.'

I knew my brother had often been at the sharp end of our mother's tongue.

'But then, when you were sick, mother sat with you whenever she wasn't working. She even cried a little.'

We both fell silent. Neither of us could remember the last time our mother had cried.

It was hard to keep talking about our mother, so our conversation turned to gossip. My brother was great at telling stories which made us forget our worries,

'Doug, one of the cooks, put his favourite picture of a very famous actress above the oven. Her name is Betty Grable, and Doug says he will marry her one day. Anyway, a few days ago, an ember from the oven set the picture on fire – you should have seen Doug!'

Hans ran around, imitating the irate Doug, waving his arms and legs as he tried to save his beloved Betty Grable. I couldn't stop laughing and neither could Hans.

'The picture was burned to a crisp, but Doug kept it! He said as long as he can remember her, she's still with him.'

The antics of the guys that Hans worked with were hilarious, and all of them spoke positively of their lives in America. It seemed a perfect place to make a new start.

Hans and I no longer felt at home in Germany.

Too many horrific events and experiences had stolen our birth country from us, just as it had stolen the mother we knew.

Perhaps America was the answer. But first, we had to survive the war. As we would discover, the end was closer than any of us thought.

A few days later, I was packing my clothing to return to Rosa's when I was disturbed by an odd rumbling sound of noise. Voices shouting but distorted by distance.

I peered down through the open window. A sudden, much nearer shout stopped me in my tracks, then another, and another, a weird hollow banging following each cry.

I strained my ears to hear what was being shouted.

'Hitler is dead, Hitler is dead!'

A soldier ran out of one of the hospital tents. He was banging a saucepan and shouting again and again, 'Hitler is dead!'

I heard a whistle blowing as the cry was picked up by others. Tents opened, and soldiers, nurses and patients who could walk spilled out, some dancing, many holding each other and shouting with joy. Some people were sobbing, overwhelmed.

'Hitler is dead, the Soviets have stormed Berlin!' someone cried out.

Dr Steve appeared outside the canteen and began to excitedly question one of the soldiers.

I stood and stared at the commotion unfolding below me. I felt relieved that the war would soon be over and glad the fighting would stop, but a big part of me was anxious and apprehensive. Hitler had held my country, my family, my life in his grip for so long. Our 'leader'. And now he was no more. Visions flickered through my head, too fast for my thoughts to catch up. Ruth and her family, my many happy days in the German Women's League, my father dancing with my mother in his brown uniform. The Jews being transported from my home town to the camps. Disgust and self-loathing rose like acid scarring my brain, my stomach heaved. I swallowed hard and tried to push the images away. But one thought would not leave me: what would happen to my family now?

Arms grabbed my shoulders from behind and I screamed in fear, but it was only Hans.

'The war is over, Greta!' he cried, pulling me into a bear hug and jumping me up and down on the spot.

Suddenly it all felt wonderful. We rushed down to Dr Steve. We followed him into one of the larger tents, where there seemed to be a bit of a party.

Two bottles of brandy were shared, tiny shots spilt into tin mugs full of black coffee.

'May we all go home very, very soon!' Dr Steve raised his mug as the patients and troops echoed his call.

Hans and I looked at each other, our smiles frozen on our faces. Where was home?

CHAPTER 12

When the celebrating faded, we realised the death of Hitler heralded danger for my family and for all Germans.

The tentative relationships between many of the town's residents and the troops at the hospital had seemed genuine. The US military hospital had become almost a benign presence in the town. Everyone had more food, and we were safer. It seemed like bridges had been built between the occupying Allies and the townspeople.

After the announcement of Hitler's death, the atmosphere changed. There was a simmering hostility towards the Americans and Allies that came from an awareness they were no longer an occupying force, but the victors of the war.

It didn't take long for hostility to become an explosion of aggression.

The son of one of the townspeople, a young boy named Klaus, had become friends with an American private called Daniel Smith. For weeks, they exchanged banter back and forth. Daniel called Klaus 'his little buddy'. The day after the news was announced that Hitler had been killed, Daniel and Klaus were sharing a joke and some chewing gum outside the administration tent. Suddenly the young boy grabbed Daniel's gun and shot him in the heart.

Klaus then ran through the tented town, firing shots indiscriminately into the air and at soldiers and medics who crossed his path.

'Come on, you Jew loving Yanks,' he screamed, 'Come see what a member of the Hitler Youth really thinks of you. You will never defeat the German people.'

As Klaus stood defiantly brandishing the gun, a single shot cracked and echoed around the square. High above, a US trooper situated on the town hall roof fired at the young boy's head. Klaus dropped to his knees instantly, his mouth open in surprise that death could be that quick and easy at twelve years old. He hit the floor and never moved again.

The tragedy of Daniel and Klaus sounded the death knell for our work with the Allies. Dr Steve and the senior officers decided no German should work at the hospital again. With the ending of the Second World War just days away, violence was crackling under the surface between the defeated and the victorious.

Dr Steve called my mother, Hans and me into his room at the town hall. He held out a copy of the *Stars and Stripes*, the military newspaper for US troops. He showed us reports that hostilities would soon formally cease and the US, British, French and Soviets would take control, based at the Allies' headquarters in Berlin. The doctor was grave as he spoke.

'As you know, all the recovering wounded are now being sent from here to permanent hospitals. Patients will be shipped back to England and onwards to the USA. This means all military hospital staff will be moving to another location shortly.'

Dr Steve looked resigned as he sat down behind his desk. 'I have thought this through. It's too dangerous for patients and not appropriate for any of you to continue working at the hospital, especially after the incident with Klaus.'

My mother rushed to speak, 'But Dr Steve, I thought we would all be able to travel with you and the hospital to the next place and continue our work?'

She gave Dr Steve that look from beneath her eyelashes: attractive and defencelessness, which had worked so often in the past. His reply was cold.

'Helga, that's impossible. It would appear with the ending of the war that revenge and sabotage is still a priority for many Germans. I won't risk any of my men or patients, despite your family's help over the last weeks.'

I knew we needed the protection of Dr Steve and the Allies more than ever, so I burst out, 'Dr Steve, please can we go with you to the next posting and then find jobs there?'

He replied in a clipped voice, 'What you must all have learnt during this war is that nothing is stable or consistent. Your time working here is over.'

There was a brief silence. Dr Steve bent under his desk and brought out a bag of food and handed it to my mother. We were dismissed. The doctor resumed his work, waving his hand to signal we should leave. He didn't look up as we left.

The walk back to Rosa's was terrible. A couple of American soldiers were leaning against a wall having a smoke. As we passed, one of them spat in my mother's face, leaving brown spittle on her cheek and eyelashes.

'German whores!' yelled his friend, shaking his fist, 'What's wrong with you people? The war is over, but you send your children to kill our boys!'

We hurried past, silent and afraid.

As we rushed on, we could hear him screaming, 'Dan Smith was my friend and a good guy, you bastard whores!'

My mother rushed us through the narrow streets, before stopping suddenly and pulling us into a doorway. She gave me the sack of food and told us both to run back to Rosa's as fast as we could.

'I will meet you there later.'

I watched her disappear down a cobbled side alley and knew instantly where she was headed: Al Malone's billet. My mother didn't return that night. She arrived mid-morning the next day with news.

'We are leaving today with Manfred. He is giving us a lift on his cart.'

Saying nothing else, she walked to the door and I followed her to the tiny outhouse we used for bathing. Hans and Rosa sat silently, drinking weak coffee at the kitchen table. Shutting the door, my mother began to sluice water from the cracked jug over her arms and then in between her legs.

She told me angrily, 'I stayed with Al Malone last night in the hope he could get us all safe transport to Berlin. This morning when I woke, he and his men had already left.'

Her face twisted in rage.

'To think I slept with that brute all those weeks and for what? It makes me sick just thinking of his hairy paws all over me.'

I stepped forward to comfort her, but she shoved me aside and continued, 'As I was walking back across the square, Dr Steve stopped me. At least he was a little more helpful.'

My eyes brightened; I knew Dr Steve would not let us down.

My mother sneered, 'Don't be too cheerful, men never deliver what they promise. Dr Steve said Manfred could take us to the next Allied supply dump. It's on the road to Berlin.'

We had no choice but to leave the town, as once the Allies had left, food would be scarcer and the townspeople less than welcoming to strangers like us, especially ones that had worked for the Allies.

My mother's voice broke through my thoughts.

'Come on, we have to leave within the hour. Manfred will not wait.'

Time was short but saying goodbye to Rosa was important to me and Hans. She had been so kind, like a grandmother to us both. Rosa refused to travel with us, as she said she was too old and wanted to stay in the town where she had been born. Hans and I kept taking turns to give her a cuddle, not wanting to let go. Deep down, we knew we would never see Rosa again. My brother and I had said too many goodbyes in our short lives.

Unlike us, mother was impatient to leave. She briefly thanked the old lady and left the house without another glance. Slowly, Hans, Rosa and I followed mother's hurried steps across town to the cart. I took my mother to one side as Rosa gave Hans one last embrace.

'Why are we going towards Berlin?' I asked.

'It's best for us to stay with the soldiers. There is always plenty of food and we may find other jobs.'

I must have looked uncertain and was about to speak when I was silenced by her sharp words, 'Don't keep asking such stupid questions.'

She glanced over at Hans and moved closer to me, 'Your father is dead. He is never coming back. I will tell Hans later when there is no one around, but we can never talk about your father again, is that clear?'

'There, she has finally told the truth,' I thought.

It was on that day my father truly died.

There was little time for sentiment, as I also understood that the next part of our journey could well be the most dangerous. With a quick goodbye to Rosa, we stepped up into the awaiting cart.

Manfred, our driver, was a gnarled-faced farmer, terse with a wide, toothless mouth and an even wider brimmed hat. His ageing piebald horse was tethered alongside a boarded-up tavern. The old man used his horse and cart to move equipment back and forth between the hospital and supply depots. This would be Manfred's last trip, so we were fortunate to get a lift.

Pointing at the tavern, Manfred told us, 'Many a time I had a good beer in that establishment. Let's hope life will come back to this town now the war is over.'

He sighed, 'War is futile. Only ordinary people suffer.'

As he fussed with the cart, balancing crates and sacks, he muttered to himself, 'I've lived through two wars and I've had my fill of fighting and what it brings.'

Mother sat in the front of the cart with Manfred while Hans and I squeezed into the back, which was filled to the brim. We noticed that secreted underneath a couple of blankets was a crate of booze. Apparently, Manfred was also part of the 'black market' supplying alcohol to the soldiers and to anyone who had dollars or items to barter.

The thin, almost skeletal nag raised its weary head. Manfred shook the reins, and we moved towards the path heading out of town. There were miles of countryside to navigate before reaching the safety of the supply base. We all knew that we had to keep as quiet as possible and any conversation must be kept to a whisper. The last thing we wanted or needed was unwanted attention from anyone. Hans and I bounced about in the back of the wooden cart, the road uneven due to the heavy use of military vehicles. We both had to hang on tightly to each other.

We watched as the tented hospital where we had made so many memories became just another part of the backdrop. Hans and I waved furiously until Rosa was just an outline and then a tiny dot that disappeared to nothing. The sun was warm, making the skin on our faces tingle; we even got slightly sunburnt.

As the sun moved higher into the sky, we came across a tiny hamlet that was empty of everything and everyone. Not a sound came from the buildings, no bird or creature moved. It was full of ghosts. Shortly after, Manfred pulled on the reins and the thin horse stopped. The old man shared a hunk of cheese and a bottle of the wine from the crate, his tone brisk despite his generosity. My mother drank the red vinegary-tasting booze with relish; both Hans and I hated the taste but didn't want to offend the old man.

'A few more hours and we will be at the supply dump. Captain Mankowitz is mostly in charge, he is the one you need to speak to.'

With that, the old man made his way to the horse with a handful of crumbs and a bucket of water. The elderly beast quickly took both, and, soon after, we were on the road again. The steady rhythm of the horse's hooves was hypnotic and strangely calming. As the sun moved across the sky and shadows fell, the road forked, and we moved into woodland.

Suddenly, four burly US soldiers barred our way. The biggest soldier approached, his granite face relaxing as he recognised Manfred. Clasping sausage-shaped fingers around the reins, the US soldier guided us slowly to the supply depot. The horse and cart were led into a clearing where wooden buildings and tents were heavily camouflaged with dense netting. This made it almost impossible for the base to be seen from the road or sky. Dozens of tents, four sheds, a huge, barn-like building, and several outhouses, including a hastily dug latrine, was the extent of the supply depot.

At least six troops circled the largest building to stop looting, keeping vital supplies and equipment safe. I watched as my mother put her fingers through her hair, moistened her lips, and pinned on her most beguiling look. We stopped at the largest tent and Manfred went inside with the US soldier. A small, tubby man with jet black hair bounced out, as if on springs, and shouted back at the old man.

'Manfred, get your German butt out here and help me move this stuff. We need that radio equipment unloaded pronto.'

Smiling broadly at my mother, the swarthy-faced man walked towards the cart. He held out his hand and, with a gentlemanly flourish, introduced himself.

'I am Sergeant Alex Sanchez, ma'am. Dr Steve sent word you and your kids were coming. He told me how many of our boys you helped nurse back to health.'

Looking over my mother's shoulder briefly, he gave us a small salute, 'Pleased to meet you, Helga, Greta and Hans.'

With a theatrical wave at the buildings and tents, he said 'Welcome to my world!'

'I am in charge of the depot. Captain Mankowitz and the cook left for

Berlin yesterday, so we could really do with some help in the kitchen.'

The stocky sergeant didn't stop talking for a moment as he carried boxes in and out of the tent. His buoyant personality was contagious, and Hans and I couldn't help but grin as he chatted to us over his shoulder. In the next two minutes, we learnt Sanchez was a devout Catholic who missed his mother's wonderful cooking 'more than anything else about home', and that he was glad the cook had been sent to Berlin because 'his food was diabolical'.

Sanchez mimicked vomiting and gestured us to follow him into a nearby tent.

'Look! Behold our magnificent kitchen!' he laughed, gesturing to a tiny stove, worktop and sink.

'Meals for a minimum of thirty men are made here.'

Hans was suddenly in his element and started to clean up, moving the utensils into a more useful arrangement. He asked Sanchez a series of questions about the food stores, giving the young sergeant barely seconds to answer each one before moving onto the next. My brother's time working in the kitchens of the field hospital had given him not only culinary skills, but a huge enthusiasm for baking.

Smiling broadly, Sanchez put his fingers to his lips and kissed the air, before announcing, 'You will be our saviour! One so knowledgeable about cooking, you will become a top chef, I don't doubt it. I cannot wait to try your recipes.'

Hans and I joined in the laughter, and our mother kept her flirtatious smile intact, but her eyes flashed disdain at Sanchez's effusive tone and gestures.

Sanchez ran through the basic layout of the camp. Some tents were used for sleeping quarters, others for the administration of supplies. One of the sheds was used for maintaining vehicles and another for storing medicine and medical supplies, which was locked and with guards on sentry. This was not just to keep looters at bay but also to deter the troops from stealing opiates. During my time at the mobile hospital, it had become apparent that morphine and similar drugs were often used by soldiers to ease fears on the battlefield instead of physical injuries.

The sergeant took us to a huge barn-like shed and we all watched as two soldiers opened massive wooden doors. Hans and I gasped and stared. Stacked floor to ceiling were tins, boxes and sacks of food, enough to feed a town for months.

'All of this is heading for Berlin very soon,' said Sanchez, 'I'm just waiting for the transport.'

Winking at us, he said, 'That's when you can hitch a ride with us to the capital.'

As we finished the tour, Sanchez told us about his four sisters and two brothers, and how his family had come to America after his grandmother emigrated from Mexico to California. Whenever he talked about his grandmother, he would roll his eyes, cross himself and say a prayer. Occasionally he'd burst into song, crooning incomprehensible lyrics in Spanish. Hans and I giggled so much our sides hurt. My mother's bright smile stayed in place when Sanchez was looking at her, but when he wasn't, her expression was contemptuous.

When we arrived back at the main tent, Manfred had already left. Though my family had not known Manfred for long, I felt a moment of panic at his departure, as I realised we were with strangers once again.

'Come into my office,' said Sanchez, proudly showing us his desk and small filing cabinet. Back home, his brothers and sisters were domestic labourers. Sanchez was seen by his family as having prospects with his important military job. In the midst of the office furniture was a neatly made bed. I immediately knew why Sanchez's office also doubled up as his bedroom and it had nothing to do with shortage of space. Sanchez, catching my gaze, seemed embarrassed and muttered,

'Some of the guys don't take kindly to Mexicans, so I sleep here. I am not supposed to sleep alongside the white soldiers.'

Sanchez stopped talking and then glanced at us, a German family, suspiciously until I replied, 'Sanchez, my family more that most understand discrimination not just personally but professionally. When I was working at the field hospital, I nursed some black soldiers and what was known as 'coloured' men. Most of the white American soldiers refused to share a tent with their badly-wounded black or 'coloured' comrades, despite Dr Steve's intervention.'

Sanchez visibly relaxed and a wave of words tumbled out as he confided, 'In America, Mexicans are only given the most menial jobs, and in the army, we are considered not as good as white soldiers.'

Sombrely he told us, 'There has been a bit of bad feeling since Captain Mankowitz's departure.'

I was alert as Sanchez carried on, 'The captain recognised my skills and put me in charge as the highest-ranking solider left at the depot. But you might hear some talk about me and my background, take no notice. Mexicans are the best and bravest, as you shall see.'

Hans and I exchanged looks as we remembered how the black and what was known as 'coloured' soldiers had to eat separately in their tents at the hospital.

They were not allowed to mix with the white US soldiers in the canteen.

I was brought firmly back to the present as Sanchez offered to escort us to where we would be sleeping.

His embarrassment gone, he entertained us with stories of his distant relatives who lived in Spain. We learnt that his grandfather had been a famous matador, or bull fighter.

We were to sleep at the back of a small shed. We watched as the energetic sergeant moved boxes of bandages to make space. Hans and I were open-mouthed when Sanchez retrieved some new woollen blankets from the store adjacent and gave us one each. Brand new blankets that were totally clean and smelt of nothing and no one else. Hans and I kept rubbing the wool against our faces as it felt so nice.

The sergeant bid us goodnight and we made our beds and settled in. Hans chattered excitedly about our new friend, but mother interrupted, her eyes closed.

'He's a homosexual, Hans.'

Hans and I stopped talking and looked at each other uncertain. We had no idea what that word meant.

Our mother made only one more comment.

'I can't stand men like that, if you can even call them men.'

CHAPTER 13

We rose before dawn each morning to prepare food for the day. We fed the soldiers when they came off their shifts, so hot food was available most of the day and often during the night. This meant a lot of cooking, cleaning and hard work, and it kept us busy. There were lighter moments, as we got to know the soldiers and learn about their lives in America.

It was certainly less demanding than my job at the mobile hospital, and I enjoyed the respite.

Days melted into one another as my family became accustomed to a new place, new environment and new jobs.

Seeing my brother's obvious talent in the kitchen made me proud. Hans was in his element devising tasty meals, which were greatly appreciated by the hungry soldiers. I could easily picture my brother running a successful restaurant in America. During his time at the mobile hospital, he had gained a lot of insight into American food and tastes. Most importantly, Hans loved to cook and saw it as a vocation.

When he was cooking, my little brother was transported to a happier place.

One day, Hans and I were dishing up lunch when Sanchez burst into the canteen, jumping onto a table as he tried to play a beaten-up trumpet. The tubby sergeant had won the instrument from a military bandsman in payment for a debt over a card game. Everyone stopped what they were doing to see what the fun-loving sergeant might do next.

One private muttered as he went back to eating his breakfast, 'What is that smartarse Mexican going to tell us to do now?'

Sanchez shouted in his loudest voice,

'I have just got news from HQ in Berlin. The war is officially over! The war in Europe was declared officially over on May 8th, 1945!'

He repeated the message twice and began to dance a jig on the table.

For a heartbeat or two, there was absolute silence, then a roar rose up as the men shouted and laughed, stamping their feet in time with Sanchez. Men shook hands and clapped each other on the back. Others sat in corners crying, some were even praying.

Sanchez continued to dance and blow on the trumpet, before he jumped down and whisked the ladle out of my hand, pulling me and Hans into a dance around the canteen. My mother had been outside peeling potatoes, and came into the tent as we whirled round with Sanchez.

Her face was white and shocked, but she shared a tentative smile. After a few minutes, she came over to join us, opening her arms wide, then holding us tight.

'It's over,' she said, in a thin and tired voice, 'It is finally over.'

Hans and I relaxed into her embrace. It had been such a long time since she showed us affection like this. My mother was so thin, her bird-like bones dug into my flesh. I pushed my face into her golden hair and, for a moment, lost myself in the familiar scent of my childhood, of love, of home.

In an instant the moment was over, and mother pushed us both away, grabbing Sanchez's sleeve as she twirled around and around the tables and benches.

'What does this mean?' she said to him.

Sanchez picked her up and swung her around and said, 'It means, pretty lady, that in a short time we will be heading for Berlin and then back to the good old USA!'

'Yes, but what does it mean for us?' she demanded, but Sanchez had picked up the trumpet again and was blasting out a tuneless ditty.

She shook his arm again and asked, 'Yes, but what does it mean for my family?'

Sanchez still didn't hear her as he continued playing the trumpet and telling everyone over and over that 'the war had ended!'

That evening, the soldiers celebrated but mother, Hans and I retreated to our make shift bedroom at the back of the shed. We knew drink and men could quickly become a deadly mixture, but we slept without incident and the next morning we were back in the kitchen serving up food for the soldiers.

The air was buzzing and all the troops were upbeat and smiling. It was infectious and it felt like the bad times were finally ending.

Sanchez came into the canteen, rubbing his head.

'My mouth is as dry as the desert in Nevada, and my head feels like it might explode.'

The soldier was terribly hungover, but his smile was ever present.

'Don't worry beautiful Helga and Greta and handsome Hans,' he said. 'When the order comes for us to go to Berlin, you are coming with us. Dr Steve said weeks ago he would arrange all of that. But at the moment, our orders are to stay here and carry on with our duties.'

My mother beamed and gave Sanchez a coffee and a large portion of eggs and pancakes, before sitting down beside him.

I knew what was coming.

With a familiar doe-eyed gaze, she said, 'Thank you so much Sanchez for all your kindness. As a mother, I appreciate you helping to keep my children alive. It's so hard being a woman on her own, and you have been the perfect friend.'

With bleary eyes, and shovelling food into his mouth, the sergeant shook his head, trying to smile and chew at the same time.

Mother lowered her gaze and furrowed her brow, suddenly looking panicked and sad.

With a distressed look, she concluded, 'I am just so worried about what will happen to us when we reach Berlin. Did Dr Steve say anything about that? We do not have a loving family like yours, sergeant. There is no one in the capital we can stay with.'

Sanchez was still very hungover, and in his compromised state it took a while for him to understand the responsibility that was being placed upon his shoulders.

The young man opened his mouth to say something, then stopped.

Leaping up from his seat, he reached down and swept mother into his arms.

'I'm sure Dr Steve will be in touch,' he reassured her lightly, 'Of course I will help wherever I can.'

Stepping back, 'Don't worry, I will sort something out. Our lady will show me the way.'

My mother replied with a kiss to Sanchez's sweaty brow and then made her way back to the counter where I was serving food. As she did so, she wiped her lips with distaste. My mother had hopefully paved the way for our family to be safely transported to the capital with the US soldiers and had pushed for some form of accommodation when we arrived. I knew she disliked Sanchez intensely, but, as always, she was prepared to sell her soul for our safety.

I went back to preparing food, but my mind stayed on my mother and her performance with Sanchez. Part of me admired her, but a larger part despised how adept she had become at manipulating people. I hated that she had been raped, had sold her body to Al Malone for food and supplies, had simpered to every man she could, to get her own way.

Helga had become a whore in every way. I hated myself for thinking of my parent in that way. It made me feel both guilty and angry at the same time. I knew in my heart I was also a hypocrite. My mother had done terrible things to keep her children alive, but I was beginning to loathe her and what she had become. I never showed this dislike towards my mother. Ever obedient, I smiled when she wanted or needed agreement. I, too, was acting a part as the mostly biddable daughter and help-mate.

When the announcement of the end of the war settled in across the camp, nothing much really changed. We were in limbo till we left for Berlin. Our menial jobs continued at the supply depot: cooking, cleaning, washing dishes, putting supplies on trucks, and taking supplies off trucks.

We would not be going to Berlin anytime soon, and I was glad. Our chores, though repetitive and mundane, were dependable and trustworthy. Even cleaning ovens and kitchen equipment and serving food had a peaceful, meditative quality. I found safety in the routine, while the thought of Berlin and the fearful uncertainty ahead brought me out in a cold sweat.

Weeks passed, and Hans continued to cook while my mother and I helped in the canteen. We were in a secure bubble, we all had enough to eat and were gaining strength. I started to put on weight and Hans grew a few inches, but my mother, though she ate like a horse, remained thinner than ever.

It was a Sunday when we heard from an old friend. A visiting chaplain, Father Major Wainwright, held a Sunday service for the soldiers. We were not invited, so I watched through a small opening at the back of the tent. I was reminded of the Sunday services of my childhood and I relaxed into the feeling of home as the chaplain invited the men to sing hymns and offer thanks to God.

Lost in a rare moment of peace, I did not hear her footsteps approaching.

'What are you doing?' Sharp fingers dug into my flesh as my mother pulled me away.

'My family do not get involved in all that stupid stuff. Waste of time. Pah!' she dismissed. 'Rituals! Where did they get any of us?'

For once I retaliated, 'Well you got married to father in a church, was that just a ritual too?'

A crack like a whip spun me around as her hand smashed across my face and I staggered to the floor, just missing a tent peg through my hand. Only one tear dropped from my eye, as I watched her slender figure stride towards the kitchen.

Hans looked up from emptying a bin and ran to me.

'Greta are you OK?'

Under my breath, but within earshot of my brother, I said, 'She is a bitch, I detest her.'

Hans helped me up, shocked.

'Never say that Greta, we are a family and must care for each other,' he said. 'She has been through a lot.'

I answered, 'And so have we.'

I brushed mud off my overalls and headed towards the canteen with Hans, but we didn't make it far before Sanchez ran over.

'Come quickly, quickly. Dr Steve is on the radio, and he wants to talk to both of you!'

We dashed to the radio office, where Private Jones was sat hunched over the buzzing radio.

Suddenly, we heard the crackling but familiar voice of Dr Steve.

'Hans, Greta, I am glad you are keeping well. I am now in Berlin. This is just a short message. I should not even be talking to you.'

There was a humming sound as his voice became distant and then clear again.

'Stay away from Berlin, try to go somewhere else. People are starving, the city is full of rubble and destroyed buildings.'

The crackle returned with background noise of men and vehicles, until Dr Steve's voice was clear again.

I shouted through the small mic, 'Dr Steve, I hope you are well too. We have no one in Berlin. Can you help? Can you tell us where you are staying, and we could come and stay with you?'

There was static and then complete silence. Hans and I looked at each other. There was a sense of joy at hearing Dr Steve and his promise to help, and shock that our conversation was so brief. Fear crossed Hans' face as he realised that our destination, Berlin, was not going to be a good place to stay.

Private Jones looked at our faces with sympathy and said, 'He only had a short time to talk. I am sure he will be in touch soon. Next time I speak to Dr Steve, I'll tell him you have no family in Berlin and see if he can help.'

The young soldier turned to smile at Hans and said, 'Maybe I can get an extra portion of that wonderful stew you make when I'm working the late shift!'

Hans promised to send over extra portions of everything he made, if the radio operator could just pass on our message to Dr Steve.

My brother protectively put his arm around my shoulder as we walked back to the kitchen, and, with a steely look, reassured me, 'I'm sure Dr Steve will help. It's going to be OK, Greta! Perhaps eventually he could sponsor us in America?'

In that moment, Hans' face was so full of hope. I smiled briefly at him saying 'OK', a term that he used liberally in his conversations now. He had picked it up, along with other sayings, from the American GIs. 'OK' was a positive word and I had to remain positive for my little brother, even though he was now nearly as tall as his sister.

As we entered our workplace, Helga was glowering over a pot of vegetables and meat. She said nothing to us, nor we to her, not even to tell her about Dr Steve and his warning. She would be angry that she been excluded from the radio call and would probably take her frustration out on me or Hans. My face was still red from her slap and I did not want to repeat the experience.

I realised that Helga's vicious behaviour was caused by the terrible stress she was under and the uncertainty of our family's future. But reasons or logic did nothing to temper my dislike and growing indifference towards my mother.

War had changed me, too.

CHAPTER 14

As Dr Steve advised, we stayed at the base with Sanchez. Weeks passed. Trucks came and took supplies away, and slowly the stash of food and medicines diminished. Buildings and sheds were dismantled. The depot was shrinking. Our world was being taken apart once more, and soon we would be moving to another place where we would have to start again.

Still no word came from Dr Steve, despite many radio communications from Berlin and the US HQ. Every day I would pass the tent when Private Jones was on shift and ask him if there was any news, but despite the radio operator's support, Dr Steve seemed to have disappeared.

One afternoon, Private Jones told me, 'Greta I am getting terrible reports back from Berlin. It's a total barren landscape, the city has been bombed hundreds of times. My counterpart in Berlin tells me there are only few habitable buildings and people are stealing and running wild. Is there not another place you can go?'

I shook my head. Where could we go? Berlin seemed the only option. Life on the road for a single-parent family was far too dangerous. The capital, and the hope of help from Sanchez or Dr Steve, seemed the only option.

Our duties in the canteen were lighter, as the men at the base were gradually moved onwards. We were re-assigned to help Sanchez with the inventory of supplies and packing up the food and essentials for the trip to Berlin.

A few more weeks passed and at times I felt we could stay at the supply depot for months. Finally though, we were on the move, as one very hot spring day Sanchez called us into his office. Sweat pouring from his forehead he told us,

'We will be moving out completely within four days.'

He brushed away greasy hair from his brow nervously as he turned to my mother.

'Helga, you and your children will be coming with me on the last truck out of here.'

He held up his hand as I tried to speak and find out more information,

'There has been no further word from Dr Steve. I will try my best to help you. I have colleagues in Berlin, and I am going to see if they can find you some accommodation. I can offer you no promises, as I have been unable to get hold of them either.'

Helga – I had not spoken the word 'mother' since she had hit me – replied in a sugary tone, 'Thank you so much for caring for us. We will help you to pack up and get ready for the journey.'

Sanchez offered her a small shrug, as Helga pushed on, 'Thank you for finding us a place to stay the city.'

Sanchez turned to her sharply. 'Helga, you twist my words. I said I would try, but I won't promise something I can't achieve.'

He kissed the cross that hung around his neck, and I was reminded of the cross that Chuck's mother had given him. Suddenly, the tent began to spin. I grabbed onto a chair and willed myself back into the present. Hans saw my face go pale, and, alarmed, held on to me.

I whispered, 'Don't worry, I'm just a little tired and it's so hot in here.'

The tent stilled, and Hans and I went about our daily routine, whilst Helga continued to cajole a squirming Sanchez. She was nothing if not persistent.

During those last days at the supply base, Helga urged both me and my brother to eat as much as possible and sleep as much as we could. We all had to be healthy and fit for the forthcoming journey.

Four days later, we were on the move. The last remaining tents were taken down and packed away with kit bags, weapons, supplies and the kitchen equipment, as the last of us prepared to leave the camp. All that remained of the base now was yellowed grass and dusty earth.

Sanchez brought the three of us to sit in the front of the lorry with him. It was exciting to see the road ahead, though we bumped and jolted over pot holes in the damaged roads.

Hans looked green and I felt the same. That morning, Helga had forced us to eat a huge breakfast, telling us coldly, 'I don't know when we might eat again.'

Distracting us from our churning stomachs, Sanchez chatted incessantly and kept Hans and I entertained with his stories and gossip.

'I read Clark Gable recently flew over Germany,' he announced, and my attention leapt at the mention of my favourite movie star crush.

'He joined the US Air Force and has become a hero off screen as well as on it.'

I felt sad as I realised Clark Gable had been one of the many bombers in the raids that had all but destroyed Berlin. War changes all men, it seemed, even Clark Gable.

My mother's face was thunderous, as Sanchez chattered on about the raids on the German capital. Sensing he should not have bragged, Sanchez became subdued.

The cheerful soldier could not stay quiet for long though, and was soon sharing a series of his usual funny tall stories, but I could no longer enjoy them as I once had. I even felt a shade of resentment at this man who I had for weeks regarded as my friend.

While Hans slept, and my mother stared out of the window, my mind span with jumbled thoughts and fears about the future. The Allies were made up of many nations who had cooperated through the war. But what would happen to that alliance now the fighting was over? My country had been brought to its knees. Would the Allies help us to recover? As I looked around, the landscape was brown and mostly bare apart from a few tufts of grass, the road potted and broken. We were the only vehicle on the road and there were no pedestrians either. The only sound was the whirring of the engine and Sanchez's ongoing chatter.

I sensed Sanchez's mood change as we neared Berlin. He was a US soldier and we were part of the nation that had lost the war. The humour in his voice disappeared as he told us, 'Although we are Allies, you must be careful in Berlin to remember that not all of the nations are the same. The areas patrolled by the Soviets are said to be very harsh, stay away from them if you can. They will not see Germans in the same way that we do.'

I felt my mother shiver as he mentioned Soviet troops, but she turned away when I looked at her. There was no point pushing her; I had enough fear of my own. Sanchez had made no mention of our fate once we got to the city, and our attempts to ask him had been met with silence or ignored.

As the day moved onwards and the sun hit its highest point in the sky, we stopped for a drink to allow our driver to rest a while.

Sanchez became stern. As we sat under a tree for shade, he informed us, 'This part of the journey has been easy. Don't be fooled. I have been told that when we turn at the next crossroad, there will be many people and troops. Helga, you and your children are not to talk unless I say so.'

Sanchez was serious, 'I will handle any questions, is that clear?'

He stared directly at my mother, his exuberant nature tempered. We agreed and got back into the lorry and drove for another hour or so until we reached the crossroads.

Long before we arrived, we smelt and heard them. The odour of hundreds of unwashed people, the sickly-sweet scent of rotting corpses, and the rumbling sounds of feet stomping and scraping on bone-dry earth. As our vehicle turned onto a much wider road, I gasped at the view in front and to the side of the truck. A huge mound of swaying, moving creatures that looked barely human: wandering, displaced people, some staggering, some walking, dazed. Between these marched pockets of Allied soldiers striding with determination and purpose. Carts dragged by skeletal nags slowed our pace. A few armoured trucks in the distance kept blaring their horns, hurrying the human detritus out of the way.

All of us were heading towards Berlin.

The four of us looked around in total shock. The pace of the lorry slowed to accommodate people weaving about in the centre of road, emaciated and dying but still willing their bodies onwards. Entire families clung to the edges of wooden carts, piled with possessions. Filthy men with straggling beards linked arms with dirt-faced women and silent, blank-faced children as they lurched forward, leaning on each other for support more than comfort. Women dragged weary feet as they cradled children in their arms or carried them on their backs. Many were bloodied and wounded. Others were so thin I wondered how they managed to stand on legs with no flesh, just bone.

Sanchez blew the horn when the lorry could not move for people, to persuade the malnourished, wide-eyed men, women, and children out of the way. In ditches on either side of the road sat other groups and individuals, some laying down, others holding out their hands in supplication. There were dozens of frozen-faced skeletons who were once living, breathing people staring sightless into the blazing afternoon sun. I looked at them in morbid fascination, looked away, and then looked again.

My mother asked, 'If all these desperate people are heading for Berlin, how will my family find accommodation or jobs?'

Sanchez, now almost unrecognizable from the friendly man we had known at the supply depot, warned her through gritted teeth, 'Shut up till I tell you to speak. Your German accent will not help your cause. You and your family could create a lot of problems for me. You should not even be in a US Army vehicle.'

We were paralysed into silence.

We passed a couple of buildings that had been destroyed by some sort of explosion. Curls of black smoke still wisped from what was left of roofs and walls. Hans and I gasped as we saw three bodies which appeared to have melted like wax, their legs and arms long, yellow and string like. The face of one reminded me of the painting *The Scream*. The head had formed an S-shape, with a strange, elongated chin. A slack, huge mouth gaped in an eternal, soundless scream. I knew of the famous painting by Edvard Munch. It had given me nightmares after I was forced to watch my father burn a copy of it in the street. The picture had been part of other possessions once owned by a Jewish banker who lived near my birth home. As a police officer, my father was instructed to burn many copies of works of art and books that Hitler loathed.

With a terrible irony, our lorry came to a standstill alongside the melted corpses, as a jam of people barred our way. Helga's eyes met mine and I knew she was remembering the day of the fires, too. Silently, she put her finger to her mouth, urging me not to speak about the terrible things that my father had done and we as his family had witnessed.

We sat in the lorry for a long time as the human traffic ahead moved at a snail's pace. The four of us kept trying to look ahead, but all the time we were drawn again and again to the grotesque waxwork-like display of what were once living individuals.

I had so many questions but did not dare speak. Sanchez's mood had visibly darkened as he edged the lorry along inch by inch, making sure he did not hit a refugee.

Eventually he said, 'I will talk, but please none of you reply or speak.

'When a bomb explodes, there is often a fire-storm. People close to the explosion will disappear to nothing. Those on the edges will remain but their skin and fat will melt. When the heat lessens, the body solidifies and the remains are twisted into curious shapes and sizes.'

The waxy corpses seemed to make Sanchez regret his harsh words.

'I am sorry I shouted. I am worried, very worried, for you and for me. Dr Steve was supposed to sort everything out so you could accompany me on this trip. There has been no word from him. You should not be here with me. I could get into a lot of trouble with my commanding officer by giving you a lift.'

It was yet another blow but explained Sanchez's sudden personality change. I tried to focus my eyes, looking at the road ahead. It proved impossible for any of us. Continuing scenes of horror played out around our vehicle. Sanchez advised us to wind up the windows and shouted for the GIs in the back to have their guns handy. Desperate people often meant desperate behaviour. Even with the windows closed, the smell was overpowering.

Women of all ages with babies and small children sat in ditches and on banks of sparse grass. Lone infants sat quietly by the cadavers of their families. Death was everywhere. Mothers were holding out their charges as, exhausted and dying, they begged anyone to take their child so that their infant might live.

One woman is etched forever in my memory, the expression on her face, the way she looked at me and the utter horror of her situation. An image that I have never been able to banish from my mind.

She was just a few years older than me, with a grimy toddler beside her and a tiny scrap of a baby in a threadbare, filthy blanket. The toddler stood and rocked back and forth, dressed in rags and in total distress, while the mother held out the baby to every passing person or vehicle, pleading in what appeared to be Polish for someone to look after her babe. As the mother held out the baby to us, I could see that the infant was dead and had been for a long time. Flies buzzed around its green and blue bloated face as the woman's toddler daughter continued to wail for food.

The four of us in the front of the lorry physically recoiled at the sight of the decomposing baby. We all turned our faces front and shifted our weight as if shifting away from any responsibility. Helga held onto our sack of food with grim determination. Sanchez drove onwards to the city.

Of course, Sanchez could have stopped and offered some of our food. I could have insisted that we helped the grieving mother. Helga and Hans could have protested, as could the US soldiers in the back of the truck. Helga could have given some of our food to the starving mother and child. She did not and I did not urge her to do so.

We had transport and spare clothes. We all had the means to save the mother and her toddler.

But we didn't.

None of us wanted to share anything, as our survival was more important than that woman, her child or anyone else.

CHAPTER 15

Eventually, in the distance, we saw the beginnings of what was once the bustling and wealthy city of Berlin. I had never been to the capital, but my parents had visited on a few occasions when they were first married. I remember my father telling me and my brother about the wonderful cafés situated alongside the Landwehr Canal, and the theatres and museums my parents visited during their trips.

The Berlin we were approaching would be very changed.

The throng of refugees and displaced people had lessened to just a few stragglers. Our lorry moved faster, so the remaining poor creatures who walked or staggered along the rutted roadside were soon left far behind. Suddenly, there was a whoosh of warm air and the urgent honking of horns as two battered US Army jeeps came alongside. Sergeant Sanchez was forced to swerve and then stop. An officer, his face caked with dust, got out of the first jeep shouting,

'Sergeant! I am Lieutenant Moss! You and your companions - get out of the truck!'

Four soldiers got out of the other jeep, their guns pointing at us to move and stand in line.

'Let's see who these people are that are taking up the front seat of a United States Army vehicle!'

Sanchez saluted, explained who he was and outlined his orders to take the truck and its contents to Berlin. As the lieutenant narrowed his eyes, Sanchez made up a story as to why he was carrying extra passengers.

'These are refugees, Sir. I picked them up on the road, they were being bothered by some soldiers. They are in shock, too traumatised to speak, and with no papers. I believe they may have come from the occupied areas. I was going to drop them off in Berlin, Sir.'

Lieutenant Moss moved closer to Sanchez and shouted in his face, 'It is not the job of a United States Army Sergeant to pick up filthy refugees.'

Once again, my family stood in line as men decided our fate. The lieutenant, clearly angry, bawled, 'I don't care for these people. I have three men, one who is wounded. They must be in Berlin by this evening. My men will ride in the front with you, Sergeant Sanchez.'

Pointing at us, Moss continued, 'Not them!'

Sanchez tried to talk but was shouted down again by the lieutenant.

'I have orders to return to my post, so you need to take these men onwards.'

The lieutenant strode over to me and pushed me in the ribs, asking, 'Who are you? What's your business in Berlin?'

Behind the lieutenant, Sanchez put a finger to his lips. Helga threw herself at the lieutenant's feet, put her hands together and looked up at him, her eyes full of pain. It was a masterclass in mime.

Moss kicked my mother away and, turning to Sanchez, said, 'I still don't care for them at all. But if there is room in the back of the lorry, you can take them to Berlin. If there is any trouble, shoot them.'

He stared at the now-heavily perspiring Sanchez and repeated, 'Shoot them. That is an order.'

Lieutenant Moss, depositing the three soldiers, strode back to his jeep. He sat and watched as my mother, Hans and I scrambled into the back of the lorry. It was a very tight squeeze.

The four GIs who had travelled with us from the supply base tried to help, shoving their kit bags into tiny spaces between equipment and boxes. Hunched and bent double, we just managed to get on board. I watched the US jeeps turn and drive away from Berlin. A huge dust cloud blown up by the spinning wheels made me cough. It was a hot afternoon. I heard Sanchez and the other soldiers help the wounded man into the front seat. The lorry dipped down as the men with their extra kit and weight made themselves comfortable alongside Sanchez. Finally, the third US soldier, with a livid black eye and a scar running from cheek to forehead, tried to get into the back of the vehicle. There was no room.

He shouted at my mother in German to move over, and she foolishly replied in our native tongue.

The US soldier, eyes blazing, spat out in English, 'My wounded buddy needs to stretch out in the front. I need to be in the back, not dirt like you.'

The soldier glared at Hans before leaning forward to grab the neck of his jumper. He dragged Hans from the lorry and threw him onto the hard road. My brother fell to the ground and watched as the soldier got into the back of the lorry.

My mother's second retort in thickly accented English angered the now-furious soldier even more.

'Please don't do that to my son! He has to come with his family, we can make enough room.'

With begging eyes, she looked at the other GIs now wedged into the back of the truck, the same men we had served food at the supply depot. They looked away.

'Get the fuck out of here, you German cunt, before I put a bullet in your brain and two in your filthy kids.'

The GI pointed his rifle at my mother's head and ordered us both to get out. He banged the side of the lorry with his gun to tell Sanchez to drive onwards. With a quick rev of the engine, the lorry moved away. My mother was still holding tightly to our sack of food as we all watched our lift to Berlin disappear into the distance.

Wobbling legs would not hold me, and I collapsed onto the ground.

My mother hauled me up, then Hans. She turned and began walking towards the city. It was a decision that would have severe consequences for us all.

Helga threw a few curt sentences over her shoulder.

'Get a move on. We have to be inside, somewhere secure, before it gets dark.'

I hesitated, looking around. Why were there no other people on the road? Was it even safe to approach the city so late in the afternoon? I tried to explain my doubts, but my mother was in charge and would brook no opposition. Automatically, my brother and I put one foot in front of the other and started to walk.

Berlin was a sprawling city and its outskirts a mile or so in the distance. At first, all we could see were the tops of a few scattered buildings. As we got nearer, the remains of many buildings and homes were scattered across the entire landscape. Tiles, bricks, wood and other debris looked like it had been scooped up by a giant's hand and thrown, haphazardly, into awkward shapes and strange places.

As we walked, I saw a photograph of a family hanging from a steel girder. They were probably long dead by now. The picture just out of reach, framed in silver, showed two smiling adults and their children. The photograph was untouched by the surrounding devastation as it swung gently in the breeze from the skeletal framework of what was once an industrial building.

Our noses were soon hit by the heavy smell of acrid smoke and dust and the rank scent of decay and death. Mother stood still for a moment and then said almost in a whisper, 'I recognise nothing. Everything familiar has gone.'

None of us knew how long it would take to navigate the bombed-out buildings. Rubble was strewn across whole area. Gaping holes in houses revealed strange scenes, empty of people, sound and life: chairs and tables set for tea, cups and saucers in place and lamps still upright. Mostly though, our entry into Berlin revealed ghost streets lined with the shells of buildings. Lone structures, which looked like they could have been offices, loomed over a few houses that had somehow survived the onslaught of battle and bombings, but on closer inspection, they contained little but the walls and floors.

We seemed to be the only people on the road, which was odd after the mass of humanity we had seen heading towards Berlin. Mother stopped to give us a drink from a flask she had secreted in her sack of our supplies. I noticed that she just sipped the water so that there was more for us.

The light was starting to fade as we came across a strange woman carrying a bucket peppered with holes.

'Willum, where are you?' the grubby woman asked again and again. 'Where are you, my son?'

Mother called to the woman in an attempt to engage and get some directions.

The frizzy-haired shoeless woman, with bleeding feet, ran away when we approached. We wisely didn't follow the deranged mother.

Then the landscape changed again. The buildings around seemed to be store rooms, out-houses or sheds, with a few cottages or houses in between. Most looked dangerously unsafe, as if they could topple over at any time. Apart from the buzzing of flies and insects feasting on the many victims buried under the destroyed buildings, there was utter silence. Just the scratching of our tired feet echoed into the emptiness that was once the outskirts of Berlin. It felt like we were the only people in the entire world. My mother insisted we walk in the centre of the road so that if a building collapsed, we would have a chance of escape, but this made us visible and vulnerable. The bluebell sky changed grey and the light to the colour of slate.

I was relieved when we came across two buildings. They were just old storerooms, but looked stable and had a roof and walls. We had to be inside and safe before the light completely disappeared.

'We will stay here for the night,' my mother told me. She shouted for Hans, who was dawdling behind. He'd found a stick and was pushing bricks and dirt around in search of treasure. As we waited for him, mother and I jumped at the sound of deep voices and the clip-clop of horses' hooves. Laughter echoed from around the corner of the building, then words spoken in Russian, something about vodka and tea. It was two Soviet soldiers. They appeared carrying guns across their backs, suddenly alert to our presence.

My mother and I turned to run, and I saw Hans disappear around a corner further up the street. Within seconds, the Soviet soldiers had urged their horses onwards, picked us both up and swung us separately across their saddles. We tried to escape but thick arms held us captive.

The horses trotted into the blue darkness of a different building. I was thrown onto the floor by the taller of the two Soviet soldiers. He had yellow teeth and sucked away on a cigarette that smelled of mould. His rock-hard arm squeezed my wrist. Out of the side of my eye, I could see Helga spread-eagled on top of a table in the middle of the building. An odd question pierced my mind and I thought how strange that a complete wooden table could have survived the intense bombing intact.

Already, the shorter, stocky Soviet who had abducted my mother had his trousers around his ankles and I saw his white rear move up and down in the gloom. Helga shouted in German, English and a smattering of Russian learnt whilst nursing Soviets at the mobile hospital.

'Please, please don't touch my baby! You can both have me, but don't touch my Greta!'

Screaming, she pleaded, 'I will do anything you want, as much as you want. Please let my baby go.'

I watched, paralysed with fear, as the fatter Soviet punched Helga in the face so hard that a front tooth flew out and landed at my feet.

Helga's strangled voice shouted to me, 'Greta, just lie there. Let him do anything he wants. You have to live.'

There was silence as I heard the whoosh of another blow to my mother's stricken face. I saw her head loll unconscious into darkness.

The Soviet with the yellow-stained teeth laughed.

I was raped repeatedly, turned over back and forth. I had been a virgin, had kept myself intact throughout the war. Now the war was over, I lost my innocence in every way. The attack went on and on. I found out later that some men in war can climax repeatedly, as if all the aggression and murderous feelings are spilled between the legs of willing or unwilling females. Perhaps this is why so many women raped in war become pregnant.

The Soviet pushed himself into every opening of my body. My eyes, face, mouth, hands were covered with his sticky semen, my legs bruised and bloodied. I stared above at the gaping holes in the roof of the building and looked at the stars, twinkling silver and gold. I concentrated on one star and looked upwards. I tried to think of being outside of my body and floating in space. I wanted to be in any time or place but here, underneath the Soviet with the stinking teeth, black fingernails and putrid breath.

Eventually it stopped. The soldier wiped his mouth on my face and his penis on my arm, pulled up his trousers, and retreated to another part of building. He sat with the other Soviet soldier and they talked and shared another cigarette. I heard them quarrelling over our sack of food and who should go with me next.

I could not move, sperm stuck to my eyelashes, lips, hands, it was everywhere. For good measure, in between his chat with the other Soviet, the taller soldier had come over and urinated over my feet.

I wet myself. My legs and thighs were blood-splattered. I kept lying there, shock and fear petrifying any movement. Helga was rousing, moaning something incomprehensible. I strained my ears to find out what the Soviets were talking about. I found out that the stocky one who had attacked Helga was called Vassilly. I never found out the name of my rapist. From what I could understand of their conversation, I suspected they were going to take turns raping us again and then we would be murdered.

In the distance, I heard a vehicle and voices. My heart was beating so fast I thought it would leap out of my chest. If there were more Soviet soldiers, the rapes might continue for hours until we died.

A gunshot cut through the voices. I heard English.

'What the hell have you fuckers been up to?'

Another voice followed, 'You two Ivans! If you don't move away from those women and come over here, I'm going to shoot you dead, both of you.'

He repeated the warning in Russian. The two Soviet soldiers scrabbled to their feet and moved towards the outline of six men standing in the doorway of the storeroom.

In broken English, the Soviets answered.

'These are just German women, they mean nothing. Why don't you have some fun, too?'

The English soldier, with a strange accent I didn't recognise, shouted,

'Get out of here! What do you take me or my men for, animals like you?'

Vassilly and his comrade became belligerent.

'German soldiers killed my entire village, my parents, too! They are fascist beasts!' growled Vassilly, 'Why should I care for German bitches?'

There was a lot of pushing and shoving as the tall Soviet and Vassilly were kicked and man-handled out of the building by four of the Allied soldiers. Vassilly grabbed the sack containing what was left of our belongings as he went.

The smell of my rapist was everywhere. I could taste him in the air that I was gulping down, and my skin seemed to have absorbed his very scent. I was unable to move a muscle. I shut my eyes as I heard an Allied soldier's tread move towards my prone body.

I sensed a man bending over me. I could feel his breath on my face. I willed myself to die or faint, but I remained conscious of every beat of my heart and of each ragged breath escaping my bruised ribs.

'Lassie, you're safe now,' a voice said. It was the man with the strange accent.

'My goodness, you're only a child.'

He made a sound like a cough, and there was a short silence before he said, 'I'm Jock McKenzie of the 15th Scottish Division. These are my men.'

Another silence followed before he said, 'Don't be afraid, we won't hurt you.'

I kept my eyes closed tight and held my breath.

When the voice came again, it was soft, almost a whisper, 'My great grandparents were Highlanders, child. I promise you, we respect women.'

I had no idea what a Highlander was, but the word sounded strong and reliable. Before I could answer, I felt a hand in mine and suddenly Helga was by my side. She had crawled from the table to comfort me.

'I'm here, my Liebling. Don't worry, it's over now.'

My mother spat on her dress and wiped the sticky fluid from my eyelashes and face. She was trying to smile, to reassure me, but she had no front upper teeth, a split lip and an eye the size of a golf ball.

Mother gathered me in her arms and whispered the phrases she used to say to calm me when I was young and unwell. She rocked me back and forth, assuring me that she was close.

Helga turned her face to Jock and said in English, 'Thank you for saving us.'

Her voice whistled through her missing teeth.

Jock introduced his fellow soldier, Jamie, another Highlander. Jamie and Jock took off their jackets and handed them to me and Helga to wrap around our shame. My top and skirt were shredded, and Helga's dress had been ripped from neck to knee.

I looked up and saw my brother peering around the doorframe. He came slowly over and, through gritted teeth, said, 'I curse those Soviet bastards and their families and children. I should have stayed and killed them. One day I will find them and slit their throats.'

My mother went to comfort Hans but he continued with his rant, a mixture of guilt and anger, explaining, 'When I saw the Soviets capture you, I ran for help, as I figured that with their guns -'

He gasped for air, 'I ran through the streets but there was nobody about. Then I saw the lights of the Highlanders' patrol lorry.'

Jock intervened, 'Your brother begged and begged for us to come. We were not sure at first whether it was a trap. There is still a lot of animosity and resistance towards the Allied forces. But I could tell that Hans was a good kid and of course we wanted to help.'

The Scottish soldier with the lovely lilt to his voice placed his hand on Hans' shoulder and told him, 'You saved the lives of all your family. If those Soviets had got hold of you, they would have shot you straight away. You did the right thing coming for our help, laddie. Never be in any doubt of that.'

Hans moved towards me and took my other hand. His once soft, young face looked like granite. The red-haired giant of a Highlander lit a cigarette and offered a drag to all of us. Hans took the lighted butt, gave a long pull and exhaled deeply. He had clearly been smoking for a while, but for once Helga did not reprimand or chastise. She was as traumatised as I and did not refuse the proffered cigarette either. After sharing a cigarette, Jock and the other soldiers kept a respectful distance as my little brother supported me and Helga out of the building.

The anonymous, dirty storeroom in Berlin where I had not only lost my virginity but also the last remnants of the girl called Greta.

CHAPTER 16

We drove around with the Scottish soldiers for several hours, as they patrolled the city trying to protect its inhabitants. Highlander Jock and his men had orders and were not supposed to be back at their billets until dawn.

The Scottish soldiers did their best to keep peace in a city of chaos and vengeance. I sat stone-faced as Helga continued to hug me, and Hans clasped my hands. Jock and Jamie had placed us at the very back of the lorry, safe but also in the pitch black. It was neither comforting nor frightening for me; I had completely shut down, unable to think, speak or reason. Fresh water was offered to us in a bucket to wash our faces and hands, and two blankets to replace the men's uniform jackets.

Jock made sure that two of his men guarded us at all times, while the others went about the task of searching buildings for rogue German soldiers or anything criminal taking place that needed a firm hand or a bullet. Occasionally we heard a shot fired, running feet and then silence.

As the blackness turned to navy blue and glimpses of light entered the dank darkness, the canvas flap opened and Jock, grinning, came towards us. He thrust a tin mug up to my mouth and pushed opened my lips with the metal rim.

He ordered in a no-nonsense voice, 'Drink all of this as quickly as you can.'

He stood over me. I obeyed and gasped as a fiery, burning taste filled my mouth, throat and stomach. It was strangely comforting. Jock had a bottle of whisky and filled up the cup again and gave it to Helga, before finally offering a half-size measure for Hans. He laughed as he told us,

'We have just relieved a very overweight publican of his contraband and I thought you could all do with a stiff drink!'

He glanced at us, saying firmly, 'I know I could,' before he took a great glug from the bottle.

The warmth of the spirit gently eased my petrified limbs. Helga started to relax a little and Hans' hand softened within mine.

Jock told us, 'We have just an hour to go before we finish our patrol. Then I will take you all somewhere safe and warm where you can sleep and regain your strength.'

He looked sad as he watched the three of us huddled together like frightened animals.

Taking the mug back from Hans, Jock said, 'Those Ivans are vermin. Trouble is, the city is full of all sorts of men like that. They hunt in packs for women just like you, vulnerable and alone.'

He asked Helga, 'Where were you heading? It's crazy to come to the city during darkness.

'If only you could have waited until morning. The city is much safer during the day when there are more people about.'

I moved away from Helga, out of her embrace. I knew we should never have attempted to come into Berlin so late in the day. No wonder there was no one else on the road.

Hans explained, 'We are looking for work and a place to stay.'

Jock told us, 'There are thousands, if not millions, of people like you and your family, all fleeing various horrors and looking for work and a place to live. Everyone seems to be in the wrong place, everyone -'

His voice trailed into silence, but, after a moment, he tried again.

'For example, look at me and my men. We shouldn't be in Berlin, but we got caught up in -'

He stopped abruptly. Realising he shouldn't be saying so much about the Allies' movements, he began again.

'Anyway, perhaps I shouldn't talk about the past. You have all experienced enough. You were lucky to find the 15th Scottish Division. We are brave, genteel and know how to treat ladies and their children!'

He offered the whisky again and we all had another drink. Helga, tight-lipped and suddenly suspicious, declined, but both Hans and I gratefully swallowed another mug. My first real taste of strong alcohol didn't make me feel drunk at all, just less frozen.

Jock's warm brown eyes met mine, 'I know of a place I can take you for a couple of days. You can all get some sleep. It's very clean and the people there are friendly. It's just twenty minutes' drive from here.'

To try and lessen the tension, Hans piped up, 'What are Ivans?'

Jock answered, 'Ivan is the British Army's nickname for Soviet soldiers.'

We all looked puzzled. Jock sat next to Hans, but before he could explain more, the men who had been on foot patrol returned to the truck. The conversation about 'Ivans' was brought to a close. It was time for the Scottish Highlanders to head back to their HQ. As the truck picked up speed, Jock tried to set us at ease by talking about his home in the Highlands, where his grandparents owned land. His exotic accent matched his stories of wild majestic mountains, beautiful woods, stags and the clean air during the snows.

The Highlander towered over the rest of his men, 'Six feet, six inches in my stockinged feet,' he told us proudly.

'I took part in the annual Highland Games before the war and the King of England watched me throw the hammer.' Another puzzling insight into a Highlander.

The truck jumped and bumped as we made our way into the city centre. I could just about hear the noise of vehicles and voices as the city started to wake. Light and shadows danced through the tiny gaps in the canvas. The lorry screeched to a halt. We had reached our temporary home. Jock gently helped us out of the vehicle, and we were ushered into an impressive mansion. On either side of the building were several similar residences. Though tired-looking, their windows still shone in the daylight and the buildings were obviously habitable.

We approached a huge door. A bullet-scarred, brass plaque on the wall read 'Hotel Berlin'. As we walked through the entrance, we were transported into the most opulent place I had ever seen. I saw marble floors, an ornate and sweeping staircase, and an almost complete chandelier in the centre of the ceiling. Hans stood open-mouthed at the extravagant décor. Still alert to any potential threat, I was observant, watching, waiting and speculating on what this new place may mean for my family and our future.

Behind a large, plush reception desk stood the most glamorous woman I had ever seen. She looked like a film star. Full-busted, her silk dress whispered as she moved. Her bright, white hair was cut short and blood-red lipstick surrounded her perfectly white teeth. She seemed lit from within.

'This is Madam Sophie!' announced Jock, 'The head of Hotel Berlin. Madam Sophie runs everything here.'

Jock went behind the reception desk, gave the platinum blonde a squeeze and then quietly told her what had happened to us.

'Those bastards,' Madam Sophie said in German. She picked up the phone on the reception desk and spoke in Polish for a long time. I could understand a few words but not enough to make much sense of it. Once she had finished, the blonde came out from behind the desk and grabbed hold of Helga's hands.

'I do understand what has happened to you and your daughter,' she said, looking down, 'I understand from personal experience.'

Madam Sophie shook her head as if she had revealed too much, then continued brusquely.

'Jock is a good man and he has been very kind to me and my ladies and residents. I now return that kindness by being kind to you.'

Pushing Jock playfully towards the front door, the dazzling Madam Sophie shooed my family towards the sweeping staircase which dominated the entrance.

'Come with me, come with me,' she insisted. We dutifully followed.

Hans was mesmerised by Madam Sophie's hips as they swayed in hypnotic motion towards the stairway. I realised that Hans was growing up and part of me recoiled from my brother's burgeoning sexual interest. Jock said goodbye and blew a kiss to Madam Sophie. As he headed out of the front door, he almost collided with two giggling, attractive girls who looked like they had come straight from a party. Their dresses billowed as they entered the lobby, and both were carrying bottles.

'They've got bottles of champagne!' Hans whispered to me as we craned to look back at the young women.

I remembered a photo I'd seen in a magazine of film stars drinking champagne on a sandy beach near Hollywood. The people who lived here must be very wealthy, I thought.

Helga was inscrutable. She didn't say a word. Hans and I were different. Though deeply shocked, I was hypnotised by the overwhelming sights and sounds of Hotel Berlin and what was on offer.

Expensive paintings lined the walls, and intricate, carved bannisters of wood and wrought iron swept upwards. It was like walking into a dream. Everywhere looked so ordered, so normal.

How did this building survive so much bombing? It was as if the war had completely passed over Hotel Berlin.

We were taken through various winding corridors as Madam Sophie explained the hotel had been used by top-ranking members of the Nazi party during the war. Since then, it had become a place where the top brass of the Allied forces would come to stay, party and drink.

'The Hotel Berlin has survived the war!' Madam Sophie said with a short, bitter laugh, 'A bit like me.'

She opened one door and then another to reveal the most wonderful bathing area I had ever seen. A large, white, roll-top bath was in the centre of the room as a maid, a young woman who I guessed was no older than fifteen, was testing the temperature. Steaming water poured from gold taps in the shape of fish. Towels were draped over chairs, and a large bottle of scent and a bar of soap sat on a small, white stand. A big window was shuttered with grey boards. An ornate lampshade hung from the ceiling.

'As you can see, the Nazis did not scrimp on themselves. Even as the German people starved, they lived a good life.'

Madam Sophie spat out her words in distaste as the maid continued with her chores.

'This is Lisa. She will help you to get washed and clean while I sort out some clothes for all of you.'

Eyeing us one by one, she told Lisa, 'I am sure there are clothes to fit all of them reasonably well in the Blue Room wardrobe.'

She looked sympathetically at my bedraggled family.

'Lisa, give them the delousing treatment first, and then once they are washed and clean, I will put some clothes in the adjoining bedroom. Burn what is left of their own clothes straight away.'

Yawning, she said, 'I'm now going to bed. These all-night get-togethers are exhausting.' She turned to Lisa, 'Don't disturb me until this evening.'

Madam Sophie gently told us, 'Don't worry, you are safe here and soon the memory of last night will be just that - a memory. It's the future we now must look towards. At least we are alive. Far too many have died, and we have to live for them!'

With an airy gesture, she swept out of the room and left us to the bathroom and its delights. The bath was big enough for both me and Helga. While we eased our bruised bodies into the soapy water, Hans was taken to the Orange Room to bathe and sleep.

When the bath water was cold and grey, we wrapped ourselves in the sweet-scented robes left for us by Lisa and made our way to the adjoining bedroom. A huge double bed beckoned. We climbed into bed and felt the luxury of white fine sheets and a mattress that was like a cotton cloud. Though exhausted, we could not sleep. Every physical movement caused me and Helga some pain or ache: a reminder of the rapes.

Then the flashbacks began. No words were spoken but I could see by the expression on Helga's green-tinged face, and my own white pallor reflected in the mirror on the wall next to the bed, that both of us were reliving the events of the previous night. I shut my eyes and tried to think of other things, people or places. It didn't work.

Lisa appeared, carrying a tray containing two tall glasses. 'Please drink all of this,' said the maid, 'It's a sleeping draught that will give you a much-needed rest.'

The glasses were filled with a dark liquid that smelt and looked like whisky, though it had a strange aftertaste, but both Helga and I drank gratefully.

The young woman paused for a moment before saying, 'Don't be afraid, this is a good place.'

Her head hanging low and looking shamefaced, Lisa whispered, 'I was raped, by many different men, my family killed. This medication will really help.'

Helga and I drank every drop, and, within minutes, both of us were asleep.

134

CHAPTER 17

The sleeping draught worked well, perhaps too well, as both Helga and I slept for the entire day and night. I woke to the sound of voices in the street. Groggy, I got out of bed and made my way to the window. Pulling back the curtain, the bright summer's day blinded me until my eyes focused on the street below. People hurried in all directions, cars and military vehicles filled the road.

Our room was on the second floor. As far as the eye could see was a city of black and grey. Most of the beautiful buildings that had survived the war were walls without roofs, surrounded by flattened areas filled with bricks, wood and debris. Here and there, I could see a few blocks of houses and shops that seemed to be almost complete. Bombing can be absolute, but it sometimes creates strange patterns where lone houses or buildings are left untouched and standing randomly.

I could tell by the large houses and wide streets around Hotel Berlin that we were staying in a prosperous area. The mansions next door to the hotel and the townhouses along the street remained intact. Even in the last days of war, the wealthy and their homes somehow always survive.

Suddenly I glimpsed the reflection of my white face in the glass. Immediately I saw the Soviet soldier, his grimy, gurning face above me. I jumped and cried out, my hand flying over my mouth. I tried to force myself to think of something else, repeating my times tables, then counting every item in the room, describing each one in my mind again and again. Slowly, I erased the image of the Soviet's face.

Despite my distress, Helga did not stir from her deep, almost coma-like sleep.

I pulled on the clean robe Lisa had left on a chair and went towards the heavy oak door. As I reached for the handle, Lisa appeared with a tray bearing a pot of coffee. Smiling, she gestured me to the table at the far end of the bedroom.

'Let's sit together and talk,' she suggested, 'or not talk, depending on what you want to do?'

We both sat down on a red velvet sofa. It was so soft and clean, and I couldn't stop myself from smoothing the material repeatedly. It was also another way to distract myself from intrusive thoughts.

The maid, freckle-faced, rounded, and cheerful, made herself comfortable next to me and confided, 'Of course, I could talk instead. I'm very good at chatter and conversation, according to the other members of staff.'

She laughed as she poured out rich, black coffee, adding milk and several spoons of sugar. I took a sip and sank back into the sofa. I sighed softly and looked around. After the terrible places we had been living, this new bedroom was like paradise.

Lisa touched my hand and said, 'I'm glad you're taking it easy. My coffee is good?'

I nodded, and she continued, 'We get nice food and things here, as our customers are very rich and well connected. Hotel Berlin has always attracted such people. The guests change, the nationalities change, but what doesn't change is the fact that they have money, don't mind spending it and can access any goods or favours they need.'

Waving her arm, she told me, 'Outside of the hotel, Berlin is savage and cruel, but here, if Madam Sophie likes you and you work hard, it's a good place to live and work.'

The chatty maid kicked off her shoes and wiggled her toes. 'My feet are throbbing! I've been up since 4am this morning, cleaning rooms, running errands, and mending clothes. It's very busy at the moment. We have a lot of people staying here.'

My face darkened and I started to shake. Lisa noticed and came closer to hug me. Strangled sounds came from my chest which I had no control over, then dry sobs erupted from my mouth. These eventually turned to liquid tears that flowed down my face like a river in flood. Now I understood the tears that poor Joanne had shed. Even my noisy sobs did not wake Helga, though they went on and on. Lisa held me as I cried out my fear, pain and anger. She embraced me as if I were her precious child and didn't let go. When the earthquake of shock finally stopped, my eyes were dry and my throat so sore I could not speak. Lisa poured another cup of coffee and urged me to drink.

It was now the maid's turn to talk about her journey to Hotel Berlin.

Lisa came from a tiny hamlet in Poland. When Germany invaded, the Nazis raided her home, killed her entire family in front of her and then raped her. All her neighbours and friends were destroyed. Lisa, because of her youth, was sent to Berlin to service the men of the German Army. These brothels were set up by the officers who took a cut of the takings.

Lisa talked about the horrors of her experiences in a flat, matter-of-fact voice, as if it had happened to someone else.

'There was an officer, very high-ranking, who took a liking to me. I will not say his real name, but I called him 'Diabeł', the Devil. He liked me as I was so young, and he often got me to dress even younger. What he did to me and made me do was the Devil's work.'

She continued in a monotone, 'I did everything and anything he and the others demanded of me. I had no choice.'

Lisa's sunny demeanour had vanished, and she abruptly ended her story.

'I will tell you more, perhaps on another day, if you want to know.'

I nodded, though I knew Lisa would probably never talk of it again. This seemed to be a skill used by everyone that had suffered atrocities. Tell your story once and once only, then move forwards. It was a trick I had seen used multiple times in the mobile hospital by wounded soldiers patched up and sent back to battle.

Colour returned to Lisa's cheeks as she explained, 'There is an old saying: the 'Diabeł' is never nearer than when you are talking about him.'

Lisa got up and started to busy herself with tidying the room, smoothing cushions, and clearing away the coffee cups, muttering to herself, 'We don't want any rubbish like him here!'

The young maid came over to me, took hold of my hand and put it to her face as she told me, 'This is a secure place for women like us, as we understand each other and what we have all lost.'

Putting her shoes back on, she said briskly, 'Today is a new day and a new start and we must both think of good times. We are young, good-looking and talented! The world will get better, and we will get better.'

Shaking her head as if to remove the past, she said, 'Now come with me.'

I followed Lisa through the back corridors of the hotel down to the kitchen, keeping my gown firmly wrapped around my skinny frame. It was far too big and kept slipping off, and I had to keep holding the hem up so I didn't trip.

We arrived at four large windows that opened outwards onto a terrace and small courtyard garden. A rose bush grew beneath the windows, climbing the frames. Scattered within the vibrant green leaves were crimson roses the size of dinner plates, their heavy heads in full bloom. Their scent was rich and overpowering.

Lisa smiled as she brought a flower to her face, feeling its petals, 'Aren't they wonderful? Despite everything, roses still grow in Berlin.'

She told me, 'This is Madam Sophie's private garden area. She never allows us to cut these flowers, except to deadhead them. She says they are a symbol of life, and while these roses keep blooming, we will bloom too!'

We sat on the tiny balcony for a long time, surrounded by the scent of roses. We chatted idly but mostly sat quietly and, for the first time in months, I felt less lonely. Lisa knew and understood what had happened to me, as she was near my own age and we shared many similar experiences.

Hans appeared, wearing a uniform of sorts: a new pair of black trousers, a clean white shirt, and a black apron.

Lisa explained, 'Your brother is an entrepreneur and has talked his way into a job here at the hotel.'

Smiling, she said, 'Hans has many American-themed recipes that he shared with our chef, who is now very taken with your brother. From today, Hans will be our general help.'

In response, my brother gave me and Lisa a formal bow, then rushed to my side and embraced me. I felt his thick hair tickle my forehead before nausea rushed over me. I recoiled from Hans and pushed him away. He stumbled, falling to the ground, his eyes stricken. Lisa came to our aid, helping my brother up from the ground.

She told him, 'Hans, you must learn that your sister is still very shocked after what has happened, and any sudden movement will startle her. In time, things will settle down again. Your sister still loves you and always will, but you have to be gentle with her and your mother for a while.'

Hans looked upset as he walked away stiffly and returned to his chores. I was mortified. I had never felt uneasy with Hans, he was my beloved brother.

Lisa straightened her skirt and became organised, 'I must go back to work! And you must go and see your mother and support her, too.'

When I got back to the room, Helga was still snoring and continued to do so for the next couple of hours. It gave me time to bathe, and I filled the bath to its brim with water so hot even the steam made me gasp. I laid down in the cauldron and scrubbed my skin again and again. Looking at my naked body brought the worst thoughts and feelings. The scratches, vivid bruises, bite marks and the clear signs of the Soviet's thumb prints on my neck and around my throat were reminders of the assault. Now I understood my mother's furious washing in the river, the need to feel clean, to make myself clean, and to banish any physical sign or smell of the rape.

I lost track of time, but when the pain of my repeated scrubbing became too much, I got out of the bath, dried myself in a white towel, and dressed quickly. Lisa had left clothes for me and Helga draped neatly over an armchair. I put on bloomers and a vest, then chose a simple but pretty yellow dress with a pale green cardigan to match, and white socks and sturdy boots, which were slightly too big. I sat down and looked at myself in the large mirror of the dressing table, the first time I had seen my reflection so clearly in many months.

Did I look different? I stared at my face to see if the assault had outwardly damaged me in any way. I saw a pretty, thin girl in her teens, with dark circles like rain clouds under sad eyes. She wore a worried frown. Did I look like this before our journey? My reflection reminded me of the scared fawns we had often stumbled upon in the woods with Rufus.

I stood and twirled in a circle, watching myself in the mirror. It was a lovely dress, but I felt empty and odd, as if all my feelings had been removed. I swished the yellow dress back and forth hoping the softness of the material and the clean smell would raise a smile, or a spark of emotion. But there was nothing.

I stopped as the livid bruises on my thighs were revealed.

Looking for another distraction, I sat down again at the dressing table. There was a large powder puff, and I pressed it to my face, just softly, but it was enough to send out a cloud of talc into my face. The powder made me cough and sneeze uncontrollably. This sound woke Helga, and from across the room she began to laugh, a high-pitched sound forced out of tired lungs.

'That reminds me of when you were little and used to sneeze whenever I was baking, as you would put your head over the flour as I sifted it!'

She opened her arms and I rushed across the room into them. We stayed like that for a long time.

As the sun began to set again and the noises in the street outside faded, Lisa appeared with a tray, bearing three plates of food. Behind her followed Hans. Apologising, I went over to my brother and touched his arm awkwardly. I managed to give him a quick hug, but it was harder to embrace him than it was Lisa or Helga. I realised it would take a while before the easy-going relationship I had with my brother would return. The rape had taken away so much more than my virginity. From that day, Hans was careful about showing me any physical contact, always asking me beforehand if he could kiss me on the cheek or wrap his arm around my waist. The spontaneity we had always shown towards each other was lost, leaving both of us unsettled, often distant.

We ate the meal, which was just a few fresh vegetables and dehydrated potatoes drenched in a thick gravy, but it was the best we had eaten for a long time. We talked about anything other than the night before our arrival at the hotel. It was yet another horrific event that would never be mentioned again. Instead, we chatted about practical things. Helga and I were stunned and proud that Hans had already secured a permanent job at the hotel. With his ready charm and obvious work ethic, his skills had not gone unnoticed. My brother's position was the lowliest at the hotel, doing the jobs and shifts considered the most unsociable or dirty.

With his new job came a small bedroom, no bigger than a broom cupboard, next to reception, which allowed Hans to be 'on call' day or night when guests arrived or departed. His job was to carry luggage, clean shoes and boots, run errands and do any chores that were needed. Hans knew it would be hard work with long hours, but it guaranteed meals, accommodation, and, of course, a small payment at the end of the week.

My enterprising brother had already made firm friends in the kitchen. Speaking between mouthfuls of food, he excitedly told us, 'I watched the chef prepare dinner! He has worked in the best hotels and even cooked for King Christian of Denmark.'

Puffed up, he continued with pride, 'Chef Weber says, if I show talent in the kitchen, he'll give me some lessons. This is another step towards my restaurant in America! I'm already learning so much. Chef Weber must make the most inventive meals from the sparse rations available. There are no markets and very few shops in Berlin anymore, and the residents have been hungry for months.'

I glanced sadly at my brother, a child with an old man's head, an old person's view of the world.

Hans rushed on to tell us, 'Even though Madam Sophie has lots of connections and can obtain a lot more food than those outside, kitchens in hotels have to work with a much smaller variety of foods and budget. Imagine what great learning this is for me and my future career as a chef!'

I so admired my brother's determination, but Helga just kept eating, her conversation sparse and to the point. I watched as she stuffed food into her mouth, chasing vegetables and crumbs around her plate. Hans continued to share his plans with us both.

'Mother, I overheard some of the guests talking. They were saying that many people in Berlin and across Germany are travelling to America looking for a new life. When we have enough money and the time is right, we should all leave and go there, too!'

Helga snorted. 'Pipe dreams and useless talk. We all must find jobs in Berlin. Did you find out if Madam Sophie wants any more staff at the hotel?'

Hans' voice was more subdued as he answered in a flat voice,

'According to Herr Schmidt, the head waiter, Madam Sophie is always looking for permanent staff as people keep leaving due to lack of papers or moving onwards due to their shady past. A lot of them are illegal refugees.'

Helga and I looked at each other. In a low voice she warned us, 'Our past is gone. We are an ordinary German family. I was born in Switzerland, I am a widow and we have lost all our relatives and our home in the woods. If you must, tell people that Rufus and Joanne were your grandparents, that their house was our house. That is our life story, is that clear?'

Hans and I nodded.

Helga said, 'We will never have this conversation again. You both know what you have to say and what you must not say.'

The evening had turned sour. Helga's face was pinched and angry. I faked tiredness, and Hans scrambled quickly to his feet, muttering about getting some sleep before his next shift. He reached out and lightly touched my shoulder as he said goodnight.

I climbed into bed, closed my eyes and hoped that sleep would soon enfold. Helga's sharp tongue interrupted,

'We must see Madam Sophie tomorrow and persuade her to give us both a job! She is a whore, but I know how to charm whores.'

I put my hands over my ears to shut out Helga's spite. I squeezed my eyes shut and willed images of Jenni the goat, Joanna and Rufus to fill my mind, instead of an ink, dark building and a nameless Soviet soldier.

CHAPTER 18

The next morning, we were called to Madam Sophie's apartment on the fifth floor, at the very top of the building. The servants' rooms were wedged into the attic space above the kitchen and stables, their only view the backyard or store rooms. Madam Sophie's apartment looked out over the whole of Berlin, as there were fewer buildings of height left standing. The hotelier's rooms were only accessible by a private stairway or very small lift. Only trusted members of staff and those with an invitation could enter.

The entire top floor was secluded, but some of the corridors revealed traces of war. Holes in the ceiling had been hastily patched and there were men painting the walls and sanding the floors. In the main part of the hotel used by guests, bullet holes were hidden by paint or a curtain. The ambience of Hotel Berlin was essential for its survival and profit margin.

Madam Sophie's apartment took up several rooms, but the rest of the floor was known as 'the offices'. Quite what happened in them was unclear. When Hans asked other members of staff about the top floor, they either feigned disinterest or gave him a look that implied it was better not to know. For the time being, my curiosity was limited by the need to ensure Helga and I could also secure a position at Hotel Berlin. Hans had told us the night before that Madam Sophie had a reputation as a tough businesswoman. Despite her initial kindness, Helga and I would still have to prove our worth to the hotelier and to her business.

I looked at Helga as she arranged her face into a passive, unthreatening expression, though her eyes remained icy. She knocked at the large oak door with determination. I knew she would not take kindly to deferring to a woman she viewed as 'lower status'.

'Come in,' a distracted voice called from inside.

Madam Sophie was sitting behind a desk in a corner of her apartment. It was strewn with paperwork, ink pots and files.

The rest of the room consisted of a dining area for guests. A huge oak table, which would easily seat twenty guests, had as its centrepiece a silver candelabra. Three large windows stretched from floor to ceiling, faced by two comfortable-looking sofas and several armchairs. Gone were the reds and vibrant colours of the guest rooms, instead the walls were painted in calming cream and greens. It felt relaxed and quiet here, far removed from the bustle and noise of the lobby and restaurant. This part of the hotel had an old world and sophisticated charm. Many of the soft furnishings, though comfortable, were rather shabby and a bit worn, the best saved and used for paying guests.

The room was full of light. I could see the houses opposite and beyond; many streets had been flattened, while strange pockets of houses, shops and buildings were untouched. The view was stark and haunting, like a painting devoid of bright colours, leaving only grey, black and brown. Hundreds of civilians were moving about, busy and intent and, of course, military vehicles and personnel weaved through the streets and avenues. The city was alive with the movement of many people, all in a hurry to move onwards.

I quickly brought my attention back to the room and to Madam Sophie. Doors were open throughout her apartment and I spied a large bedroom with a bathroom, then another room full of mirrors, and rows of dresses and shoes.

The carpet was not worn but appeared dusty as if it had been shut away in a dark, dank room. Colourful scenes of pre-war Berlin dotted the room, framed in wood or silver against the light green walls. The apartment was understated and tasteful, very different from the overblown embellishments of the guest rooms. It appeared that while the hotel's customers preferred plush furnishings, Madam Sophie had a more traditional style. The platinum blonde looked up and gestured for us to sit. She continued to write.

'It's good seeing you both looking so much better,' she said. 'I have to finish this urgent paperwork. I am afraid settling bills and organising the running of the hotel is essential and often means tedious tasks like these.'

Quickly, her pen scratched across various documents: a signature here and there, a cross right through, or a hastily written note, as she worked her way through a pile of papers.

'There is coffee on the table, would you pour us all a cup? I am nearly finished.'

Helga and I made ourselves comfortable on chairs of crimson velvet, shot through with gold thread. I couldn't stop smoothing the material with my fingers as it felt so good. The texture and softness reminded me with a pang of our dog Mia's coat. Like everything I had ever loved, she too had disappeared. As the invading Allies had approached our home town, the constant bombings and smell of burning on the wind had spooked her and she had run across the fields, never to be seen again.

I was shaken from my memories by Madam Sophie calling out, 'Jacques? Jacques? Where are you, you lazy boy?'

A door opened from a panel that looked like a bookshelf behind Madam Sophie's desk. A tall, young man about eighteen years old appeared. He had a baby face that was almost cherubic. He wore an ill-fitting jacket and trousers and was carrying two ledgers. I noticed that his clothes were of good quality but didn't fit his lopsided body. He had a scuttling gait, and his appearance struck me as odd.

'Madam, I have just been through to the main office and found the papers you needed.'

The young man spoke English in a high-pitched tone, with a strong French accent.

'It took a bit longer than I anticipated,' he apologised, and I saw that his teeth were crooked and grey as he spoke.

'Ah, yes, put them down there,' Madam Sophie waved toward her desk, handing the lanky Jacques a batch of letters from her desk. Barely had they left her hand before the papers were flying through the air and to the floor, as Jacques' clumsy fingers lost grip. I noticed Jacques was trembling and rushed to help him, picking up the papers and putting them in numerical order. The sheets were written in German, French and English. I recognised many of the words. Some of the correspondence detailed contraband like alcohol, as well as soap, items of food and clothing that had long disappeared from everyday use. There were notes about guns and ammunition, and even medical drugs like morphine were mentioned. I hid my shock and smiled tentatively at Jacques, and his smoky grey eyes looked back. I conversed a little with him in English and French and he seemed surprised and pleased that I had a grasp of several languages.

Madam Sophie thanked me and then told the awkward young man, 'Jacques, that will be all for the next hour or so. I will ring down later when you need to take those letters across the city.'

She added, 'Remember to take Horst and a weapon with you, I heard you had trouble with Frau Schmidt the other day. The gangs are running riot in that sector.'

Jacques gave a small bow to the hotelier, bowed twice to me and left the room. With her work now organised to her satisfaction, Madam Sophie joined us for coffee. Sitting opposite us in a large leather armchair with huge brown buttons, she placed her feet, encased in dark blue satin, to one side. She sipped with the delicacy of royalty and placed a cigarette into a long, jet-black holder. To me she looked like a goddess.

Madam Sophie told us, 'Jacques is very changed, he is from the camps. His father was a German Jew, his mother French.'

She paused for breath as she dragged on her cigarette.

'He was experimented upon, terrible, terrible tortures which I can and will never repeat.'

She shuddered before she said, 'Thank you Greta for being kind to Jacques. Please talk to him if you see him around the hotel. He is a genius with accounting and languages, and even with his many differences, he has a good heart.'

Madam Sophie then drew her attention to Helga and came straight to the point.

'I know you don't like me Helga and, truth be told, I don't like you either. But Greta and Hans are good children, so you must have some qualities.'

I could feel Helga bristle with indignation next to me. I placed my hand on her wrist and pinched it in warning to be quiet.

'Greta reminds me of myself when I was her age: beautiful, bright and resourceful. She is friendly and has great potential. I believe she can be a great asset to me and the hotel and so can Hans if he works hard.'

She carried on in a rush, 'I am getting a team together to help run Hotel Berlin so that it takes us all successfully into the next decade.'

Helga tried to talk but I cut in, 'I don't know what to say, Madam Sophie, except thank you. We will all work hard, be tactful and make Hotel Berlin the best hotel in Germany. In fact, the best hotel in Europe!'

Madam Sophie laughed, a huge belly laugh that was at odds with her elegant appearance. She laughed like a working man in the fields. She slapped her hand on her knee and said, 'There you are Helga, she is just like me! Full of it!'

Helga gave a sickly smile and asked, 'Will there be work for me, too?'

'Of course there is a job for you here in the hotel, you're their mother. I would not separate you as a family. There has been too much of that.'

She leaned forward and said to Helga with a warning, 'But many different nations work and visit Hotel Berlin. You will have to respect them all, Helga, without exception, is that clear?'

Helga continued to bristle but, recognising our good fortune, merely said, 'Of course.'

Madam Sophie then opened her arms, as if to encompass the whole world, and said, 'War makes monsters of many people. Individuals we pass in the street every day in Berlin probably have blood on their hands, is that not right Helga?'

The hotelier lit another cigarette and waited. Helga and I were both taken aback and hoped that Madam Sophie did not know about our past and my father's role in the Nazi machine. We kept silent, hoping it was just a rhetorical question. The clock on the mantelpiece ticked away the minutes. The hotelier scrutinised us both carefully. No words were spoken. The clock continued to tick away the time. Both Helga and I looked down at our laps, sitting like statues.

Eventually, Madam Sophie spoke, softly.

'There is also good to be found. Take Jacques for instance, his camp was liberated by the Soviets. A Cossack took Jacques under his wing, fed him, clothed him and brought him to Berlin and my doorstep.'

Helga and I gasped at the mention of the Soviet Army. As Madam Sophie continued talking, I had to force myself to listen.

'Without that Cossack, Jacques would be dead. That member of the

Soviet Army befriended Jacques. He saved that young boy's life and gave him the opportunity of a future.'

Glaring at us both, the blonde said in a hard voice, 'If a man from a Russian background, or a member of the Soviet Army comes into the hotel as a guest or customer at the bar, you must treat them with respect, is that clear?'

Gulping for air and trying to keep the panic out of my voice, I replied, 'It will be very hard Madam Sophie, it's so soon since -'

The blonde's eyes became as sharp as her tone as she held up her hand.

'Of course it will be hard. It's always hard for us women who have been raped, beaten and used. But as women, we must make a stand for our future. God willing, Greta, one day you will have children and be the bearer of the next generation. We must put the war behind us, live, and move away from our terrible experiences. We have to be more than victims! We are the builders of the new Europe, a new country, one that does not discriminate.'

Madam Sophie's words struck me like a thunderbolt. I was the next generation, and however I chose to live my life would affect how my children interpreted theirs.

Helga suddenly stood up, shouting, 'I will not serve a member of the Soviet Army till the day I die! I want to kill that whoreson that raped my girl! She was untouched, you know, a virgin!'

Helga glared at Madam Sophie, who replied in a clipped tone, 'We were all virgins once.'

I could see our jobs, accommodation and lives disappearing down a black hole, and intervened, 'Madam Sophie, I will work hard to be the best member of staff you have, so will Hans. Perhaps for a while, there might be work for Helga away from the guests?'

Madam Sophie was quiet for a few moments, weighing up our usefulness to her and the hotel.

'Helga, you can help in the kitchens and laundry, away from the guests. Greta, you will be working with Lisa initially. Let's see how you and your mother get on.'

She sighed. 'Before you go though, I want you to recognise something. It may help for you both to look at matters in a different way.

I was badly hurt by Germans – your countrymen and women – for three years. I was beaten, raped and tortured. I will never bear children. I didn't think I would even survive. My whole village was destroyed by the Nazis and then I was used as their whore. Yet here I am, offering jobs to you, a German family.'

Helga's eyes glittered like black jewels, but she said and did nothing except sit down. She seemed to disappear into the sofa, while I felt stronger and bigger. What Madam Sophie had said hit a nerve within me. She talked a lot of sense about people, but, most importantly, Madam Sophie believed in me. Now I had to believe in myself.

The hotelier was an observer of people and watched our reactions closely without giving away her own. She reminded me of the sphinx; an enigma that I wanted to get to know. The stunning blonde was ambitious, and I wanted to be part of her adventure. Staring at her, I realised I too was observing Madam Sophie, so in some ways we were alike.

The coffee had become cold and Madam Sophie pushed her cup away in distaste. Looking bored, she let out an exasperated sigh. I could see that she had reached her limit of listening to her new staffs' emotional outbursts, and the businesswoman came to the fore. She pointed to a table by one of the windows.

'Over there are your uniforms. Helga, report to head housekeeper Frau Schoenberg at 5am tomorrow in the laundry room. Greta, you are to meet with Lisa in the kitchen at 4am. There is a small bedroom in the attic which you can both share.'

She waved her hand, 'Now leave me, please. I have lots of work to complete.'

We picked up two neat piles of clothes: black skirts, white shirts, aprons and, for me, a frilly head piece to be worn every day to keep my blonde hair in a neat bun. I thanked the inscrutable Sophie once again for our jobs and we left her sitting in a cloud of cigarette smoke and French perfume.

We made our way to what was now our attic bedroom. It was small and contained two single beds, a stand with a jug and basin, a tiny cupboard for our clothes, a mirror, a bedside cabinet, and a stool. The beds had sheets and even two blankets. A very small window looked up to the sky, which had turned turquoise. It was going to be a very hot day.

I was keen to try on my skirt and blouse. I gave a twirl in front of Helga and asked her, 'What do you think?'

I circled again and watched the black material move like a gentle wave around my legs. I still felt disorientated and detached, despite our good fortune, but my head knew I had to keep going. Our jobs at the hotel were the opportunity my family so needed.

Helga sat unresponsive on the bed. I dragged at the collar of the shirt and pulled out the waistband of the skirt. They were both loose on me.

'I'm sure a few weeks of good food will soon fill this out!' I joked to her glum face.

'Helga, try your uniform on, the material feels so fine.'

Words fell from her down-turned mouth, 'How dare that woman say you are like her? She is common as muck!'

I had had enough of Helga's spiteful tongue. I went over to her and placed my hand over her mouth. Helga tried to hit me, as I ducked and tried not to hit her. We tumbled to the floor and struggled there for several minutes in a strange, mock fight.

Eventually, I put my face to hers and told her quietly, 'I don't know where you get this venom from. We have secured good jobs, accommodation, food and it's safe here. Yet you are still not grateful.'

Helga's reaction was swift, furious and fierce. In a moment, she was trying to pull my hair out, kicking with her feet. I favoured my father and was now taller and bigger than Helga. It didn't take long for me to pin back her arms. I pulled her upwards like a sack of potatoes and placed her gently on the bed. All the fight left her. I moved away and sat down on my bed, feeling shocked and disgusted at our behaviour.

Helga's words to me were chilling, 'I'm not sure I recognise my daughter anymore. In fact, I don't have a daughter anymore.'

It was a turning point in our relationship, a major fracture that would never be mended.

As I sat there rubbing the bald patch on my head where Helga had ripped out a clump of hair, there was an urgent knocking at the door. It was Lisa, who had the room next to us. The little maid came bustling into the room.

'Helga! Greta! Please stop these arguments! I hate it and Madam

Sophie will not approve. She likes the hotel and its staff to be calm and ordered, as that's what our guests have come here for, to escape the outside world.'

She looked at us both with wide eyes, 'There has been too much fighting.'

Lisa looked upset, so I went over to her and tried to ease the tension, 'Helga and I were just letting off steam. It won't happen ever again.'

I stared at Helga. I could no longer think of her as my 'mother'. I urged her to reassure Lisa.

'Isn't that right, Helga, we will never fight again?'

Helga agreed, 'No, we must never fight each other again, I'm so tired of all the fighting.'

Lisa urged us to keep to our agreement and told us, 'You have experienced the terror of Berlin already. Outside of the front doors of the hotel, it's like a bear pit. The Allies are barely keeping control of the looters, rapists, criminals, revenge attacks. Murders happen daily. We are safe here in the hotel, don't ruin the chance Madam Sophie has given you.'

She swallowed hard as she said, 'I hear that some of the Allied soldiers go women hunting at night and go into houses, tracking females down to assault and even murder. They look on us as their sport. If a person disappears or is found dead in Berlin, who is going to care or worry? Just another dead body.'

Lisa's words and pale face evoked horrific images of the many dangers of the post-war city. She told us, 'None of your family would want to live for too long outside the walls of the hotel, so please work hard and keep quiet.'

Helga retreated to her bed and pulled the covers over her head. I felt deeply ashamed of my outburst and decided to put some space between us. I made my way with Lisa to the 'Boot Room' where Hans was busy working. He looked up at us as he spat onto a cloth and began to rub at a pair of beautiful, black leather shoes that glinted in the daylight.

'Look at these, sister! They are shoes made in Milan, Italy, and soft as Jenni's nuzzle.'

Hans put his face to the leather, smelling the tang of wealth and power.

'These shoes must have cost a year's wage and more. Just imagine having that much money!'

Hans was deep in thought as he worked through the shoes and boots of the hotel's guests. Lisa fetched us all a glass of water and we sat around talking for a while about the hotel and the range of guests that came through its doors. Lisa described a woman called Fifi who was the image of Greta Garbo. A 'friend' of a high-ranking member of the Allied forces, she dressed head to toe in French couture and wore a fur stole. She began to impersonate Fifi as we laughed.

Lisa found humour in the worst possible situations. A brilliant mimic, she could have easily become an actress, effortlessly copying the eccentricities of the older guests. She could imitate voices, gestures and walks with absolute precision. Taking a tablecloth, she wrapped it around her face and body and became the character she was impersonating. Spending time with Lisa and Hans was light and fun, and all the bad things that had happened somehow shrunk a little into the distance.

When I felt less agitated and hoped Helga had calmed down, I took a glass of water up to our bedroom, along with a tiny piece of stale cake left in the pantry. Handing over my peace offering, I told Helga how sorry I was.

Helga acknowledged my apology, drank the water and devoured the cake within seconds.

Even though it was only 5pm and the sun was shining through the skylight, she said a curt 'goodnight', turned her back and went to sleep.

CHAPTER 19

The following weeks and months were tough. I began to experience vivid flashbacks.

A car backfiring or a man's gruff voice could suddenly take me back to the warehouse, to the face of the Soviet soldier leering over me. The images were so real. I could smell him, taste his mouth on mine, and feel pain, so much pain. It was like I was being raped over and over again. I would shake and sweat, becoming frantic with fear. Fortunately, I usually managed to crawl away somewhere quiet. I would then wait until the worst waves of anxiety had passed and then return to the task of being a chambermaid.

Lisa described these moments as 'turns', and the staff at the hotel recognised and accommodated them. Most of my colleagues had suffered trauma and its emotional aftermath in their own journeys to Hotel Berlin. If Lisa or the other staff members spotted my distress, they would gently manoeuvre me out of the public areas of the hotel, into a place devoid of people and guests. My favourite refuge was the walk-in cupboard that held the hotel's clean sheets, towels and linen, where I could take time to recover while folding sheets and ironing. I found this tedious but exacting chore strangely soothing. Concentrating on the fine details of the lace napkins seemed to quell the fear. The slow back and forth motion of the iron as I pressed downwards on yet another sheet or pillowcase brought me back to the present and the security of Hotel Berlin.

One day, after a particularly bad episode that left me gasping for breath, I staggered to the cupboard, where I stayed, ironing, for three hours. As one maid took away the starched and ironed sheets, another one carried in a pile of freshly-laundered, but creased, linen. Ironing at Hotel Berlin was a never-ending task. With so many guests coming and going and Madam Sophie's precise standards, I could have spent all my days in that tiny space ironing from morning till night.

When panic lessened to mere ripples, I would admire the neatly stacked freshly-laundered linen, the air filled with the light perfume of clean, clean sheets. The small room smelt of fresh flowers and order. The whiteness of the sheets and the smell of soap somehow made me feel cleaner too.

It was always Lisa's voice that pulled me back to the hustle of life outside the cupboard, saying the same words,

'Greta, look at all those sheets you have ironed! I do believe you are the hardest worker in the entire hotel, I would say even in Berlin, for getting the linen so smooth and crisp. Madam Sophie will be so pleased with your work. Let's have a drink and gossip about the new guests.'

She would then lead me from the cupboard to the kitchen, guiding me through the public areas of the hotel as we bobbed a curtsy to each guest we passed.

It was on such a day, after another three-hour ironing marathon, that one of the guests caught my eye as he passed us in the hall. A tall English man dressed in a dusty uniform, he had a small moustache like Clark Gable and was a man of rank, a colonel.

Lisa confided, 'He is so handsome!'

All I felt was a frozen fear, and replied, 'He is nothing.'

As we made our way to the kitchen, Lisa ignored my comment and just carried on talking.

'Luis the waiter told me the colonel was a very brave man in the war and is staying at the hotel as a special friend of Madam Sophie.'

She looked at me with a knowing expression.

'You know what I mean by special friend?'

I knew exactly what she meant. Madam Sophie would be sleeping with the good-looking colonel. I felt sick. Lisa continued her chatter as we clattered down the wooden stairs to the kitchen. A pot of stewed, weak tea and a couple of biscuits waited for us on the table. I listened half-heartedly as she shared tittle tattle about the guests, as for once it didn't interest me. Trauma had drained me and all I wanted to do was sleep. My shift was over, so I finished my tea, made my excuses to Lisa and went straight to my room.

Slowly, with the combination of a routine filled with hard work and the comfort of living in the hotel, overwhelming feelings of anxiety lessened. I started to concentrate on my friendships and life outside of the hotel.

On our one free afternoon a week, I would accompany Lisa, Jacques and Hans and we would walk arm and arm through the city.

The famous buildings that had somehow withstood the bombings and the remnants of once-mighty structures that had made the city skyline famous were now being embraced within new buildings. Some temporary and haphazard, some more permanent. We strolled past soldiers digging ditches to reconnect water mains, gas and electricity.

All had a sense of new beginnings.

The people of Berlin were adapting. They had no choice but to welcome the Allies and we were all sick of battle. The war was officially over, and it was time to start again.

I was starting to blossom and, at times, was a very boisterous youngster, full of nervous energy, enthusiasm and ambition. Time spent outside with Jacques, Lisa and Hans meant being young and in the moment, and looking outwards. I forced myself to speak and converse with everyone Jacques introduced to me. Despite some shaky starts when my anxiety peaked, I eventually found my voice and it was often loud and full of mischief. I also recognised the value of the contacts that Jacques had within the city and how they could further my family's ambitions. When Lisa and I chatted to waiters in bars, to friends and colleagues of Jacques, I saw the appreciative look in men's eyes. It left me cold, but their interest was useful and often made me feel powerful.

A hope was growing inside me. When these tiny pin pricks of light appeared, I tried desperately to hold on to them. By contrast, Helga felt like part of the past. Day by day, I was moving away from her dominance, her traditional views, her old ways.

Helga never ventured far from Hotel Berlin, preferring to sleep in her room or sit in the kitchen reading books she borrowed from the hotel's library. Wealthy guests from all over the globe would often leave books, novels, magazines and newspapers. After years of only books sanctioned by Hitler, my mother devoured these once forbidden items with an avid enthusiasm. I was secretly glad that she did not want to come out with us. I preferred being alone with my peers with the freedom to enjoy a glass of wine or smoke a cigarette without admonishment. It made me feel grown-up and helped to rebuild my confidence.

After another argument with Helga about my attitude, I complained to Lisa, 'Doesn't Helga realise I am nearly 15 years old? I don't need her to tell me what I can and can't do.'

Lisa told me, 'I agree your mother is not the easiest person to get along with. But she is your mother.'

In a rare display of sadness, she confided, 'I wish I still had a mother.'

Muttering, I told my dear friend, 'You would not want Helga as a mother, no one would.'

Lisa looked alarmed at my stern tone, so I stopped talking and just puffed on my cigarette as we walked arm and arm through the streets of Berlin.

Flashbacks receded to become occasional night terrors as more pleasant times and experiences filled my head.

If Helga had flashbacks, she did not tell me about them. We were no longer close. When I returned to the hotel, she never asked what I had done or where I had gone. When we both had a day off, she showed no interest in spending time with me or Hans. While we became outgoing and optimistic, Helga withdrew into herself. As Hans and I grew, Helga seemed to shrink in height, but she was piling on weight. My relationship with her began to centre on work more than family, and it was the same for Hans. Despite always being her favourite, she rebuffed and dismissed my little brother until he gave up trying. We left her alone.

One morning I woke to find Helga being violently sick. She had been vomiting on and off for a few months and was looking very peaky, frequently complaining of being tired and complaining about her swollen ankles. A few times I took shifts when she was unwell. I put her illness down to greed: Helga ate everything on her plate, and anything left over on everyone else's. But on this morning, she couldn't stop being sick. I rushed over to help and pulled back her hair. Her vomit looked like raw egg and smelt awful. When she finally finished, I gently pushed her back onto the bed and fetched her a cup of water.

Since we arrived in Berlin, various diseases had been reported. With so many people living in bad conditions, half-starved people wandering the streets, and new people arriving in the city all the time, outbreaks of deadly illnesses were common. So far, the staff and guests in Hotel Berlin had been unaffected. I worried that Helga may have picked up something contagious, but when I felt her forehead, she didn't have a temperature.

'Do you think you ate too much last night?' I asked, glancing at her rounded stomach. 'I haven't seen your tummy look like that since you were carrying Hans!'

Helga was getting fatter by the day. I was joking, but when I looked at Helga's face, it was furious.

'Yes! I'm pregnant with that Soviet's bastard!' she spat.

I reeled with the information. Helga was pregnant from the rape?

I gasped and held out my hand to comfort her. She shrugged me away, covering her belly with the sheet, her face full of anger.

'You need to help me get rid of this,' she punched her stomach hard as she said it, then did it again several times. I grabbed her hands and held them, staring at her. My head spinning with shock, I asked, 'What do you mean?'

'The maids were talking about a midwife who lives nearby who helps women like me,' Helga let out a bitter laugh, 'Trouble is, she wants American dollars. Lots of them.'

Helga glanced at the floorboard near my bed, where Hans and I hid small amounts of our wages each week that we were saving for the future. Reluctantly, I pulled up the board and retrieved our meagre savings from a sock, tipping the contents out onto Helga's bed.

Snatching the few coins and a couple of notes, she told me, 'That's not enough.'

I opened my mouth, feeling angry at her ingratitude, but an urgent knocking came at the door. We looked at each other, and I shoved the chamber pot of vomit under the bed while Helga tidied her hair. Helga quickly hid the money inside her nightgown. I realised our savings were gone for good. I opened the door, it was Hans.

'Is everything all right?' I ushered him inside as he said, 'I heard you both shouting. What's going on?'

I forced a smile and said, 'Helga's been sick. She ate too much cake last night!'

I gave a hollow laugh. The room smelled of vomit. Hans looked from me to Helga. He did not seem convinced.

'What are you doing here?' demanded Helga, 'I thought you were helping in the kitchen this morning.'

Hans sighed and smiled, 'Yes I was. But more maids are needed in the ballroom. It's a terrible mess after last night. The party celebrating the soldiers returning to England didn't finish till 4am. Lisa asked me to come and fetch you both. She knows you are both on the late shift, but she really needs your help. Three of the other maids are busy sorting out the Imperial Room as apparently there are important guests arriving at lunchtime.'

Helga got up and poured water into the bowl on the bedside cabinet, washed her face and sprinkled moisture onto her greasy hair. She looked dreadful.

'Go and tell them Greta will be there to help in a few minutes,' said Helga, swaying slightly.

Hans left, and I began to dress quickly, watching my mother out of the corner of my eye.

'How much more money do you need, Helga?' I asked as I prepared to leave.

'Much more,' she hissed at me, 'Maybe six times what you have already saved.'

CHAPTER 20

In the following weeks, Helga tried various remedies to get rid of the baby. Part of me recoiled from the fact it was a baby conceived by rape, and another part of me was disturbed that a baby brother or sister of mine would never have the opportunity to live.

I ran her several steaming baths, filled with almost boiling water, and watched her scream with pain as the steam clouds touched her skin. I bought a bottle of gin from Jacques, mumbling about a surprise birthday party for one of the maids. I knew he wasn't convinced but, like all of us, he asked few questions. None of these methods worked and we still didn't have enough money for the midwife.

One morning, I was changing the beds in the State Room when Lisa came running in.

'Helga has fallen down the stairs! You should go to her, Greta!'

I arrived to find Helga leaning heavily against one of the waiters. Her right eye was already turning black and she was limping, unable to put any weight on her left ankle. The waiter carried her to our bedroom, where she immediately fell asleep.

Despite all her efforts to miscarry, Helga did not bleed, and the child stayed glued to her womb. Pale and tired, she was still gaining weight, and even a big cardigan did not hide her huge stomach. Fortunately, with her job in the laundry and occasionally in the kitchen, she was away from prying eyes or curiosity, but time was running out. It would not be long before Helga's pregnancy could no longer be hidden, and I was at a loss how I could make enough money to pay the abortionist. After days of worrying, I made up my mind to talk to Lisa and then to Madam Sophie. We needed help.

Almost immediately, my decision was overtaken by something even worse than Helga's unwanted pregnancy. Hans disappeared.

At first, I did not notice anything unusual. I had not seen Hans about the hotel for a day or so, but I'd assumed we had been working opposite shifts. We sometimes went a few days without meeting each other if he was working the night shift. It was Frau Schoenberg, the housekeeper, who alerted me to Hans' absence. She stopped me in the corridor as I moved from room to room changing linen.

'Greta, your brother was supposed to greet some guests this morning, but he didn't appear. Do you know where he is?'

I opened my mouth, but she didn't give me a chance to answer.

'I let him have his afternoon off yesterday instead of Thursday. He said he had errands to run for your mother, but then he didn't appear for his shift last night, so we covered for him. I thought he had been waylaid or had just gone out enjoying himself.'

My heart jumped as she told me, 'But this morning there was still no sign of him, so Georges the night porter went to his room and his bed had not been slept in. This is so unlike Hans.'

I was unable to speak, instead questions tumbled through my head. Why would Hans take his afternoon off on another day and not tell me? Why had he not come back to the hotel? I found it hard to form words and when I did speak, they rushed out in short bursts.

'I don't know where Hans is. Do you think he's missing?'

I tried to push down the growing sense of dread as I told the housekeeper, 'I don't know of any errands he had to run for Helga.'

I looked around the corridor as if I could conjure my brother from thin air. There was no reason on earth why Hans would miss work. He loved his job and would never let the hotel or his colleagues down. I threw the sheets I was carrying into Frau Schoenberg's arms and ran to find Helga. She was in the laundry, sitting in a chair and mending a green dress. Barely glancing up, she began to complain.

'Madam Sophie has found more work for me, now she knows how neat my sewing is. I have to mend her clothes, even her underwear.'

I rushed over and grabbed Helga by the throat.

'Hans is missing!' I shouted into her shocked face, 'Where did you send him? What did you make him do?'

Her sweating, round face was horrified, sleeves tight around her fleshy arms. I shoved her back into the chair.

'Where is he?' I screamed again.

Helga stumbled over her words, panicked, 'I don't know! I don't know anything of this! He's supposed to be working in reception today.'

I stared at her and realised she knew nothing. Helga looked as frightened as I felt.

'Frau Schoenberg told me Hans took yesterday afternoon off to do some errands for you. He didn't return last night or appear to start his duties this morning.'

'That's a lie! I would never send my boy out alone in the streets like that, it's too dangerous!'

Helga struggled out of her chair, shouting, but I barely heard her. My eyes scanned the room as I desperately tried to understand where my brother had gone. When I turned back to Helga, she was slumped on the floor. She had fainted. I yelled through the door to one of the chambermaids.

'Suzanne, can you look after Helga? She has collapsed. My brother is missing.'

Leaving Helga with the chambermaid, I ran to my brother's bedroom, desperate for clues. Opening the door on the tiny room no bigger than a broom cupboard, my heart sank to see my brother's neatly made bed. On top of it was his recipe book. His meticulous scrawl across the front page read 'Ideas for my American Restaurant'. My heart was beating so fast I thought I would choke. Hans never went anywhere without his recipe book. I was certain he was in serious trouble.

'Miss Greta?' I span around to see one of the butlers, Fred, in the doorway, 'Madam Sophie would like to see you.'

Hans' disappearance had soon filtered to the top of the hotel.

Fred guided me to the hotelier's apartment. By the time we arrived, I was visibly shaking. Madam Sophie was waiting for us, looking pensive. As we walked in, she put down her cigarette and steered me to a chair, before pouring out and handing me a large brandy. I forced the fiery liquid to my lips, draining the glass in two large gulps. As she crossed the room to her desk, I saw Jacques was present. He stood behind Madam Sophie's chair with a notepad and pen as she began to speak.

'I am hoping your brother has got into some sort of scrape. I have information from Jacques that Hans has in the past run errands for people outside of the hotel - for the military and even some small-time crooks. If I had known this, I would have discouraged it immediately.'

I listened, open-mouthed. Hans running errands for criminals? It didn't make sense. My brother could be a bit mischievous, but he would not knowingly put himself in harm's way.

'I don't understand,' I whispered.

Madam Sophie turned to Jacques, 'Find out where Hans went and what has happened to him. I don't care who you have to bribe.'

She turned back to me, 'I have grown fond of you and Hans, I will do what I can.'

As Jacques left the room, Madam Sophie urged, 'Have another drink and then go back to work. Work is always the saviour.'

'But I need to go looking for Hans!' I burst out, 'I need to see where he is, to talk to his friends and colleagues -'

She put up her hand and talked over me. 'You must not do anything of the sort. Jacques is doing that. He is the best person for this job, he knows lots of people, so leave him to do this. The last thing I want is you going AWOL in Berlin too. I will also make some calls and see what I can find out. Now, I want you to do something for me.'

'Anything,' I replied, 'Just bring Hans back!'

She smiled sadly before replying, 'Go to the Orange Room and make it the cleanest room you have ever serviced, before helping the other maids. When you are finished, go to the linen cupboard and iron.'

Madam Sophie walked over and held my trembling fingers in her steady hands.

'I should have some news for you by the end of the day.'

Walking toward the door, I suddenly turned, remembering, 'Helga?'

'Don't worry about her,' Madam Sophie told me, 'I have made arrangements for your mother, she is being cared for. You have to be the strong one now, Greta.'

'Of course,' I stuttered.

I was dismissed. Madam Sophie was kind but underneath she was steel. Hotel Berlin and its survival meant everything, and without its success none of us would have a livelihood or even a future.

I worked like an automaton for the rest of the day, trying not to think. I cleaned the rooms to perfection, then escaped to the linen room, but ironing no longer soothed me. It was just a round of mindless repetition. Frightening thoughts and horrific scenarios about Hans looped through my mind. I pushed them away into the place where all my trauma resided.

Every so often, Lisa's head appeared around the door of the linen room to see me grimly ironing. My dearest friend never spoke and neither did I. There were no words that would help.

As the day turned to evening, there was still no sign of my little brother.

CHAPTER 21

At the end of the day, Lisa came to the linen cupboard and took me back to Madam Sophie's apartment. The hotelier asked me to sit next to her on the sofa. Jacques, as always, was in attendance. They both looked grim. The room began to darken as I sat listening to her findings.

'I am afraid there has been no sighting of Hans. I have learnt that he was given an errand by a low life called Heinz who occasionally uses the hotel bar. He works as a freelance fence for many of the gangs and he has also disappeared. Should he reappear, he will be questioned and then never allowed access to the building again.'

She spoke quickly, 'According to Jacques and his sources, Hans was instructed to carry a package into the most dangerous part of the city. We believe he was carrying weapons.'

She looked hard into my eyes, 'I understand neither you nor your mother knew anything about this?'

'Of course not!' I replied, confused. 'We would have stopped Hans from doing anything so stupid and dangerous.'

There was a silence and I asked, almost to myself, 'Why the hell would he risk so much?'

It didn't make any sense. I had so many questions but, for some reason, my fear of the answers didn't allow me to voice any words. My mouth opened and shut. Madam Sophie leaned closer to me, her eyes brimming with concern.

'This is very hard for you to hear Greta, but you need to know the truth. Hans was trying to get money to help with your mother's predicament. He had been offered a lot of money for running this errand.'

I had that awful feeling of falling. I clutched the arm of the sofa. I realised Hans had heard every word of the argument between me and Helga a few weeks before. He must have been outside the door the whole time we were talking about Helga needing money for an abortion. I summoned up all my energy to ask the dreaded question.

'Hans is dead, isn't he?'

Madam Sophie drew me to her and rocked me gently back and forth. I was numb.

'If you had come to me when you found your mother was pregnant,' she told me, 'I could have helped, I know doctors.'

After a short silence she said, 'In fact, I can still help with your mother's situation.'

Turning to Jacques, she instructed, 'Get Dr Strang to meet me here within the hour.'

Jacques slipped out of the room.

Madam Sophie looked at me intently as she told me, 'Greta, we will continue to look for Hans. As you know, the city is still dangerous, filled with chancers, missing people and refugees. It will be hard, but I promise I will do my best to find your brother.'

Despite this kindness, I knew Hans was probably dead, laying under some rubble in a disused building, his body being eaten by stray dogs and flies. I tried to block the thoughts from my mind. To hang on to a thin glimmer of hope that perhaps Hans had been knocked out and had lost his memory and was stumbling around in the city somewhere. What I did know and believe was that Madam Sophie and Jacques would do their best to find him, whether he was alive or dead. My life, which had just started to have colour and meaning, in an instant had become sepia toned and dulled.

Bringing me back to the present, the hotelier informed me, 'Your mother has been so distressed that we have kept her sedated all day. Lisa is very good at administering just the right amount of sleeping draught.'

Her voice was no nonsense, 'I want you to be very strong and make a decision for your mother and your family.'

Madam Sophie was grave, 'Dr Strang will be here very soon. He can help your mother to safely terminate the child. He is a qualified surgeon and I have used his services in the past.'

She looked at me, her manner indicating that she too had personally used the services of the surgeon.

'What is your decision?'

There was no choice. Helga had been on the verge of a mental breakdown since she had discovered she was pregnant. With the disappearance of Hans, she had become mad with grief. Helga hated being pregnant with the Soviet's baby. It was unwanted. It would be a disaster for my family. I knew if the pregnancy continued it would push my remaining parent into an abyss of blackness from which she would never return. I was also unsure how safe the baby, once born, would be with Helga. There were numerous tales in the city of women killing babies born of rape and unwanted liaisons.

Whilst Helga was under sedation, it made sense for the baby to be aborted.

'Go ahead,' I whispered.

Madam Sophie nodded, 'Good, I will make all the arrangements.'

Looking at me with concern she said, 'Now you must rest, too.'

The hotelier pulled a small bottle from her pocket containing the all-too-familiar liquid. Tipping a quarter of its contents into a glass of brandy, she watched as I drank greedily. I never wanted to wake up again and, pushing my fingers inside of the glass, licked the remaining contents in the hope that it would put me into a permanent sleep of no return. At that moment I just wanted to die.

Within a few moments I started to feel sleepy and looked with glazed eyes as I watched Jacques return. He sat in a corner and silently started to scribble away in his accounting book.

The last thing I remember is Madam Sophie reassuring me, 'Jacques will watch over you whilst you rest, you will not be alone.'

Then there was nothing.

Whilst I slept, my mother had the abortion. On that day I lost my beloved brother Hans and an unnamed sibling that never had the chance to take its first breath.

CHAPTER 22

I woke dazed and groggy in my bedroom. Helga was sitting in a chair opposite. She looked awful, with a bleached complexion and an odd, vacant gaze. As my eyes adjusted, I saw Lisa pouring water into the basin perched on the bedside cabinet. Dipping a cloth into the liquid, she washed Helga's face.

Lisa looked towards my stirring figure and told me, 'Jacques sat with you for hours and when my shift was complete and I could care for you, he carried you to your bedroom. You have been asleep for nearly two days, Greta. You were exhausted and needed to rest completely.'

I tried to sit up, but it was too much of an effort. Lisa hurried over and, pulling me upwards, placed a pillow high behind my shoulders.

'There, it will take an hour or so before you're steady on your feet. I'm afraid Madam Sophie is not as good at measuring the medication as me and she gave you a much larger dose.'

Trying to smile, Lisa told me, 'Dr Strang insists that your mother gets up from her bed during the day to avoid complications.'

Helga, seeing me awake, tried to talk to me but her words were slurred. Lisa told me that she was drugged for the pain and trauma she had suffered. I was glad. With Lisa's help, I managed to totter to the chamber pot. My bladder was bursting.

I drank a cup of water containing a handful of herbs. My dear friend Lisa informed me that the herbs were from the garden and great aids to nerves and recovery. I sat down at the small stool next to the mirror, and Lisa slowly patted my hair in an effort to make me look less dishevelled.

Helga's reflection in the mirror was almost transparent. I glanced fleetingly at my own image: a strong-boned girl with mauve patches circling her eyes. Willing a smile to my dry lips, my eyes crinkled just like Hans' and, for a second, I saw my brother. I pushed away thoughts of him and the aborted baby before they had time to overwhelm me. The sleeping draught had left my usually racing mind dulled, as if everything was in slow motion. I went back to bed and dozed.

*   *   *

When I next woke, Lisa was helping Helga to slowly move around the room, before placing her in bed and giving Helga yet another glass of medicine. Once my mother was settled, Lisa turned her attention to me. She got me out of bed and washed and clothed me like I was a small child. I was dressed in a lovely white, clean shift embroidered with tiny flowers around the neck. Lisa brought out a red silk wrap which obviously had once belonged to Madam Sophie. When I was neat and tidy, she pushed me gently towards the door.

'Come with me, there is coffee waiting for us.'

We walked slowly up several flights of stairs. I swayed as if drunk. It took me a moment to realise we weren't going to Madam Sophie's apartment. I realised we were heading to the 'offices', rooms we'd seen when we first arrived, but which I'd never visited.

Lisa opened a large wooden door and we entered a room lined with shelves filled with books. Leather chairs and a chaise longue were tastefully placed. It was a place of work but also contemplation. Jacques sat behind a desk, quietly scribbling into a ledger. He appeared to be compiling the accounts for the hotel. As soon as he saw us, he stopped working and stood, showing me to a comfortable chair, whilst Lisa sat next to me on a wooden stool. Jacques' eyes were soft and pensive as he prepared strong, black coffee. I watched as he spooned in several sugars and then presented me with the drink. It was so hot it burnt my lips.

Lisa handed me a pill and I took it without question. Jacques and Lisa chatted about the hotel and guests, waiting for the tablet to work. By the time I had drunk my coffee, I had a strange sensation of floating, feeling out of step with reality. When it was obvious that I was relaxed and compliant, Lisa quietly told me, 'Greta, a lot has happened since you and your mother have been sedated.'

I tried to straighten up, but it was too much of an effort. Lisa rushed on before my hopes were raised.

'We have not found Hans, but Jacques thinks he knows what happened to your brother.'

Jacques leant towards me and took my hand.

'Hans went to the other side of Berlin with a package containing guns. There was a fight between two rival factions. Your brother was caught up in gang conflicts, and we must assume he has died.'

He looked at the floor before turning his caring gaze back to me, 'I am so very sorry, Greta.'

I was unable to cry, the loss too great to comprehend or accept. There was just a gaping void of nothing. I absorbed all the information that Jacques and Lisa imparted. I didn't ask any questions, or demand evidence or confirmation, I just listened to what had happened to my lovely young brother and learnt that I would never see him again.

Then there were more shocking revelations. Lisa held my arm as she spoke,

'Greta, I want there to be no lies between us. You need to know what has happened to your mother and her current health.'

I stared blankly at her.

'The baby was near full term, it could not have been the consequence of the Soviet's rape. Your mother must have conceived much earlier. By the time the surgeon realised this, he had to continue. Your mother was bleeding so much, she would have died if he had not. She is very ill and may never fully recover. She will need a lot of nursing.'

Lisa patted my arm softly, 'She does not know how old the baby was, Greta. I think we must keep this from her?'

So, the baby was not from the rape. The child must have been Al Malone's, the US Army sergeant who had left us behind. I knew that even if she had been informed about the paternity of her baby, Helga would still have gone through with the abortion.

Lisa looked into my eyes.

'Your mother may die, Greta. I don't think it's wise for her to know about the baby or what has happened to Hans. What do you think?'

I shrugged and nodded. I was bone weary; the medication was making me slow. I was unable to process the full horror of what had happened to my family in just a few short days. Just one question bounced back and forth in my foggy mind, how would I survive this? As the tablet's sedative effects flowed into my system, I became still and unable to form words.

Lisa told me in a comforting tone, 'Jacques and I will help you get through this, we are your family, too.'

I could not speak as the drug worked its magic and kept me awake just enough to listen but not aware enough to become distressed. Jacques and Lisa sat with me for a long time in the enveloping silence. To ease the tension, they began to chat about everyday subjects, like the weather and how soon it would be winter again. Their chatter flowed in and out of my head, then disappeared like melting snow.

Eventually, Lisa and I made our way back to my bedroom. When we got there, Lisa showed me a list she had written for Helga's medication and nursing.

She told me, 'The tablet I gave you will wear off in the next few hours. From tomorrow you will start to take care of your mother. She needs you to nurse her and it will be good for you both.'

I remained mute as Lisa helped me into bed. She stayed with me all night, snuggling up to me in my tiny single bed as Helga snored in the background. As the anaesthetic effects of the tablet disappeared, Lisa held me as I shook with shock. Neither of us mentioned Hans, the baby or the war. Instead, my dear friend talked about frivolous things to distract and distance me from my losses. She described the dances being held at the NAAFI – an eating place that the English soldiers used. My dear friend had been seeing a British serviceman, and he had given her a precious movie magazine. By candlelight, Lisa read me stories about a beautiful English actress called Vivien Leigh and her handsome husband, Laurence Olivier. She showed me photographs of film studios and actors in London, and behind-the-scenes pictures of a play in a place called 'the West End', written by a man with a cigarette holder called Noel Coward. He was a famous writer in Britain and the USA. Lisa read until I slept. There were no dreams that night, just more blackness.

The next day, Lisa helped me to organise the room and repeated the medical care that Dr Strang had ordered. The hotel also provided material for the huge pads needed to stem and soak up the blood that continued to drip and sometimes gush from my mother's empty womb. I washed these pads daily and hung them to dry over chairs. The room, despite copious amounts of disinfectant and soap, smelt awful. Lavender and other scents were used to hide the rank, earthy smell from the abortion's leftovers.

Once all the instructions had been given, Lisa left for her shift, placing the movie magazine from the previous night firmly in my hands.

'Whenever you are starting to go into a dark place, read one of these articles out loud and keep reading till the blackness has been pushed away.'

Helga woke as Lisa shut the door.

'Greta? I need the pot.'

'Just coming mother,' I said, 'I am here and I'm going to make you better.'

* * *

Nursing my mother was both exhausting and welcome, as there was very little time to think or feel. From that morning I began to think of Helga as my mother again. I don't know what changed. Perhaps I felt she deserved the title, or perhaps it was because I needed a mother. We both needed each other. For the next two weeks I hardly left her side: bathing her, medicating her, and talking for hours. Occasionally I would hug her, and now she was so desperately ill, she welcomed my affection. Mother never mentioned the baby or the fact it had gone, that her stomach was flat and empty. She never asked about Hans. As the days turned to weeks, there was still no sighting of my little brother. Although I knew he was dead, it was difficult to accept that my young brother – once so full of life – was gone.

My mother, drugged with morphine on Dr Strang's orders, was a compliant patient. Long conversations were not easy, but we had short, and sometimes meaningful, interactions. These moments were a salve to my wounds and, I hope, to my mother's pain. I read to her from the film magazines and my mother seemed to enjoy the stories about the make-up and dresses the Hollywood stars wore, their special pets and expensive cars. The tales from New York and Los Angeles transformed the small world of her bedroom to a vista of colour and fun.

'You could be a film star, you are so lovely,' she told me as we looked at photographs of Irish actress Greer Garson and stills from a film called *Mrs Miniver*.

My mother asked if she could brush my hair. Gently placing the brush through my thick hair, she sang a lullaby from when I was a child. It was a rare loving moment between mother and daughter.

She only talked about Hans once.

'Hans is so unlike your father and for that I am glad. Such a sweet and loving boy.'

My mother then shut her eyes and said nothing else for the rest of the day.

I was no longer medicated; it was not needed. It was a full-time job caring for my mother and every night I slipped exhausted into bed and slept soundly. Lisa visited most days and her gossipy tales often made me laugh, but it was a manufactured laugh. I felt no pain, joy or anger. I was a vacuum where a joyful child had once resided. Even food was tasteless: I ate biscuits made especially by Chef Weber but felt no enjoyment. I may as well have been eating cardboard.

When I heard that Georges the head porter had died suddenly of pneumonia, I expressed sadness but felt nothing. Even though Georges had been so friendly to my family and especially kind to Hans, the porter's death didn't register.

*   *   *

Another week passed and we had a special visitor, Madam Sophie. My mother was in her chair, a green hue around her eyes and lips, her face shrunken with weight loss. There was something different about Madam Sophie's demeanour as she sat alongside my parent talking about the happenings in the hotel and daily life. Light, fluffy chit-chat made my mother giggle, a rasping rackety sound that filled the room. The two women who had disliked each other so intently now seemed to have come to a mutual understanding.

When she left, Madam Sophie gave a bottle of brandy and a new night gown to my mother and wished her well. That evening, lying in bed wearing her new linen shift, my mother told me, 'Greta, I love you. Always remember that.'

With those gentle words, she fell instantly asleep. I sat on the tiny stool and looked up towards the small window as sunset swept the sky. An image of my little brother popped into my head: Hans gathering autumn leaves in the garden at our home, placing them into a huge pile and then throwing around and around my head. I remembered him laughing as he baked pastry with Chef Weber, proudly telling me his cakes were the best in the city, as the chef patted him on the head in agreement. My brother had such dreams and hopes for a better life and future.

Quickly, I pulled myself away from thoughts of Hans. I knew if I allowed my grief full rein, I would never function again. I began to wash my mother's bloodied pads in a small bowl, rubbing hard with a slither of soap to make them white and useable again. After many weeks, my mother had stopped bleeding and now just small spots of congealed blood remained. I hoped she would regain her health. It would be an uphill struggle as she was so poorly, but I was a good nurse and if she was determined enough it was possible for her to recover.

When I had finished the washing, I stretched and checked on my mother. She was in a deep sleep. I decided to head to the kitchen, hoping to meet Lisa or another of the girls for a quick catch up. Now mother's health was improving, I would have to start pulling my weight at the hotel again. I needed to get up to speed with all the new happenings with the staff and guests. I also wanted to see Jacques, in case he had news about Hans. My brother's body had not been found, so there remained a possibility that somehow, somewhere in the city, Hans had survived.

Jacques was putting on his coat as I rattled down the stairs into a cloud of steam which was rising from the pots bubbling away on the top of the oven. His eyes shone when he saw me.

'Hello Greta, how are you today?'

Jacques' kindly manner always made me smile and I told him, 'I'm feeling stronger. I will be able to start work soon, as mother can be left for longer now.'

Adjusting his hat, Jacques said, 'That's good news.'

He paused for a moment, then said shyly, 'I'm just going for short walk. It might be a good idea if you came too, you have been inside for too long.'

He looked so expectant; I could not refuse.

'My coat is upstairs,' I said.

'Don't worry, you can have mine if you are cold.'

Holding out his coat, Jacques escorted me out of the kitchen and into the busy road that ran along the back of the building. I felt no qualms about taking his arm as we both stepped outside into the fresh air. The noise and bustle of people and military vehicles was a shock after the claustrophobic and cloying air of my bedroom. Jacques saw my discomfort and put a protective arm around my shoulder. It was comfortable.

We walked for an hour meandering around the city streets and then made our way to the river. There was no need for words. The sights, smells, and noise of the city were at times overpowering: people dashing around and cars hooting their horns. It was a city starting to revive and a good distraction from my mother's sickbed.

I was struck by the difference in the city. In a few short weeks, Berlin had changed again. Pipes were being laid to connect more businesses and homes with gas and water. More shops had opened and there were even a couple of markets selling furniture, old clothes and other items obtained from bombed-out buildings. There were also more people around, and fewer of them were in tatters, but reasonably dressed. Of course, the military were everywhere, patrolling or busily involved in repairing roads and essentials.

As we walked back to the hotel, Jacques answered the question I didn't dare ask.

'Greta, you know I will do anything to find out what happened to Hans. He meant a lot to me and of course you mean a lot to me, too.'

He saw my desolate face and said, 'I am sorry to upset you. I should not have mentioned this. I don't want to ever hurt you.'

I looked at him and saw for the first time the love he had for me in his eyes.

'Of course I know that Jacques,' I answered, stuttering, 'It's just, just, that-'

I could not cry; it was too painful. Jacques reached forward and hugged me to his bony but strong frame. I accepted his embrace and did not recoil from his touch.

I looked up at his smooth, baby face and told him, 'I know that Hans is dead.'

Jacques cuddled me close and replied, 'Hans is now safe from any pain and from any hurt. Think of it like that.'

I tried to nod but couldn't move. People on the street pushed past us, but Jacques continued to hold me in arms. Eventually I started to move my wobbly legs in an effort to walk. Jacques held me all the way to the hotel. We went through the back door into the kitchen and he sat me down with a strong cup of coffee, staying by my side for the next hour or so, his arm gently around my shoulders. I realised Jacques was the one man I could allow close. He never made me feel afraid or threatened.

When I was calm again, he told me, 'I will always look out for you, Greta. You have my solemn promise that I will take care of you.'

Looking at his lopsided, scarred face, I kissed him gently on the cheek. Jacques blushed to the roots of his hair. I did not love Jacques; I never would or could. It wasn't because of the scars he had sustained from being tortured – that meant little to me – I just didn't think I would ever feel love again for another human being, especially not a man. Loving a man meant eventually having sex and the thought of that made me feel physically sick.

CHAPTER 23

Slowly I resumed my duties at the hotel, working split shifts and nursing my mother in-between each one. Though the bleeding had stopped, she was becoming increasingly weaker and was no longer able to get out of bed. She drank lots of water but barely ate. I felt as if she was distancing herself from me and from life, as if she had no strength to continue. She had given up. The sleeping draft continued to be administered by Lisa, and my mother now mostly slept. I was not needed, and work within the hotel became more of a priority.

Having the structure of part-time work was essential to my well-being. It also gave Madam Sophie the clear message that I was still an employee and would continue to work whatever happened. I could not become sucked into the terrible decline that was now my mother's fate. Work always was the saviour and my go-to whenever trauma hit.

As we returned from a shift changing beds on the second floor, Lisa distracted me from thoughts of my mother's sickbed with news of her latest dalliance with another English soldier. She described the afternoon dances the soldier was taking her to, and it sounded like a great place to have fun. I was trying to smile at Lisa's adventures as we headed towards mother's room to check on her.

I opened the bedroom door to find my mother slumped on the floor. In her outstretched hand was a half-empty brandy bottle, and a few pills were strewn beside her. Quietly I went to my mother's side. She was cold and had been dead for a few hours. Gently I picked up her tiny, almost weightless, body and placed her on the bed. I got into bed with her and pulled the covers over us and hugged her for the rest of the day and night.

Lisa sat watching and waiting until I was ready to let my mother go. Then she called for Dr Strang. When the doctor had completed his examination, he assured me, 'Greta, you've been exceptional in your care for your mother. Unfortunately, even in a hospital she would have died, she had just lost too much blood. I tried my very best to save her, but it would have been beyond the greatest surgeon. I am so very sorry.'

With a tip of his hat, he left. I did not feel any blame towards Dr Strang. I reserved my anger for another man, Al Malone; he had impregnated my mother and left her with the consequences.

Madam Sophie had been wonderfully supportive during my mother's final days and now set about arranging the funeral. A simple coffin was brought to the basement and my mother lay in splendour with a beautiful silk shift provided by the hotelier. I visited my mother as often as I could in a room lit with one, stark bulb, her coffin surrounded by bottles of wine and various packages.

I held my mother's hand and talked to her about everything and nothing. Over the next two days I watched as red blotches appeared on her neck. Her body stiffened and then became soft again. I combed her hair and put lipstick on her mouth, but the once vibrant woman who was my mother had gone, leaving only an overcoat of skin and bones.

Madam Sophie kindly secured a burial place for my mother in a small churchyard outside the city. I knew Helga would have liked that and I was truly grateful to my employer, who never told me how she had managed to arrange such a quick burial and locate a plot. With so many casualties and the constant threat of disease, most corpses were buried in large, anonymous pits outside the city. It must have cost the hotelier a lot of money to secure such a place for my mother's internment.

On the day of the funeral, we travelled in Madam Sophie's black car, Jacques and Lisa either side of me, dressed in black, both holding one of my hands. As we left the hotel, Madam Sophie appeared. I was surprised and touched that she planned to join us.

'Here Greta, I pressed and dried the very last of the roses from this season.' She placed two heavy but dusty blooms into my hands.

I knew that one was for my mother and the other for Hans.

'Though your mother and I never saw eye to eye,' Madam Sophie said, 'I must admit I had admiration for the way she kept fighting for you and Hans.'

The hotelier sat stiff-backed in the front of the car as I shrunk into the leather seat at the back, hoping to disappear forever. I ached to be with my brother and mother. The chauffeur drove in silence, and for the next hour we followed the horse and cart transporting my mother's coffin. We arrived at a quaint little village of a dozen or so houses, dominated by an old church. Its steeple stood intact, tall and defiant against the sky.

With wobbling legs, I got out of the car and was greeted by a white-haired priest. He took both my hands and offered his condolences in a German accent that held the twang of the mountains. Behind him, I could see there could be no service in the church. The building was only a frame, the windows and doors ripped off and the remains of pews just shards of wood, splintered like a yawning face. The wind blew pages of what were once prayer books around in furious circles, scooting them across the graves in the distance.

The priest said, 'I am afraid it's very unsafe, so we cannot go inside.'

Clutching the faded roses, I walked unsteadily as Lisa and Jacques held me up on either side. Madam Sophie walked behind us, her head down, stunning in a black velvet cape and veiled hat. Four men appeared, dressed like farm labourers, and they took the coffin from the cart, swaying as they walked in slow practised movements towards the hole where my mother would lie for eternity. I stared at the coffin, imagining my mother inside, her tiny-wasted body drained of life and pale as snow. The walk to the grave seemed to take forever. It was close to the walls of the cemetery, and a large tree overhead waved its skeletal branches. We gathered round the grave and I looked down into the darkness, the hole in the ground that would embrace my mother. The priest chanted, reading from his dusty Bible. Words that meant little to me fell from his mouth, the sound only a background noise. I watched his lips moving into circles like a gasping fish, opening and then finally closing like a cage.

Crows cackled overhead and I trembled as the coffin was laid to rest in the ground. I dropped the roses into the open grave, and they landed side by side on top of the coffin. I stretched my arms, looked at the sky and shouted so loud that for a moment even the crows stopped their incessant squawking.

'Where are you Hans? You should be here with me, standing at our mother's grave. I am not an only child! Where are you?'

Madam Sophie moved as if to silence me, but I said no more. Lisa started to cry, but I did not. I was a hollowed-out shell.

The biting wind blew through the graveyard like an angry man. The service ended abruptly and, with a firm handshake, the priest left with the farm workers. I saw Madam Sophie join them at the steeple door and she passed a pile of notes to the priest. Her hands waved instructions to the men to fill in the hole containing my mother. I pictured the dark earth being shovelled on top of her coffin, sealing my mother into the ground, and shook my head to make the images disappear.

We returned to the car. On the way back to the hotel, Madam Sophie sat with us in the back of the car. The journey flashed by in what seemed seconds. When Hotel Berlin came into view, Madam Sophie broke the quiet by telling me in a firm manner, 'Greta, now you must rest.'

She patted my hand.

'Tonight, all of you will join me for dinner to celebrate your mother and brother. We will eat and drink and talk of many things. I will see you all at 7pm.'

Slowly I dragged myself up the steps to my bedroom and scrabbled to open the door. It was locked. My heart began to beat faster. I rattled and pushed at the door, trying to open it. Lisa appeared beside me and, taking my arm, said calmly, 'Come with me, we are going to share a room. All your things are in the wardrobe next to mine.'

She saw my stricken face. I felt like I was drowning, thinking about my mother's clothes and the few items she had collected over the months of employment, her precious keepsakes.

Lisa rushed on, 'Don't worry, your mother's clothes are all packaged in a box under the bed next to mine.'

She took a breath before saying, 'Madam Sophie thought it a good idea for you to have Hans' things too, and they are in another box.'

My hand finally fell from the doorknob of my old bedroom where I had shared so much and so little with my mother.

'All of your mother's and Hans' belongings are safe in my bedroom. When you are ready to open the boxes, you can decide what you want to keep and what you want to leave behind.'

Leave behind? I didn't know what she meant. All I could think about was that now Hans' belongings had finally been packed up. It meant Madam Sophie and Jacques had given up all hope of his return. Somehow, I had to accept that, too.

Slowly Lisa steered me to her bedroom, laid me down on my new bed, and placed a cover over my shivering body. I could see the edges of the boxes containing everything that was now left of Hans and my mother stashed under my bedstead. I was so cold, I felt I would never be warm again, yet I must have slept instantly.

I woke to the clatter of a jug hitting the basin. Lisa was sluicing down her body with a cloth. It was dark and a candle cast huge black shapes that danced over the walls. The servants' quarters did not have the luxury of electric lighting; that was saved for the paying guests.

'Greta, I'm glad you're awake. We are due to go to Madam Sophie's for dinner soon.'

I shook my head and pulled the covers over my face. Lisa took no notice.

'It will do us all good to talk, eat and drink. As Madam Sophie says, it's a celebration of your mother and of all of us too!'

I watched as she pulled on her best dress, straightening the seams and looking at herself with approval in the mirror. Determined, she approached the bed.

'Helga and Hans would be very proud of you. Like all of us, you have to keep going until you can smile and laugh again.'

Lisa kneeled beside me. 'You never saw me and what I was like when I first arrived at the hotel after seeing everyone murdered. I still find it difficult to comprehend, or even to recognise, that it happened. So, I understand your pain, trauma, the numbness and grief.'

Punching the air, she said, 'But you have to keep getting up in the morning, keep working, keep upright, putting one foot in front of the other. For them as well as yourself.'

I said nothing as she looked at me.

'Otherwise, Greta,' she continued, 'what has been the point? What was the point of your mother giving birth to you, raising you and then bringing you here in hope of a better life?'

I knew Lisa was talking sense and thought of the horrific events that had also brought my friend to Berlin. Yet the little maid continued to grab life with both hands and take the opportunities.

Now she expected me to do the same.

As she pulled me up from the bed and started to wash my face with fresh water, she assured me, 'We have each other and will help each other always. It will change and slowly get better, I promise.'

I said nothing but allowed her to dress and tidy my hair. I was a robot, no longer human, a walking, talking vacuum. Surely too much had happened for me to ever be normal again, whatever normal meant? After Chuck had left, after the rape, even after Hans had disappeared, I still felt some emotion, but this odd state I now lived in was like being behind a glass wall, disconnected from everything and everyone on the other side. I hoped Lisa was right and that it would eventually get better.

Lisa ignored my silence and carried on in her usual busy manner. Brushing my hair till it sparkled, I let her do everything to make me presentable. It all seemed too much of an effort.

Finally, she pushed me out of the door.

'Come along! Jacques and Madam Sophie will be waiting, and there is some very good news that she has to tell you.'

This snippet of information once would have piqued my curiosity. Now I didn't question what the good news would be, it barely registered. I allowed myself to be taken upstairs to the hotelier's private apartments.

Glancing through the windows, I saw it was the blackest of evenings. It was winter, the first without my mother and brother.

CHAPTER 24

We were greeted by Jacques, who ushered us both through the entrance of Madam Sophie's apartment. Instead of taking us to the familiar, grand room I had visited before, he veered left through a smaller corridor. We passed several locked doors until we came to the far end of the suite. Jacques knocked briefly, and the door was quickly opened by an elderly woman with the most vivid orange hair I had ever seen.

This room was smaller and cosier than the main room. I noticed that the furniture was well-used, and the drapes were threadbare in places, unlike the guest rooms on the lower floors. Madam Sophie gestured for us to sit on a huge sofa nearby. It had seen better days and smelled of dog, with stray hairs dotting the material.

The old woman reappeared to serve us drinks from a silver tray.

'This is aunt Sybil!' said Madam Sophie.

The woman gave an old-fashioned curtsey and handed me a glass of champagne.

'I call Sybil my aunt because she is so precious to me, she is my only family,' Madam Sophie said, staring at me.

'Even tough women like me need proper friends. Sybil has saved my sanity many times.'

Sybil turned and smiled at me with a penetrating stare.

Madam Sophie told us, 'She has made a wonderful meal for us. Thank you, Sybil, you can finish for the evening.'

The old woman left as quietly as she had appeared.

Madam Sophie explained, 'She can no longer talk, her tongue was removed. A drunken SS officer took exception to her red hair. Sybil mostly stays in this part of the apartment. She never goes out of the building, despite my encouragement.'

Jacques said, 'Sybil is well educated. Her father was a Professor of Law, she was once an accomplished pianist. Now she seems too afraid of the outside world to enter it anymore.'

He looked at me pleadingly, 'Greta, please don't become another Sybil!'

Jacques was still looking at me for reassurance, so I murmured, 'I will try my best to recover.'

He smiled. I listened as the others talked and gossiped about new guests and the hotel and added a 'Yes' or 'No' when expected. Recognising my depression, Madam Sophie raised her glass and announced, 'To Helga and Hans.'

We drained our glasses in memory of my mother and brother.

Despite food restrictions and a lack of variety of ingredients, our meal was excellent. I was not hungry but made myself eat, agreeing that aunt Sybil had first-class culinary skills. Lisa began to talk happily about Hans and the many conversations she had with him in the kitchen. She recounted his determination to open his own restaurant and the triumphs and disasters he had concocted in the kitchen. It was good to remember the happy times we had all shared. Our conversations became livelier as two, then three bottles of champagne, were consumed. I relaxed and began to laugh when it was expected of me. I hoped by playing the part, I would eventually feel like me again, feel anything again.

At the end of the meal we relaxed into the huge sofa and Madam Sophie gave us all a brandy. I never refused alcohol as I knew its powerful sedative effects usually stilled my racing heart and mind. That night I was unable to get drunk, however much I consumed. As the clock moved towards midnight and slipped into another day, Madam Sophie stood up and waved some papers in the air. Lisa whispered to me that this was the 'good news' she had hinted at earlier.

'Greta, I want to present you with this.'

Madam Sophie, slightly unsteady on her feet, urged me to stand beside her. I rose and walked towards the mantelpiece where the hotelier proudly presented me with a sheaf of documents.

'These are your official papers, for the new you and for your new life.'

I looked blankly at her as she pointed out the words on the pages.

'It says here your name is Greta Bless, you were born in Switzerland and are now eighteen years old.'

She paused for dramatic effect as Jacques and Lisa looked on, grinning.

'These are your official papers and will help you travel anywhere you want.'

She bowed as she finally placed my new life and name into my hands.

I looked at the paperwork, which must have cost a fortune to obtain. I should have been so happy, but instead there was a gaping abyss.

Lisa, recognising my difficulty, whispered, 'Madam Sophie gave me my papers yesterday!'

Seeing my incomprehension, Jacques answered for me.

'Madam Sophie, Greta is overwhelmed by your kindness and generosity. Let me say thank you on her behalf. Greta has had a day which started in deepest tragedy and has ended with such a prize, the ability to move freely across Europe or anywhere in the world.'

Madam Sophie weaved her way back to a chair by the fireplace and asked Jacques to light her another cigarette.

'Of course, it has been an exhausting day for you Greta. I do understand. There has been too much to process.'

Looking around the room she told us, 'Now all of you have official papers, it means you can travel with me in the future, say to Paris or another country. There will be no issues.'

Madam Sophie smiled at us in turn, 'The future is looking bright. I want you to be the core of my staff and help me make Hotel Berlin profitable and famous both nationally and internationally!'

So much had happened in a short time. It was hard to take in. This new and positive information was blunted by the pain of losing my entire family. Official papers meant freedom of movement and with a new identity I could become a different person, yet without my mother and brother, without my family, it meant so little.

I noticed everyone was looking at me. I tried to reply but my mouth would not form the words. There was just too much to think about. Once again, Jacques stood up and started to talk.

'Madam Sophie has asked me to tell both of you, there is more good news. Lisa, you are being promoted to senior house maid. This promotion means more responsibility and higher wages, as well as training new staff. Both Madam Sophie and I know you are more than capable of this role.'

Lisa giggled and ran over to Madam Sophie and gave her a kiss on the cheek. The hotelier returned the kiss. Jacques walked towards me as I stared at him blankly.

'Greta, you will be Lisa's assistant before becoming our receptionist. You are more than able to do these jobs. Your knowledge of several languages will help us welcome guests from across Europe.'

Suddenly, it happened, the dam broke. I began to cry. Huge sobs racked my frame as I cried for my mother. Then I cried for my brother and the life he would never live. I cried for my unknown, aborted sibling, for my father, and for the life we had once known and shared. My tears carried on for a long time and Lisa and Madam Sophie retired to bed. Jacques sat with me, holding my shaking shoulders until I eventually slept. When I woke, I could hardly open my red and swollen eyes, tiny slits in my tear-stained face. My mouth was dry like sandpaper. Jacques stood over me with a glass of water which I gulped down. His jacket covered my legs.

'What's the time?' I finally croaked.

'4am,' Jacques replied.

I pulled my aching body upwards and put my feet on the ground, but it swayed beneath me, a reminder of the alcohol I had drunk.

'I have to get to my room, I start work in less than an hour.'

Jacques moved towards the sofa and sat beside me, 'Madam Sophie says you are to rest today and start work at your new position tomorrow. You can sleep here for a while longer.'

As the room was spinning, I laid back down and slept.

*　　*　　*

The opening of the curtains woke me as aunt Sybil entered the room with a pot of coffee and toast. Jacques had fallen asleep next to me, and he winced as his twisted body complained. I watched as inch by inch he uncurled his shattered legs, and with a supreme effort managed to crawl onto the floor. Pain was etched on his round face. He dismissed my offer of support and, after several minutes, eventually stood upright.

Seeing my concerned face, he told me, 'I'm like this every morning. Until I start moving in earnest, it takes a while for my legs to start working again. It's a legacy from the beatings.'

Jacques was never one to talk too much about his past, and he quickly changed the subject as he waved my new official paperwork under my nose.

'This is good news for you, Greta. It means freedom.'

I smiled thinly. Over breakfast, we talked about the previous night. I learnt about some of Madam Sophie's plans for the future of her business. Eventually, she wanted the hotel to become 'legitimate' and was already working to move away from the black market once the city became stable. Jacques was sourcing more reliable – and legal – channels to access food and supplies for the hotel. The high-class courtesans, who so often frequented the hotel's bar and rooms, were slowly being persuaded to seek other venues.

Jacques stood up and stretched his complaining limbs as he walked to and fro across the floor explaining Madam Sophie's 'five-year plan'. I had to force myself to concentrate. Suddenly, he stopped talking and pulled me towards him, stroking my hair. I didn't move.

He told me, 'Today is the day for no more secrets between us Greta. You must know I love you, and I always will.'

I held my breath and said nothing.

'I know of your experiences of men and how harshly and violently they treated you and your mother. I just wanted to say that there are good men, better men like me who will always care for and respect you.'

I looked up into Jacques' eyes and told him, 'I could never be frightened or worried by you Jacques. You are a gentleman.'

Jacques smiled briefly then let me go. He sat down and put his head in his hands as I sank into a chair next to him.

'I am going to tell you something that must never be shared with another,' he said. 'Only three other people know about this and two of them were SS guards in the camp.'

I felt my stomach lurch as I prepared myself for another secret.

With short, sharp breaths, Jacques told me what happened to him in the camp: the tortures, executions, and degradation he had seen and experienced. After a long silence, he told me the true extent of the trauma he had suffered.

'I am a eunuch, Greta, unable to have sex or ever have children. The SS castrated me in the camp.'

I stared, unable to utter a word.

'I thought I would die from the bleeding,' he continued, not meeting my eyes. 'Then they broke both my legs and reset them deliberately in this twisted manner.'

In monotone he continued, 'I survived.'

He shrugged his shoulders in surprise. 'I, like many of my fellow inmates, was an experiment. That's why my voice is sometimes high, that's why my face is so smooth, with no beard. I am no longer a man.'

I burst out, 'Jacques! You are the best man, the bravest, kindest, and most intelligent man I know.'

Jacques let out a long sigh and then, smiling weakly, declared, 'Don't you see, Greta? Amongst all of this pain, we have found each other. The love I have for you is pure and forever.'

I took hold of his face and kissed him on the lips.

'I will always love and care for you, too. Thank you for telling me,' I told him.

Jacques' face turned scarlet, touched with a joy that I had never seen before.

The day after my mother's funeral had brought even more pain and terrible revelations, but it made my relationship with Jacques deeper. I understood why I felt so at ease with him, he was not like other men. I could have friendship, affection and even love without any strings attached. For the first time since my mother had died, I felt a glimmer of hope as I realised that Jacques trusted me completely, and I trusted him. He quietly filled my coffee cup and quickly moved the conversation back to the hotel and Madam Sophie's plans for a new management structure.

Lisa, Jacques and even Madam Sophie had suffered, too. How could I turn away from life and living, when they had been through so much and were still trying? I realised these people were now my family, and they were looking upwards towards the stars instead of down at the gutter, each determined to make a better life.

I had so many reasons to carry on living. So that day I decided I would do just that.

CHAPTER 25

I became Madam Sophie's star employee as I never stopped working or complained, no matter how many hours I put in or how many shifts I was offered. I needed to be totally spent before I could lay my head on the pillow and then welcome the oblivion of sleep.

In the early days, I hurt so much it was hard to look beyond the next hour, let alone the next day or week. The pain a constant heavy blow in the middle of my chest. I really was heartbroken.

Work was the only salve, so I filled my days with chores and mundane, repetitive tasks while brightly pinning on a welcoming smile for the steady stream of guests. Gradually, I learnt to manage my grief until it became part of me instead of controlling me. Yet everyday feelings still did not return; my laughter was forced and I experienced no feelings of joy or happiness. Those emotions seemed to have been wiped out from my being.

Over time, I learnt to adapt to this new emotional landscape without my family, though it was terrifying and draining. Somehow, despite the terrible blows I had experienced, I kept living and breathing.

I had to learn to live as a new me. Slowly I developed a new version of myself so that I could move onwards. Two years passed. I now lived in a future in which my mother and brother no longer existed. I had irrevocably changed.

Outside of the hotel, big changes were happening that would influence Madam Sophie, her business, and, of course, me.

The Soviet area of Berlin was now under communist rule, and strict regulations were being enforced. Fortunately for us, Hotel Berlin was in the English Sector. We heard gossip from people who had families in the Soviet-run part of the city. They told us Stalin wanted a buffer from Western states that opposed his communist rule, and that he wanted Germany to remain weak. I listened, but bereavement made me self-centred and introverted. I was just glad to be in the part of the city run by the Western Allies. This area of Berlin had a lively atmosphere. A corporate spirit had followed with the influence of the Allies and their finances. The streets were filled with businessmen and women looking to make money. Many of these intrepid entrepreneurs visited the bar at Hotel Berlin or stayed in its rooms. Berlin run by the Western Allies was a city full of potential.

I worked relentlessly in my new role and soon became head receptionist, whilst Lisa was promoted to assistant housekeeper. At our ages this would have been unheard of in any other time, but war made women of us quickly. Jacques remained my dear friend, and he never talked about his injuries again. Though it was a secret that could have divided us, it made our relationship stronger.

After many months I began to socialise during my time off with Lisa and her new boyfriend Dan, an English officer she had known for a few months. Occasionally Dan would bring a friend along and the four of us would go dancing. These nights were always innocent, an interlude from all my chores at the hotel and devoid of any romance or intimacy. The Allied soldiers were polite and treated me with the utmost respect. I allowed these young men who were far from home to twirl me around the floor and felt no fear or anything much.

I began to laugh again in response to jokes and anecdotes, my laughter sounding like splintered glass. Rarely I would experience a momentary spark of what seemed like being happy, as I moved around the room with a handsome soldier, but within a few seconds it would disappear. Despite Jacques' and Lisa's support, the black pit inside of me remained, and nothing and no-one could fill it. Even the announcement of a trip to Paris with Madam Sophie, Lisa and Jacques in the spring did not spark much enthusiasm. Instead I was apprehensive about our planned eight-week trip to the French capital. Madam Sophie now had a booming business in Berlin and had bought a run-down hotel in Paris, part of her five-year plan to expand.

Lisa couldn't stop talking about our visit. She sashayed around our small bedroom, parading the new clothes Dan had bought for her.

'Just think, Greta, we will see the Eiffel Tower, and help launch Madam Sophie's new hotel! It will be wonderful to meet our French guests and to work with new staff. They say it's the most romantic city in the world, let's hope we have time to walk along the Seine and meet some attractive Frenchmen!'

She collapsed into giggles. It was impossible not to understand Lisa's delight about our trip, but she soon noticed my dark expression.

'Hey, what's the matter?' she said.

I looked at her and words began to tumble from my dry throat.

'I'm frightened of travelling, frightened of being in another country, Lisa! What if the French don't like us? It's safe here in the hotel. I have had too many changes and I don't want to go.'

I frowned. Lisa kissed me on the forehead and pulled me toward her ample frame.

'Greta, of course you're going to be a bit fearful, as it's going to be a new and different place. But France is now free of war, you have a new identity and papers. Madam Sophie has sent Jacques many times to Paris to find this new hotel. You will see, we'll have a wonderful time.'

'Eight weeks is such a long time,' I answered doubtfully.

Lisa laughed, 'We both know eight weeks will pass in a flash with the amount of work and organising needed to launch the hotel!'

I knew Lisa was right, but it was over two years since I had been anywhere beyond Berlin. France had been occupied by my country and the Nazis. My accent was still strong, despite my papers stating I had been born in Switzerland.

Seeing my uncertain expression, Lisa said, 'Madam Sophie has made lots of money here in Berlin. Her investment in this hotel and other properties means she will be welcomed by the people in Paris. The French want to put the war behind them, and Madam Sophie will create jobs and money for the city.'

She jumped onto the bed, pushed her thick curly hair from her eyes and told me, 'We'll be safe with Madam Sophie and Jacques, it's going to be almost like a holiday.'

She wagged her finger at me. 'So I don't want any more gloomy

195

thoughts or words, we're young and going to the city of love.'

Lisa reached under the bed and brought out a package wrapped in brown paper and string.

'This is for you. Please smile and be happy! It's a gift from Madam Sophie for your birthday.'

I looked quizzically at her as she told me, 'You will have to remember this, as it's the new birthday given to you on your official papers, today you are 20 years old!'

Of course, the papers did not reflect my genuine birthday. I was not 20 years old, I was barely 17, but I accepted my new age and my new birth date.

I opened the package and found inside a blue dress made from the most exquisite material, stylish and flattering. Tucked inside was new underwear and a dainty pair of leather shoes. Lisa helped me on with the dress.

I had barely glanced at myself in two years, apart from checking my uniform or hair. I stared in the mirror and saw for the first time the beautiful girl I had become. I had my mother's shining, white blonde hair, and my pale blue eyes were framed with thick black lashes. Dark arching brows framed my heart-shaped face.

Lisa clapped her hands, 'See how pretty dresses can change you inside and out!'

I gave a genuine, wide smile for the first time in a long time. The feel of expensive material against my skin and the fine cut of my new dress made me see myself afresh. It did feel nice. Reflected in the mirror stood a stunning young woman, the woman I had become.

I told myself 'I really am pretty' then, shocked at myself, added 'I'm too vain!'

Lisa replied, 'Vain! You're not vain. You're one of the most stunning young girls I've ever seen, so lovely you could go to Hollywood and make your fortune in the films!'

I listened to Lisa resume her chatter about Paris and our trip by car and then by train to the French capital. We would be leaving at the end of March. I was grateful for the gift from Madam Sophie, which felt more like a reward for my hard work over the past two years than a birthday present. Despite my firm friendships, I often felt terribly alone. Eight weeks in Paris would be a huge change from my daily and weekly routine in Hotel Berlin. It felt like a leap too far, and yet from the day I first wore the blue dress, the pain seemed to lessen. I found myself concentrating on the opportunities ahead and put away thoughts of my mother and Hans.

I took off my blue dress and hung it in the wardrobe alongside Lisa's new clothes. I turned to her and asked, 'Do you still want me to go to that tea dance with you and Dan tonight?'

Lisa brightened, 'Yes! Dan's good friend and colleague Jack is coming too. Dan says he is a bit reserved but very nice. Are you OK about that?'

'Yes, I know what it's like to be a bit shy. I hope we can make this Jack feel welcome in Berlin.'

The afternoon tea dances were very popular, a chance for soldiers to socialise and meet new friends. The hall where the English servicemen were holding their dance was alongside a shed-like building called the NAAFI. Inside, all the tables had been pushed to the side. The room was packed with English soldiers, a few US servicemen, and girls, sat in groups and chattering as others danced with the soldiers. A man at a piano played popular tunes accompanied by a violin and clarinet.

Lisa and I stood in the doorway, trying to find her boyfriend. Suddenly Dan appeared. He had a boyish face, brown hair and was very attractive. He guided us to a large table where several other English officers and a gaggle of talkative girls were sat. The girls were from various places: I caught a Polish accent, German, and even an Austrian dialect. Since the end of the war it had become impossible to prevent the Allied soldiers from meeting with local women. It was not encouraged, but mostly the fraternisation of locals with the Allied forces was grudgingly accepted. Young men miles from home found it difficult to avoid girls and relationships. Even marriages were not unheard of, though still frowned upon officially. Apparently, it was OK to kiss and even have sex with the German girls but not to make them respectable by marriage.

Amidst the conversations, noise and music, my attention was caught by a bespectacled man, his head lowered inside a newspaper. Whilst everyone chatted away, he seemed to be in his own little bubble. Dan showed us to our seats, next to the man with the newspaper, who I thought was clearly more interested in reading than socialising. However, as we approached, he put down his paper and stood up, almost to attention. I was shocked at how tall he was, at least 6 feet, 4 inches. The man nodded to me and he pulled out a chair for me and another for Lisa, bowing in welcome, and waiting for Dan to introduce us.

'Greta, this is Jack, my best friend and, I'm afraid, my boss. He is head of the engineering team in this part of the city and the most talented engineer in the army! He and the team are rebuilding the city and if it wasn't for people like Jack, we would have no sanitation, clean water or utilities.'

He declared, 'Jack is helping Berlin rise from the ashes!'

Jack laughed, a booming sound that made his thin frame rumble. It was the most joyous sound, like a thunderclap, and we all laughed with him. As he put his hand towards mine to shake, Jack's face split into a cheeky grin. Looking at him, it felt like the sun was rising. His warm, large hand encased my small fingers in his and instantly I felt calmer.

He had a lovely melodious voice, strong and gentle at the same time. His handsome voice did not suit his face, which sadly was large, square and very plain.

'Greta, please excuse Dan's introduction, I am just an engineer who was seconded into the army for the war and now find myself in this lovely city. Berlin needs a lot of tender loving care, just like you!'

I smiled and rolled my eyes at the cliché, but Jack's eyes locked with mine and I felt my arms tingle. The sincerity and intelligence of the thin, tall man was strangely beguiling.

Jack went to the bar and returned with tea and cakes. The dance was alcohol-free. As the afternoon progressed, several men came over to greet Jack, and it was clear from their chatter how much admiration his men had for him. I found out Jack was a highly-decorated officer and had shown immense bravery in battle. He didn't speak about his medals and seemed to be the type of man who, though naturally brave, never bragged.

While Lisa danced with Dan, I sat with Jack and talked. Conversation flowed between us and it seemed as if I had known this odd-looking English officer for a lifetime. There was no awkwardness and the few moments of silence were comfortable. From the corner of my eye, I saw

Lisa nudging her boyfriend Dan. I returned her gaze with a positive look.

*　　*　　*

My friendship with Jack was easy, and over the next six weeks we met whenever I had time off work, either as a couple or as a foursome with Lisa and Dan. Jack was no Clarke Gable; his sandy hair, pale green eyes, and large face would never set any girl's heart in a spin. But there was something about him that opened my heart. I was at peace in his company, everything seemed ordered and secure. In between our dates, Jack sent me little notes and small gifts. He was wooing me, and I liked it, but our times together were chaste and proper. Occasionally, Jack would take my arm or hand to guide me through the crowds, but that was all.

We sometimes went walking through the city, Jack pointing out various places he and his colleagues were rebuilding amongst the shattered landscape. Jack was older than me and I saw his maturity as a good thing. Although we talked a lot, silence was also easy and often a welcome escape from my busy working life at the hotel.

Jack showed just how kind and sensitive he was one afternoon when we had met for a meal. I had a 'turn' and started to panic and sweat when I saw a vision of my father in the corner of the restaurant. My father shook his head in dismay that I was associating with 'the enemy'. He was dressed in his uniform that looked so much like a soldier's. My father's anger was stamped onto his pale, wraith-like face.

I put my hands over my eyes, trying to banish the unwanted image. Jack sat with me quietly until the ghost of my dead father had disappeared. Jack never asked questions, just waited until the storm had passed.

Sometimes the disturbing things I saw were real. As Jack and I were out walking one day, a man shouted across the street demanding why a German girl like me was 'walking out' with an English pig? Although Berlin was starting to regenerate, people still held on to many resentments that war had fostered. Yet in any situation we faced, Jack remained calm and strong. Despite my growing affection for him, I remained at a distance, resisting any urge to become more involved. I knew that, despite his patience, no man would accept celibacy within a marriage. I knew he was sexually attracted to me and that eventually he would want to be intimate. Just the thought of sleeping with any man, even one as lovely as Jack, drove me into a panic.

During one of our longer rendezvous, we sat in a café opposite the river, talking for hours. Jack told me about his home and his plans once his tasks in Berlin were complete. He would leave the army and work as an engineer at his friend's factory on the south coast of England. He talked about a lovely cottage he had bought near the sea, where the garden was full of flowers in the summer. Jack had his future planned. With a good job waiting for him when he was de-mobbed and a perfect house in which to live, all he seemed to lack was a wife with which to share his idyll. He never mentioned this, but it was a natural conclusion to the picture-postcard life he would be returning to in England.

I never saw myself taking any part in his future. Though I was fond of him, I saw our friendship as transient. Jack and his easy-going nature were building my confidence with the opposite sex and I was grateful to feel more 'normal', but my future was with the hotel, Lisa and Jacques. I was heading for a good career in the hotel industry, alongside the ambitious Madam Sophie. Jack was just a nice intermission.

Jack didn't ask me about my home or family but waited for me to take the lead. I gave him scant details, telling him the name, age and place of birth on my new papers. I told him all my family were dead. I could not talk about Hans. Though over two years had passed since my brother had disappeared, with no body to mourn, part of me still had not accepted that Hans had died.

So I did not talk about Hans ever, and it was too much to contemplate as Jack and I sat near the sparkling river in the weak sunshine sharing a drink. Instead, we talked about Jack's hopes for his life back home in England, about my work at the hotel and his important job as an engineer.

When I returned to the hotel after evenings out with Jack, I often saw Jacques in the kitchen. I knew he waited up to make sure I returned safely. He would make us both coffee and then listen to my excited chatter about Jack. It must have been torture for him. In his eyes I continued to see his love for me, but I was young and selfish, and it gave me an element of satisfaction that two men were vying for my company and affection. It was a strange and powerful feeling to know that two decent men cared for me. I wanted both in my life.

I spoke to Lisa about it, as she had often juggled several men at the same time. She was insistent.

'There is nothing wrong with having two men friends you are not intimate with. They'll have to get used to you caring for both of them and wanting them for their company and friendship.'

She grinned at me, 'Men come and go but our friendship continues! We will look out for each other, forever.'

Looking more serious, she said, 'Jacques asked me if you were serious about Jack. I laughed with him and told him of course not. I mean, Jack is a nice man, hardworking and he thinks the world of you but, to be brutally honest, he's too old for you and rather ugly.'

Rushing on, she told me in a no-nonsense voice, 'He's a safe boyfriend, he's helping you to get back to normal. Jack is a passing fancy, he'll return to Britain with lovely memories of his wonderful Greta and we'll be moving onwards and upwards with Madam Sophie.'

Lisa took my arm. 'Jacques, you and I are family, the three of us will support each other for many years. Occasional boyfriends are of little importance to what we can achieve working alongside Madam Sophie. She is our ticket out of poverty to a much better life.'

Once again Lisa gave me good advice. Jacques, Madam Sophie and Lisa knew more about my past than any other person alive. Our individual experiences had forged an intractable alliance between us that Jack could not shake or replace.

I pulled myself back to the present and to Lisa, as she talked about more interesting happenings than my challenging love-life. In just a week we would be travelling to Paris. The four of us would be working and living in the new hotel in the centre of the capital. Our job was to make sure it ran like clockwork. This smaller business was called Hôtel Parisien and Madam Sophie wanted it to exceed the standards she exacted at Hotel Berlin.

Three days before we were due to leave, I conjured up the courage to tell Jack I was going. I am not sure why I left it so long. We were sitting in a small bar having a glass of red wine that tasted more like vinegar. His face looked shocked and then totally crestfallen. However, he quickly brightened and urged me to toast with him.

'I can come to Paris when I have leave!' he announced, 'It's not that far to travel for my girl.'

Expectantly he took my hands in his, but I stared at him blankly and muttered, 'I don't know about that, Jack. We will be very busy, not much time off. Getting the new hotel running and profitable will take a while.'

I took my hands away, feeling claustrophobic. Jack slumped in his chair and then brightened again as he asked in a quiet voice, 'We can always write to each other?'

'Yes,' I said weakly.

On the walk back to the hotel, Jack was pensive. I stayed quiet, surprised by the depth of his devotion and desire to see me in France. I liked being in his company but if we didn't meet, I would feel no different. I never missed Jack. As we said goodnight outside the hotel, he moved to kiss me, this time on the lips. I ducked from his embrace and ran up the stairs to my bedroom. Shutting the door, I leant against it and sighed. Perhaps it was a good thing I was going to Paris, away from Berlin and the many ghosts that haunted me here, and away from Jack.

I looked up to see Lisa parading around the room in the most ridiculous hat, bedecked with a large red ribbon and pheasant feathers. The hat was so huge it hid her face. In her mouth, she had one of Madam Sophie's cigarettes and, as she saw me, Lisa drawled,

'Dahling, what do you think of this monstrous hat? That rude woman from Geneva left it in her room. I think it suits me better than that fat cow, don't you?'

I ran over to Lisa, embraced her and joined in the laughter as she began to mimic the voice of film star Marlene Dietrich. Jack and our tense goodbye were completely forgotten.

CHAPTER 26

Paris, though still scarred by its occupation and experiences of war, was a beautiful city. I watched in amazement as our car drove through wide avenues surrounded by exquisite buildings, while little boats chugged up and down the Seine. The fashionable women and cute children in straw hats and tailored coats reflected another, more prosperous world.

The hotel Madam Sophie had purchased was in a very affluent part of the city. Many of the residents looked like they had stepped out of a fashion magazine, unlike the many shabbily-dressed people who lived and worked in Berlin. Due to the up-market location of the hotel, everything from its cuisine to its service had to be top notch. For the first few weeks, Lisa, Jacques and I saw very little of Paris as we worked seventeen-hour days, bringing the hotel and its service up to scratch.

Training the French staff to the exacting standards of Madam Sophie was often difficult. Though my French was reasonable, local and countryside accents caused all manner of mishaps. The French staff were often belligerent towards me, answering back and not listening to my instructions. Finally, after lots of shouting and arguing with various maids, cleaners and kitchen workers, Hôtel Parisien was ready to welcome paying customers.

Its guests reflected the wealth that had never left the French capital. Their elegance and unhurried appearance seemed to be untouched by war. However, first impressions can be deceptive.

The 'grand opening' was a champagne event with dignitaries from all over the city. Madam Sophie had commissioned a local artist to paint pictures of the hotel and its staff, which were proudly displayed in the reception area. On the opening day, she stood resplendent in green silk, surrounded by rich businessmen and members of the Foreign Ministry as a photographer from *Le Figaro* snapped away. As always, Madam Sophie seemed to know everyone that could be of use to her latest venture in Paris.

Within days, the hotel was a bustling hive of activity, guests pouring in from across France, many in transit to other parts of Europe or moving across the Channel to Britain. All were obviously well-off, and some were what we staff called 'down-at-heel wealthy'.

The hotel workers were mainly young girls and boys from poorer parts of the city or rural areas. With my straight back, distinctive look and bearing it was obvious I had Germanic roots, and this caused some problems. One evening, I caught Maria, one of the French girls I had trained, spitting into the tea she was about to serve me. When I rebuked her, she said, 'You say you were born in Switzerland, but you are German, and I hate the Germans.'

She was sacked by Madam Sophie despite my pleas for leniency. The hotelier warned me, 'Look, this time it was a gob of phlegm, next time it could be poison. I have seen that look before many times. Maria is intractable. That young girl will never forgive or forget.'

The opening of Hôtel Parisien was not a seamless undertaking. During the first month, there were several deputations from neighbours and local shopkeepers. There had been many complaints about Madam Sophie and her sharp business practices. There was resentment and dislike that a 'foreigner' and a woman had taken over a prime business in the capital. Shortly after, the grocer, butcher and baker refused to supply food to the hotel's kitchen. A local resident confided in Jacques in a local bar, 'Immigrants, refugees are taking all the best jobs and making lots of money. What about French people and their families? They should be running that hotel, not some foreign whore.'

Jacques assured the disgruntled man and shopkeepers that it was he, a Frenchman, who had bought the hotel, in order to assuage their anger. As the complaints and embargoes continued, Madam Sophie put on a charm offensive, inviting the moaning businessmen and residents into the hotel for drinks and snacks. Over champagne she pointed out the advantages of working with her business, that the hotel would provide much-needed income to the local economy and boost their own profits. All the while, at the back of the room were a group of large, imposing-looking men. They quietly ushered from the room anyone who was still protesting. They never returned.

I said nothing, knowing that Madam Sophie sometimes employed strong-arm tactics or bribes to get her way. The next week, supplies of bread, meat and a box of vegetables arrived at the kitchen doors. This was supplemented with tinned food, dried eggs and potatoes.

Madam Sophie told me and Lisa with a smile, 'People are afraid, our world was turned upside down by the war, now it has to right itself. And that means change, lots of change, often very quickly.'

Her eyes were cold as she said, 'Sometimes the not-so-bright have to be led by the hand and other times they have to be forced to do what will be best for them.'

I did not like this side of Madam Sophie or her business. I knew that cold, hard side of her could just as easily be turned on me if I did not come up to scratch or disagreed with the hotelier's wishes. I was learning all the time about Madam Sophie, and as the years passed, I watched often with admiration and sometimes aghast at her capacity to make money and ingratiate herself with anyone who would be of use to her personally or professionally.

Jacques, Lisa and I walked a tightrope of diplomacy in our dealings with the French staff. I learnt a great deal from my time at Hôtel Parisien, not least how to handle resentful and difficult people. After Maria was sacked, I was concerned there would be even more comments about my origins. However, once it became common gossip, the rest of the staff became almost obsequious to me. It was false and I knew it, but I played along and promoted one of the older girls, Monique, to head maid. As this meant a higher salary and career prospects, she soon became an ally.

After three weeks of non-stop work, Jacques, Lisa and I were given a much-needed afternoon off. We wandered down to Montmartre to see the famous artists and cafes. We had an exciting time mixing with eccentric characters and viewing their stunning paintings. For all my terrible experiences, I was still rather naïve and some of the paintings and sculptures shocked me to the core. Jacques laughed as I turned away from an easel holding the image of a naked woman with three bright crimson breasts.

I concentrated on some books as my blushing face cooled. A scruffy man was selling dog-eared novels and manuscripts from the pavement. Pages were missing from many of them, and some looked as if they had been rescued from a fire. Nevertheless, I rooted around hoping to find some books I could purchase for the hotel library. Deep in thought as I leafed through a French edition of Dickens' *David Copperfield*, I glanced up as a furious-looking woman was running towards me.

There was no time to shield my face as she started to rain down blows upon my head, vile language filling the still air. Her mouth was foaming, and she stunk of absinthe.

'You're a German, your bastard people killed my daughter and fried my grandmother in the ovens at Auschwitz!' she screamed.

Then a man across the street shouted, 'Fucking Germans, fucking refugees and fucking foreigners!'

He made to cross the road as Jacques dragged the woman away from my cowering body. The artist who had drawn the red-breasted woman pulled me and Lisa out of the way and hurried us down a side alley. He shoved us into the door of a dark bar where people were drinking green liquid and smoking from strange pipes. The air was heavy, almost suffocating.

'In here you'll be safe,' the young man told us, as he kept pushing us towards the back of the bar. He gestured around a corner towards a blackened door, which he opened. The hinges squeaked and a terrible smell of mould hit us as he shoved me and Lisa into the dark. We held each other tightly, our chests beating a drum roll of panic. There was a click as the door locked. We had been imprisoned in a room smaller than the broom cupboard at the hotel, above us a midnight black. I stretched my arms as far as they would go but it appeared to be a vast space of empty black. I urged the panic rising in my throat downwards and clung onto Lisa.

We heard the stamping of heavy feet and the crack of a rifle. Straining my ears, I thought I heard shouts, but the noise disappeared. All that was left was the sound of a gasping accordion coming from the bar. Perhaps twenty minutes passed until we heard the key turn in the lock and bright light spilled across our pinched faces. We both let out a sigh as the stale, smoky air of the bar rushed into the confined space. Jacques pulled us out of the cupboard and sat us down, pushing two glasses filled with green liquid into our shaking hands.

'You two have my friend Jean to thank for saving you. Small groups like that can get violent very quickly. Fortunately, with the police now active these incidents happen less often. The street is now almost deserted, the troublemakers have been dispersed.'

Jean sat opposite me, attractive in a Gallic sort of way with a saturnine face and dark brown, sleepy eyes. He stared at me intrusively and my face reddened with heat. I began to fidget uncomfortably in my seat. Jean dipped into a leather satchel hanging around his neck. He held out a vial of brown gunk.

'This is vegetable dye. While you are here in Paris my dear, best dye your hair brown. It's so blonde, it attracts attention.'

He leaned over and took my hand.

'You have a strong, distinctive profile and bearing, you're a very striking young woman.'

I slapped him away. He bowed and said, 'Pardon.'

Lisa took the bottle from him and said, 'Thank you, Jean, for saving us from that mad woman. I will take Greta back to our accommodation and dye her hair.'

Removing the scarf from around her neck, Lisa wound it around my aching head to hide my blondeness.

Jacques questioned, 'Mad woman, or mad with grief and hunger? I paid her off and she soon scuttled away.'

Staring at me, Jacques said, 'I am so sorry you had to experience that, Greta. Are you alright?'

I shrugged my shoulders, sipping the absinthe. I was shocked at the attack but unsurprised. It hardly registered except for the pain around my eye which I could feel forming a bruise. My run-in with the crazy Frenchwoman meant little compared to everything else I had been through. I put the attack to one side and concentrated on our bizarre surroundings. I decided that I did not like the taste of the absinthe, but I drank the green liquid as alcohol calmed and relaxed me. Lisa and I amused ourselves by observing the artists sitting in corners chattering like magpies, while others lay prone on benches, semi-conscious and drooling.

It was a place of brilliance and desperation. When we eventually left, Jean told me, 'I would like to paint you one day.'

Jacques gave a brittle laugh and looked annoyed.

'Take no notice of his honeyed words. It's his usual line to get women's clothes off and into his bed.'

I shuddered and walked faster.

Jean shouted to our retreating backs, 'Non, this time it's true! She is so beautiful and has the air of a lost soul.'

Lisa shouted over her shoulder, 'I don't think I want to see a painting of Greta with three red breasts thank you very much!'

Laughing and a bit tipsy from the absinthe, she urged me along as we made our way back to Hôtel Parisien.

CHAPTER 27

I hated my new hair colour, muddy brown. It didn't suit me. I looked into the tiny mirror balanced on the dressing table, moving my head from side to side in the hope the dun colour would catch the light. It didn't. I looked like a sepia photograph of myself.

Lisa had emptied the entire contents of the vegetable dye over my head and her efforts had paid dividends. I rubbed my head in a useless effort to uncover glints of my former golden locks. A purple bruise was livid underneath my left eye.

Seeing my furious face, Lisa dipped a flannel into a bowl of water and sponged my bruises. Trying to soothe, she told me, 'Soon Paris, Berlin and all the cities affected by the war must learn to think about the future, not the past. I'm hopeful that one day we will all live in harmony. Then you can wear your blondeness with pride on the streets of Paris.'

I looked at my dear friend, and though I wanted to believe her, I doubted very much if the millions of people wrecked by the war would ever forget.

My beating by the strange woman in Montmartre had not affected me. I was angrier about my hair, of which I had been so proud. I wanted to return to Berlin and the sparkling blonde that was part of that city, back to being me, whoever I was. After the attack, and the need for me to colour my hair, I started to dislike Paris. I sought out reasons to have negative thoughts about every building and shop, finding fault with everything I saw or experienced. I limited my trips away from the hotel, and whenever I had free time would only venture out with Jacques to some small local café.

Despite the blossoming trees and fine weather, I started to tick off the days until we left Paris. When a letter arrived from Jack it was a link to my tiny bedroom back in Berlin. Yet, as I opened the envelope with its familiar scrawl, and glanced over the poetic prose and his outpouring of love, I shrugged. I felt nothing. Placing the letter into my bedside cabinet, it was instantly forgotten as I made ready for work.

One night after a long shift, I was heading for my bedroom when an excited Lisa met me on the stairs and grabbed my arm.

'Come with me! Come on! There's a lovely surprise waiting for you in the kitchen!'

I grimaced. The new chef had been trying out new puddings and cakes and I was so tired, the last thing I wanted to do was to eat anything sweet or heavy, but Lisa wasn't listening to my protests. She dragged me down the rickety stairs and deposited me at the kitchen table.

The chef had gone to bed and we were alone in the kitchen. I looked around, puzzled, and was about to ask Lisa what all the fuss was about, when Jack moved out of the shadows.

I ran into his open arms. I started to sob and tell him through gasps of air about the woman that had punched me, and how much I hated Paris. Jack said nothing and stood strong and dependable, smoothing my hair and nodding. His eyes were loving, and he never mentioned or even saw that my lustrous hair was now a different colour. Jack only ever saw me.

Finally, he said, 'Greta, my wonderful girl. I could hold you for hours, but can we sit down? I have been on trains, and in cars and trucks for the last two days. I need to rest these weary bones!'

I laughed as we settled into chairs opposite each other. For a long time, we sat holding hands and just looking at each other. Jack's eyes never left my face. I felt like I had come home. We sat in the kitchen all night: talking, not talking, hugging and, eventually, even dozing. Lisa left tip toeing away, she knew how badly I had been hurting. Jack told me he had sent me many letters over the previous weeks, the most recent informing me of his visit to Paris, but I had received only one. Neither of us knew why. Apart from wanting to see me again, Jack had been sent to Paris to deliver papers to his brigadier and discuss the current situation in Berlin. He also needed to speak to Madam Sophie.

We had just two days before Jack had to return to Germany.

We were woken before dawn by the chef moving plates. He grinned when he saw us asleep and awkwardly entwined at the table.

'Hey Greta, won't you introduce me to your friend?'

'This is Jack, my boyfriend,' Jack's face lit up as this was the first time I had verbally acknowledged him as my boyfriend.

We ate bread and jam for breakfast, as Jack chatted to Chef Luca. I laughed with them as they shared a joke and a cigarette. Lisa came running down the stairs an hour later, her maid's hat askance as she tried to straighten her hair.

'Greta,' she smiled, 'Madam Sophie wants to see you and Jack.'

I was surprised. The hotelier was notorious among the staff for sleeping late. Jack and I walked hand in hand to the dining room, where Madam Sophie was doing a spot check on the glasses. She turned as we entered, 'Ah Jack and Greta. Come with me to the office, we have much to discuss.'

Jack raised his eyebrows. As we followed Madam Sophie, he told me, 'I've spoken to your boss many times by telephone since you came to Paris. I wanted to make sure you were keeping well.'

He hesitated for a moment, 'I hope you don't mind?'

I looked away. Part of me was pleased but part of me bristled with irritation. Jack was clearly deeply in love with me and I felt so much better now he was here, but I still felt unsure. I knew I didn't need him as much as he needed me, and his going behind my back annoyed me.

To say I was bewildered was an understatement, so I never answered Jack's question but let go of his hand as we went through to Madam Sophie's office. She sat down behind a large oak desk, on which stood two telephones. In the corner of the room a much smaller desk held a typewriter.

'I have learnt from my connections in Berlin that there has been a serious confrontation between the Soviets and Western Allies,' Madam Sophie said gravely.

'All train passengers and military transport between the two sectors are being searched and sometimes restricted regarding their movements by the Soviets. I understand that the Soviets may well increase this stranglehold in the near future.'

Jack listened intently.

Glancing at his face, she said, 'I expect you are surprised at the level of my intelligence?'

Jack remained silent but watchful, and Madam Sophie continued quietly,

'Jack, I am not expecting you to say anything, but your silence speaks volumes about what awaits us in Berlin. It would appear that although the war is over, a new battle is beginning. The USSR and the Soviets are jostling for supremacy over the whole of Berlin, they want to keep Germany on its knees.'

Madam Sophie lit a cigarette and leaned back in her chair,

'I have made the decision that myself, Lisa and Greta will leave Paris as soon as possible. Jacques will remain here to handover duties to Pierre as general manager and Louise as head housekeeper.'

Distracted, she stubbed out the barely smoked cigarette.

I could contain myself no longer and burst out, 'I'll be glad to leave Paris.'

The hotelier glanced at me with an icy look and said, 'Maybe, Greta. But what is brewing in Berlin will not be a picnic.'

CHAPTER 28

O ur return to Berlin was more difficult than our outward journey. The
Soviets were beginning their stranglehold on the movement of
people and goods into West Berlin, the sector run by the Western Allies.
I learnt more about the events that were unfolding in the German capital
on the journey back.

'As you know, the Deutsche Mark has been introduced into West
Berlin. This will eventually help the city and Germany to recover
economically from the desiccation of the war,' Jack told me, sighing as
he continued. 'Stalin would like to govern the whole of Berlin and keep
its people and Germany subservient to the USSR. He has demanded that
the Western Allies remove the new currency. If we don't, he will
blockade Berlin.'

Madam Sophie interjected, 'Don't worry Greta, we will be safe at
Hotel Berlin, I have every faith in the Western Allies. This will blow
over.'

Her words did not reflect her strained face. Jack squeezed my hand to
reassure me, but I pulled it away. All I wanted was to return to Berlin so
that I could wash the foul brown dye from my hair and get back to the
regularity of my life and work at Hotel Berlin. Selfishly, I didn't care
about anything else. I was tired, and I shut my eyes and ears to the hushed
conversations between Madam Sophie, Lisa and Jack as they dissected
what this stalemate between the Soviets and the Western Allies could
mean.

Despite the rising tension between the Soviets and the Western Allies,
with the help of Madam Sophie's purse and Jack's contacts we all arrived
safely in Berlin. It was a dusty and late spring morning. Relief flooded

through my body as I sat down on my bed in the small, familiar room I shared with Lisa. I felt even better when I had washed all the dreadful brown dye from my locks. The peace of being back at the hotel and its mundane daily routine did not last long. Within ten days, Jacques too was back in Berlin as the situation between the Soviets and the Western Allies deteriorated.

We had all got back from Paris just in time, as on June 24th, 1948, all the roads, railways and canal access to the sectors under Western control were blocked by the Soviets. The Western Allies still refused to withdraw the Deutsche Mark and a stand-off between the two factions began. The Soviets aimed to starve Berliners into submission. Starvation was a familiar enemy, but it had been a long time since I was truly hungry. With no outside means of transportation, food, coal, and clothing would become scarce and run out. The Soviets were hoping for panic and anarchy; they wanted the whole of Berlin under USSR rule.

Within two days of the blockade, the Berlin Airlift began, and the Western Allies started to fly in supplies, including fuel, to our sector. Over two million people lived in the Western sector, a huge number of people to keep from starvation. It took time for food to filter through, and the amounts accorded to every adult and child were strictly rationed. Though the food drops were frequent, the supplies were basic and bland; tinned and dried food became the staple. The hotel had few guests and those that stayed faced rations, too. The chef found it almost impossible to make inventive meals from the amounts awarded to each adult. Each day, week and month of the blockade meant a drastic reduction in the calories allowed for each citizen. With just enough to survive, I became thin again, everyone became thin.

One day, Lisa and I were out for a short walk during our afternoon off. We were near one of the many barricades that snaked across Berlin and separated the Eastern from the Western Sector. We were stopped in our tracks by what seemed to be a heated exchange between a Soviet soldier leaning over the barricade and a woman on the Western side holding a screaming baby, with a toddler clutching her skirt.

'Here Frau, have some milk for your baby and bread for your little boy. We have hot meat stew here for your family, also lots of tinned food.'

The Soviet with the face of a teen spoke in perfect German as he waved his bounty to a clearly distressed mother. Dressed in a threadbare frock and tattered coat, she shouted out to a small crowd who had gathered.

'Look! They're offering me so much food. My breasts have shrunk because we have so little to eat, so I have no milk for my baby. My poor boy, his belly aches for meat.'

Sensing he had gained ground, the Soviet continued in a calm but clear voice, 'Come, come over to us, and become a member of our country, it's much better than being starved to death by the West. We have lots of food to give you. The English soldiers, the American soldiers, they don't understand your hunger or care about you or your baby.'

Suddenly the woman went from a waif to warrior. Anger made her grow in height as a torrent of rage spilled from her blue lips.

'You fucking bastards, why would I go over to your side to be raped again?'

The woman leant down to pick up a brick from a bombed-out building nearby. She started to take aim as, gently, a man on the edge of the small crowd took the brick from her shaking hand and placed it back on the ground. The Soviet on the other side of the boundary stopped, ducked out of the way and disappeared. There were mutterings in the crowd, but it soon dispersed, with a few people going over to the woman to give her a supportive hug.

Lisa and I walked back to the hotel, lost in our thoughts. It was a time of great uncertainty, and we were fearful of the future but never voiced our anxieties as that made them too real. I heard whispered concerns from the staff at the hotel that another war would break out, this time between the Western Allies and the Soviets. At night I often had nightmares of the Soviets invading our sector. Jack reassured me again and again this would never happen. He and his men were busy day and night collecting, collating and distributing food supplies, putting his work to rebuild the capital on hold. Even restructuring was not seen as essential now millions of people were at risk of starving to death.

The disturbing turn of events put a bit of a buffer on Jack's passion and when we met, we often had only a few snatched hours together.

Occasionally I allowed Jack to kiss me passionately on the lips and, though it wasn't unpleasant, each time his hands wandered, I froze.

Jack didn't mind, telling me, 'It will take a long time for you to trust a man again, Greta. I know that. I can wait, for years if needed.'

But the burning desire in his eyes told another tale, and I felt torn.

The blockade meant that Jack's plans to leave the army and travel back to England were put on hold, giving me time to think about what to do next and our relationship. I turned to my best friend for advice, but her reply, for once, did not help.

'Are you in love with him?' Lisa asked.

I looked at her uncomprehending, as she continued dressing for a date with her new English friends. Dan had returned to England and she had a new beau, a soldier called Fred.

She turned to look at me.

'Does your heart skip and miss a beat when you think of him? Do you miss him when he is not around? Do you want to smother him in kisses all the time?'

The answer to all her questions was, 'No.'

Lisa's face hardened, 'Well you don't love him and don't owe him anything.'

My friend's advice left me even more muddled. I was not sure what love meant or if I could even feel it. I watched as she primped her hair and smoothed down her dress in anticipation of a fun night out.

'Fred, Steve and Peter – and all the Polish girls that work at the corner shop – are going to a bar near the NAAFI this afternoon,' she explained gleefully. 'Apparently Wolfgang's still has some booze available! It's a shame you're working.'

When Lisa left, I shook myself out of my confusion and ran down the stairs to reception. I was on call till midnight. It was a quiet shift. The days of over-indulgence for the hotel's guests had long been scuppered by the blockade. I occupied myself with paperwork and tidying up the ledgers for Jacques. When I'd finished, I tried to read a book from the hotel's library to improve my English. It was called *Jane Eyre*, a complicated story about a governess and her employer that Jack had recommended.

'It's a love story,' he'd smiled as he slipped the book into my hands.

216

I thought perhaps *Jane Eyre* could teach me about this sensation called romantic love, that so many books, songs and people exclaimed was the best feeling in the world.

The clock above the painting of Berlin before the war, struck eight and I yawned. Suddenly, I was startled by the appearance of Lisa at the hotel's entrance, which staff were rarely allowed to use. She ran into the lobby as if a pack of wild dogs was chasing her. I began to rebuke her for using the main door, but Lisa pushed past without a word, disappearing into the back office.

Fortunately, the overnight porter was in the main lobby, tidying up cushions and brushing crumbs from tables. I called him over and asked him to cover for me,

'I think Lisa is ill, she is in the back office. Can you take care of reception? I need to see what's wrong.'

His bullet-shaped head ducked up and down in reply.

In the office, Lisa sat like a sphinx. I went over to my dearest friend and kneeled at her feet.

'Lisa, what's happened?'

Her face was white as marble, her beautifully-styled hair ruffled, and her clothes dusty. She would not meet my eyes, but began to speak in a quiet, flat voice.

Six of them had gone to the bar near the NAAFI, where Fred had exchanged cigarettes and soap for a bottle of wine. Lisa was having fun, laughing and talking with people she knew and considered friends.

She and Fred had met just before our trip to Paris. He seemed nice enough when I met him. Fred had told me how much he missed home and his mother, and that his father had died when he was just twelve years old. Tonight had been Lisa's second outing with him since our return from the French capital.

Lisa, speaking in a whisper, said, 'Halfway through our second bottle of wine, we both went outside for a smoke and a little kiss.'

Her voice wavered, and a cold feeling sank into my stomach.

'There was an alleyway at the side of the bar, full of rubbish and mice. Fred pulled me down for a few kisses, it was nice. He chatted a bit.'

I stared at her. In stuttering breathes she looked at me and said, 'Greta, he pushed me against the wall and pulled my drawers down, opened his trousers and-'

She stopped for a moment, 'I said no and then no again, but he carried on.'

There was a long pause as she stared into the distance.

'I didn't know what to do, Greta. Afterwards, he kissed me on the forehead and offered me a cigarette. I pulled up my drawers, adjusted my dress, and had a puff on the cigarette. Then he took my hand and we went back into the bar.'

My hands were shaking as I listened to her.

'I danced with Fred and listened to the Polish girls laughing about some weird customer that comes into the shop.'

She shook her head in disbelief and said again, 'I didn't know what to do. After an hour or so, I got up and told them I was unwell and had to go home.'

I winced as she made a sharp sound. I realised it was an attempt to laugh.

'Fred even offered to walk me back to the hotel.'

Alarmed she told me, 'It was then that I ran. I kept running until I got here.'

Slowly I rose from my knees, reached out and held her for a while. I said nothing.

Going outside to reception, I told the night porter to take over my shift. I half-walked, half-carried my dearest friend to our room. I washed her all over, dressed her in a clean, white nightgown and laid beside her until she slept.

*　　*　　*

The next morning, we returned to work as usual. I asked Lisa if she wanted me to cover for her so she could rest in our room. She insisted on going to work. What else was there to do? She never mentioned the rape again, though I tried to give her many opportunities. It was a closed subject. Lisa had yet another scar to carry.

Lisa changed subtly, becoming more cautious. She only went out of the hotel if I was free, and I had to cancel several meetings with Jack as a result. As always, he didn't complain.

She also stopped dating. 'I am going to wait for my 'Mr Wonderful', Greta,' she told me. 'I will know when he walks into my life. There's no rush.'

I hoped that I, too, would recognise 'Mr Right' whenever he came into my life. I realised with a pang that Jack was not at the top of my list.

My meetings with Jack were now few and far between. I received notes and occasional gifts from my English soldier, but he never pushed me for a date. I knew the distance between us made him sad, especially as now I only suffered an occasional kiss. Lisa's rape had made me unsure even of Jack and his agenda. As always, he waited patiently in the background as I continued to prevaricate.

The days moved along. The Berlin Airlift continued and flights into the city became more frequent. More cargo was now coming into Berlin by air than had previously been transported into the city by rail. The Soviets lost their battle for power, and on May 12th, 1949, the USSR lifted the blockade on West Berlin. This battle between East and West had ceased.

The 'Cold War' had just begun.

With the return of goods, cargo and supplies into the Western Sector, guests, businesses and money flooded back to the city. And Jack, tired of Berlin, made a decision.

CHAPTER 29

It did not take long for Hotel Berlin to become busy and bustling with its usual cosmopolitan guests and, once again, life settled into everyday chores. Just as Lisa and I were getting used to our everyday lives in Berlin, another big change loomed upon the horizon.

Madam Sophie called an urgent meeting and Lisa, Jacques and I received orders to attend. As the three of us filed into our employer's apartment, my eyes widened at the uproar. Staff were packing furniture, books and clothing. Despite the heat of summer, there was a fire burning in the grate, and I watched as the hotelier tore up and then threw documents into the leaping flames.

Madam Sophie led us into her bedroom and shut the door.

'Sit down all of you,' she said.

We waited until, a moment later, Sybil appeared to serve refreshments. She went to sit in the corner and waited for Madam Sophie to begin.

'There is no easy way to say this, and I would appreciate you all keeping quiet until I have finished.'

With a rush she told us, 'I am moving my business to New York. I will be leaving at the end of the month and I would like all of you to come with me.'

Lisa and I gasped and looked at each other. Jacques sat impassively. He clearly knew of the hotelier's plans.

'With the raising of the blockade, more regulations have been put in place. Berlin is starting to become legitimate and its businesses must do so, too. I have been warned that my tenure here at the hotel is shaky.'

She paused for a brief moment, 'Let's just say investigations by the Allies and local police have found,' she stopped and said with a grimace, 'some discrepancies.'

Taking a breath, she said, 'So it's time to move on! I have secured another hotel in New York and we will be sailing in a few weeks.'

Lisa and I were speechless. Jacques intervened and told us, 'Madam Sophie has secured the appropriate papers and passports for all of us. We will have no problems entering America. It will be a wonderful adventure for us all. Berlin is not the place for any of us anymore. All of us have had to do many things to survive.

'We have,' he cleared his throat, 'certain associations that would not be taken kindly by the new administration or by the Western Allies.'

'It is time for a new start in a new country,' Madam Sophie said firmly, 'a new beginning, for all of us.'

Lisa burst into laughter, leapt up and began to dance.

'Greta! To think, your Hans wanted to run a restaurant in America and now you and I have the opportunity to work in that wonderful country. Your brother must be smiling down on us.'

I did not know what to say. I felt a growing sense of unease: another country, another change, another place to try and live without discrimination or fear. Surely this sudden flight to the USA was the same as the journey that brought me to the doors of Hotel Berlin?

I considered Jacques' warning with discomfort: we all had secrets we would not want the Western Allies to know about, that I would not want Jack or anyone to know about. I put those thoughts to one side and concentrated on Lisa's happy acceptance that our journey to New York was a brilliant venture. When Lisa mentioned Hans, I had a momentary feeling of joy. How happy he would have been travelling to New York! Perhaps Lisa was right, and it was my little brother guiding us in some way to live in America. However, doubts soon surfaced at the speed of our departure from Hotel Berlin. Whatever the investigations into Madam Sophie were, they must be very serious for her to want to move so quickly. And what about Hôtel Parisien and all our hard work there?

Madam Sophie smiled at Lisa, jumping around the room in delight, but I noticed how tired and ill at ease she looked, and how tensely Jacques held himself. The documents still curling into smoke in the fireplace warned me that Madam Sophie had a lot to hide from the Western Allies.

I had many questions but before I could ask them, the hotelier informed us, 'We will take a car then a train to France, get a boat to Ireland, and then another to New York. Our journey will take a couple of weeks.'

She paused. 'By the end of the summer we will be living in New York City.'

The hotelier sipped her coffee and straightened.

'I will tell the rest of the staff tomorrow there is to be a change of management. Their jobs will be secure, and I am hoping for a seamless takeover.'

She puffed out a circle of smoke. 'A new head of staff, Frau Bergen, will be arriving in five days. She will work alongside you until we depart.'

Madam Sophie left and Sybil poured us all another cup of coffee. The rest of the meeting was a discussion between me, Jacques and Lisa regarding official paperwork and the handing over of the hotel to a new owner called Herr Gunther, a businessman from Hamburg. These complicated arrangements and how they would be managed as smoothly as possible took many hours. Finally, when Jacques was satisfied that we had completed these tasks, he got up to leave. I followed him to the office behind reception. Lisa, full of dreams of the USA, raced back to our room to organise her wardrobe.

Jacques sat opposite me and laid his hands on the table, his palms facing upwards.

'I know you have lots of questions and I will answer them all,' he told me. 'But remember it might be good for you not to know too much, so let me tell you only what you need to know.'

I sat and listened to why Madam Sophie's dreams for Hotel Berlin were now like the ashes in the grate.

'Madam Sophie is in a precarious situation, Greta. Her cash flow has come from various sources, including a man called Hjalmar Schacht, known as the 'Devil's Banker'. He served in Hitler's Government. I am afraid the recent photograph that appeared in *Le Figaro* drew unwanted attention to Madam Sophie. People from her past made themselves known to the Allies here in Berlin. They are compiling a dossier.'

I struggled to take in all this new information. My heart was beating faster as I began to understand.

'Madam Sophie has greased many palms, and Hôtel Parisien has been sold. She has made a deal with some very powerful organisations in America. Nothing will happen to us now, and we will all have a clean slate in the USA.'

I didn't like what I was hearing. I knew my boss had a shady past and dealings with less-than-honest people, but I had no real knowledge of these associations. By working so closely with Madam Sophie, was I implicated in her 'deals'? And did she or her associates know about my father and his role within the Nazi Party?

My fears must have shown on my face, as Jacques declared, 'Don't worry, Greta. It's going to be fine. I have arranged everything. Your past and mine will be wiped out in the USA. What an exciting place to start again.'

Despite his reassurance, I didn't like change. I certainly didn't like the speed at which this change was happening. I left the office and went to my bedroom. Lisa was trying to put her clothes and possessions into a very small suitcase. No matter how much she tried, she couldn't get the lid to shut. Eventually she gave up and grinned over at me.

'Oh well, I'll have to find me a rich American to buy me more stuff!'

I didn't answer as she carried on, 'Just think, Greta, we'll be going to New York! We might meet Clark Gable! Or even Errol Flynn!'

Lisa's enthusiastic chatter bubbled through the evening and night, and neither of us slept well. But while Lisa was full of hope, I was filled with apprehension. I didn't want to go to America. I wanted to stay in Berlin. My last thought before sleep was 'what about Jack?'

*   *   *

The next few days were a hive of activity within the hotel. The whole staff were told of the change of management and assured of their jobs and security. Madam Sophie was busy visiting various banks and other

224

organisations. She planned on taking everything of value with her to America, including her most trustworthy staff. My mind was buzzing with the fantastic turn of events, and I retreated to the linen room whenever I could.

One morning, Jack appeared as I folded sheets. His big face broke into a wide grin as he watched me.

'Hello Greta, it's been a while.'

I continued folding and said, 'Yes?'

Jack came to stand in front of me and said, 'We need to talk, Greta.'

My heart dropped. Jack shut the door and turned back to me, taking hold of my shoulders.

'I'm leaving Berlin very soon. I'm being demobbed and going back to England.'

My eyes widened as Jack got down on one knee. He presented me with a small box, which he opened to show me a ring with a large white diamond, circled with smaller ones. It nestled in a bed of black velvet.

'Will you marry me, love of my life? Come with me and live in England. I promise I will love and adore you forever.'

Jack continued to kneel and hold the box, while I continued to stare at him like an idiot. Eventually he stood up and sighed deeply.

'I thought so, but hoped I was wrong. You don't want to marry me?'

The silence stretched between us until, dejected, Jack said, 'I will always love you Greta, and despite being turned down by the love of my life, I would still like to see you before I leave for England?'

I remained steadfastly mute.

'Could we meet for a coffee to say goodbye?'

I remained mute.

Resigned, Jack opened the door of the linen room and informed me, 'I'll be back in ten days, Greta, on the 28th. We can say cheerio then.'

The place that had saved me in the worst times was now the place I broke Jack's heart.

With his head bowed and his tall body slumped, Jack left me standing in the linen room. For the rest of the day and in those that followed, I thought about the trip to America and about Jack's proposal.

I felt I had no choice but to depart for America, where my friends were heading. I would have regular and steady work, an income and accommodation. Although I was frightened of the new venture, I could not stay in Berlin without Lisa or Jacques. I was too scared to be on my own. I made the decision to leave for America many times and then I would think about Jack and his proposal of marriage and a life in England. I felt pulled every which way.

The next ten days passed in a flurry of constant activity and preparation. Perhaps I was in denial, but I somehow forgot that the day of our departure – the 28th of the month – was the same day I was supposed to be meeting Jack to say goodbye.

I had heard nothing from the English soldier: no notes, gifts or confirmation of our meeting. I assumed he was so upset and he had decided not to see me again. Who could blame him?

The morning of the 28th dawned. Lisa and I were wide awake early, packed and ready for the next chapter of our lives. I had gradually prepared myself for the idea of living in America. I reassured myself it was the best way forward for me: there would be no reminders of the horrors of my past in a far-flung country.

At breakfast time, we carried our bags down to the reception area. Madam Sophie was bellowing instructions as two doormen carried her cases to the car. I looked around the lobby of Hotel Berlin. I thought of my mother, Hans and I arriving here, and shook away awful memories.

It was time for a fresh start.

Our bags finally packed in the car, Madam Sophie nodded to Frau Bergen at the reception desk and with hardly a backward glance, walked out of the hotel for the last time.

'Come on!' she called to Lisa and I. 'Jacques and Sybil are already in the car. Come along! We must not miss the train.'

I was following Lisa into the car when a familiar voice shouted behind me. I stepped back onto the pavement and stared along the street. People were stopping to look in the same direction as the voice became louder.

Madam Sophie laughed from the front of the car, and leaned through the window to tell me, 'Jack phoned me last night, I told him of our trip to New York. He said he would try and get here as he had something to tell you. For a plain man, he can very dashing and surprising.'

I turned back to stare in the direction of the shouting and froze as Jack jumped through the crowd into view, shouting my name. He ran to me and pulled me from the car, into a bear-like hug. I held my breath for a moment, uncertain of what to think. Suddenly a feeling of happiness rushed through me. I was glad, so very glad, that he was there.

Jack held me at a distance and looked at me.

'Will you marry me?' he said.

This time I didn't hesitate.

'Yes, yes Jack! I'll go to England with you as your wife.'

Madam Sophie laughed again from inside the car, and stepped out, looking at us with approval.

'Jack, you are one of the kindest men I have ever met,' she said. She turned to me and her smile became sad.

'Ah Greta, I hope you have a long and happy life with him.'

For the first time in weeks, I smiled widely and my laugher was light and full of sunshine.

I knew I wanted to be with Jack. He was my safe harbour and I hoped he always would be.

Jack began to cry with joy. He placed the ring on my finger and assured Madam Sophie, 'I will take care of Greta and always keep her safe.'

'You'd better!' she replied, but as she spoke Madam Sophie moved closer to me and placed a piece of paper in my hand. Whispering in my ear she told me, 'Just to be on the safe side, always have an escape plan. I have given you my address and telephone number in America. If your back is against the wall, or if you change your mind, you will always have a job with me in New York.'

My eyes filled with tears as she continued, 'I will wire you the money for the voyage anytime. My Greta, we will always be friends.'

Realising this was another goodbye, Lisa and Jacques tried to get out of the car, but Madam Sophie saw my tears and was firm, waving them back.

'No goodbyes, they are too difficult.'

With brief kisses on both cheeks, and a waft of perfume left in the air, Madam Sophie got into the car and it sped away. I saw Lisa's pale face, screwed up and covered in tears, her small hands waving furiously until the bend in the road. Jacques' face was pressed to the window, an etching of sadness.

The dust from the road filled my nostrils, replacing the smell of Madam Sophie's French perfume. Jack waited patiently until I turned and looked up at him. My English captain had the most radiant smile. I ran into his open arms. With my Jack, I had finally found a place to call home.

AFTERWORD

2005, England.

Greta lived in a small terraced house on the south coast. She had rarely returned to Germany since leaving with Jack in 1949 and considered the UK her home. Germany held too many horrific memories, and Greta told me she never felt comfortable during the rare trips to her birth country.

It was in that neat-as-a-pin house that I interviewed Greta over many months about her life and journey. I felt it was important that women like Greta had a voice as it reflected the little-known story of thousands of women during World War Two and its dreadful aftermath. Her experiences also brought into sharp focus the millions of families across war-torn Europe during 1945 and afterward.

Greta's story is sadly as relevant today, resonating with the stories and lives of millions of refugees still fleeing global conflict in the 21st century. Women and children caught up in war often suffer rape, murder, torture and trafficking, experiences as severe as the most vicious weapons used by soldiers in battle.

Today was my last interview with the elderly Greta.

Greta was dying; she had stage four bowel cancer. Her nurse, Mona, had phoned me a few days before to say that Greta wanted to talk just a little more. It would be the ending of her story in so many ways.

Greta was in a hospital-style bed downstairs, and she was now confined to this bed.

Her thick hair, still blonde, was styled in a chignon that framed her still-handsome features. Despite decades living in the UK, her accent edged through many of her words.

Gesturing to the bone china cups and teapot as I arrived, Greta asked me to pour us both a cup of tea. Even though she was no longer able to drink or eat, she had grown accustomed to the nicety of an English afternoon cuppa. Winking at me, she pointed at the many photos on the mantelpiece.

'See that smart man in his captains uniform?' she said, 'That's my Jack!'

Chuckling she continued, 'The photo next to it was taken by an army photographer on our wedding day. Can you believe that was just 48 hours after my dearest and only friends Lisa and Jacques left with Madam Sophie for America?'

The old lady let out a long sigh and fell quiet for a while.

When she spoke again, her voice wavered, 'Within a week I was heading for England. A new wife, a new life and a new country!'

The dull whirl of the morphine pump made Greta forget she had already talked to me for many hours about her Jack and their wedding. I didn't mind; every scrap of information helped to bring alive the young woman she once was, and how her experiences had formed her as a person.

I looked over at the wedding photo again and saw a tiny scrap of a girl alongside a tall, wiry, man. He was glowing with happiness, while Greta looked shy, hanging onto his arm as if for dear life.

Greta interrupted my thoughts and, with a firmer voice, said, 'Jack saved me from Berlin and the terrors of life on my own. Germany after the war was a terrifying place for a woman. He saved my life and my sanity in so many ways.'

She pointed at a different photo, a soldier leaning against a gate.

'Can you bring that one over, Christine?'

Greta's home was full of photographs of her and Jack, their children and their grandchildren. She often told me of her extended family, and of their successes and joys. I brought Greta the photograph and she held it lovingly to her bony chest. She was starting to slip in and out of consciousness, her face gradually relaxing as pain subsided.

Mona had told me over the phone that Greta's son and daughter would be arriving that night to spend the last few days with their mother. Her daughter lived in Scotland and her son in Hanover, Germany.

Greta awoke suddenly, sat up, and declared, 'Christine, your book must be about survival and how basic it is to the human condition. People must understand that Jack and many soldiers like him were the way out for us girls.'

She sighed and sank back into her pillows, 'After the war, Europe was in chaos, a bear pit. Unless you had the support of a strong or influential man, had money or connections, you were dead meat.'

She pinched her lips together before speaking again.

'Of course, I could have gone to America with Madam Sophie and my friends, but I didn't have the energy or the enthusiasm for that adventure. I needed peace, calm and lots of love, and Jack gave me all of that.'

She reached out for my hand, becoming grave.

'Make sure you explain all the things mother had to do – was forced to do – to keep me and Hans safe. I hope people don't judge her, or think badly of me?'

Greta struggled to breathe but continued, 'The rapes, her giving herself to men for food or protection, it was against her upbringing.'

Shaking her head sadly, she said, 'I was expected to be a virgin when I married. But both my mother and I had little choice. I hope people are kind when they hear about my life and what happened to my little family.'

I reassured Greta no one would judge her. I encouraged her to talk more about the happy times with Jack. She lapsed gently into sleep as I sat and waited.

When she stirred, her voice was strong despite her illness.

'Christine, I married Jack because he was kind. He was my ticket out of Germany to England, far away from all my bad memories.'

She looked at me, 'I don't know if anyone who wasn't there can ever comprehend what it was like. The land of my birth was raped and destroyed in the war, just like many of its women and men. It was barren, unrecognizable. I no longer knew Germany as my home or its people as my friends. It was often a living nightmare.'

She started to cough, and Mona came in, propping Greta up in bed to give her some relief. Irritated, Greta waved her carer away, impatient to keep talking. The chiming of the clock echoed around the room, which was filled with a lifetime of ornaments and keepsakes.

Words began to pour from her mouth in a rush.

'I knew Jack was never going to be my Rhett Butler, he would never make me swoon. When we married, I was not even a little in love with him. But you know, he saved me and made me a wonderful home here in England.'

She chuckled and said, 'With his buck teeth and gangly build he would not have got a second glance from me before the war. I was very beautiful, you know! But Jack was so loving and so in love with me.'

Leaning over to me she whispered, 'I was very damaged by the war. Doctors, even a psychiatrist, couldn't handle my case. Nothing helped me except my Jack. He was so patient and caring. He sat up with me night after night, year after year, staying with me during the nightmares and flashbacks. He never asked me what had happened, and I could never talk about it.'

There was another long pause as Greta gathered her strength. I said nothing. I knew how important it was for the old lady to let go of the past and leave it finally behind. She confirmed this with her next words.

'There are things I have told you that I have never told anyone, Christine. I need to talk more about that now. I had a lot of depression and anxiety after the war. I couldn't have sex for three years after we married. Jack helped me through all of that and more. He held my hand and was totally selfless in his adoration.'

Greta took a deep breath.

'We both wanted children, so we made a pact. We would have sex just for making babies.'

The childish wording made me realise that, in many ways, Greta and her emotions had been frozen in time. Being raped at just fourteen years old by the Soviet soldier had impacted on her mental health and perception of adult relationships for the rest of her life. Jack had been her rock and, in many ways, had given her the unconditional love of a parent. He had died seven years before from a lung condition brought about by his years working with asbestos during and after the war.

Greta tried to sit up, and I put two more pillows behind her head. She seemed to get bigger as her voice became loud and angry.

'All men change in war, war changes all men!' she shouted.

She let go of my hand and thumped her pillow.

Mona rushed in from the kitchen, but I put my hand up and told her, 'Don't worry, Greta is getting a lot off her mind.'

The old lady nodded to her carer in agreement and Mona went back to washing the dishes. The clashing of plates and saucers provided a mild distraction during the silences of Greta's confessional. The old lady was exhausted and lay back on the pillows. Her eyes softened and we sat in the quiet for many minutes before she began to talk again.

I patted her hand,

'I never really liked sex much, even with my Jack. The rape and everything I saw during my teen years made me see men very differently. The only man I knew I could trust in that way was my Jack.'

There was silence as Greta once again drifted away from me and the room, and edged away from living. With her need to tell all, she was also letting go and shedding all of those horrific experiences before she continued on yet another journey.

Mona came in and took the tea cups away. She whispered, 'Greta hasn't long. She was insistent she talk to you.'

The old lady murmured as Mona left the room.

'He never once made me do it, so we only had sex to have children, my Sophie and Michael.'

Between gasping breaths, she said, 'Once the children were born, we just cuddled in bed after that, my Jack understood.'

Greta went quiet for a time, then repeated a sentence she had said to me many times during our meetings.

'Men change in war, all men change in war,' she moaned.

'Of course, my mother changed, I changed too, but in war it's men who hold the power.'

For a long time, we sat quietly as the clock ticked away into a summer afternoon. The sunlight blazing through the window danced around on the rose-patterned wallpaper. Shadows came and went as the light moved over the furniture and photographs, and the day moved onwards into evening. I felt sad. This was the ending of a life; a life that, despite its terrors, had been lived as well and as kindly as possible during one of the most momentous and horrific times in global history. I stayed for another two hours. Greta mostly slept, occasionally sharing snatches of words, some profound, others meaningful only to her. I would miss Greta and our talks over cups of tea. She was so very tired, and I squeezed her hand in goodbye as I prepared to leave.

The old lady suddenly stirred and beckoned me to go closer. As I bent over her, she whispered in my ear,

'My Jack came to Germany to help rebuild Berlin. He was so good at making things better. And do you know what, Christine? He eventually made me better, too!'

THE END

About the author

Christine Lord is an award-winning journalist, filmmaker and campaigner from Portsmouth, England. This is her second book. Christine's LinkedIn is available here:

www.linkedin.com/in/christine-lord-463ab222/

Printed in Great Britain
by Amazon